Had he somehow stepped into a fairy tale?

Phillip blinked at the sight. Rorie was sitting at a spinning wheel, dressed in a white nightgown with a demure neckline and tiny capped sleeves. Her hair fell over her shoulders like spun gold.

As he watched, mesmerized, Rorie seemed totally unaware of his presence. Her hands were expertly guiding and adjusting the feeding of wool fleece from a cigar-size roll into the spindle of the wheel. Her eyes were half-closed, her expression dreamy. It appeared as though she could do what she was doing in her sleep. Maybe she *was* asleep.

"Do you always work by candlelight?" Phillip asked, stepping into the room.

Rorie's blue eyes widened and her chair clattered backward as she jumped up, staring at him as though he had indeed woken her from a dream.

"Just when I'm in the mood," she whispered. Then, seeming to come to her senses, she joked, "How about you?"

"I do *all* my best work by candlelight," he said.

Dear Reader,

Once upon a time we were little girls dreaming of handsome princes on white chargers, of fairy godmothers who'd made us into beautiful princesses and of mountain castles where we'd live happily ever after.

Now that we're all grown up, we can recapture those dreams in a brand-new miniseries, Once Upon a Kiss. It features stories based on some of the world's best-loved fairy tales—expressly for the little girl who still lives on inside of us.

Emily Dalton continues the series with the retelling of the romantic Sleeping Beauty and her dashing prince whose kiss awakens his lady love.

Be sure to read all six of these wonderful fairy-tale romances, coming to you every other month, only from American Romance!

Once Upon a Kiss—at the heart of every little girl's dreams...and every woman's fantasy....

Happy reading!

Debra Matteucci
Senior Editor & Editorial Coordinator
Harlequin Books
300 East 42nd Street
New York, NY 10017

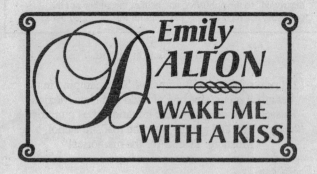

Emily DALTON

WAKE ME WITH A KISS

Harlequin Books

TORONTO • NEW YORK • LONDON
AMSTERDAM • PARIS • SYDNEY • HAMBURG
STOCKHOLM • ATHENS • TOKYO • MILAN
MADRID • WARSAW • BUDAPEST • AUCKLAND

To Gil and Sharon Pittard.

I'll never forget the Summer of '67...camping in the beautiful mountains of Colorado and New Mexico, Russell's Smokey the Bear imitation, the "mummy" sleeping bag, and gliding over the roads in a cool, blue Mustang. Thanks for the memories!

ISBN 0-373-16685-0

WAKE ME WITH A KISS

Copyright © 1997 by Danice Jo Allen.

Chapter One

"It's the biggest one *I've* ever seen," one lady whispered out of the side of her mouth.

"Theirs is always the biggest," another lady grumbled. "And the bigger the blossom—it just stands to reason—the more potent the smell. I'm sure Mr. Fairchild will pick their rose over mine or yours, Gladys. I don't know why we even bother to enter these stupid contests. The first prize always goes to those blasted Farley sisters...the old bats!"

"*Old* bats is right," Gladys agreed with a snide smile. "They must be pushing eighty. You'd think they'd be dead by now by natural causes, or at least have blown themselves up in that enchanted greenhouse of theirs. Only when they're six feet under and fertilizing daisies from the other side are *we* ever going to have a chance to win, Midge!"

Approaching the judging table from behind, Phillip Fairchild couldn't help but overhear the disgruntled conversation of two of the contestants in the Most Fragrant Rose Contest. He was appalled and amused by their vindictiveness, which seemed out of all proportion to the circumstances. And they looked so motherly and sweet! It was like listening to June Cleaver plot murder.

Before making his presence known, he glanced down the length of the long table and decided that the ladies must be talking about the three elderly women huddled around their contest entry. He couldn't even glimpse it from where he stood. But since he figured the two jealous women were exaggerating about this paragon of a rose, anyway, he was perfectly willing to wait to see it. Besides, even if it was the largest rose here today, that didn't mean it was the most fragrant. He ought to know. Fragrance was his business.

Stepping up to the table, he smiled and addressed the small audience that had gathered to watch the judging. "Good afternoon, ladies and gentlemen. I'm Phillip Fairchild."

Everyone quit visiting among themselves, and Phillip was instantly the center of attention. Out of the crowd, a little girl exclaimed, "Is that the prince, Mommy? But where's his crown?"

Behind his smile, Phillip cringed. He hated the nickname with which the media had tagged him. "The Perfume Prince" was a bit flowery and pompous for his tastes. As founder and C.E.O. of the internationally renowned Fair Lady Perfumes, and belonging to one of the oldest and richest families in the coastal south, Phillip understood how they'd come up with the nickname, but that didn't make him like it any better.

"We were lucky to get so much sunshine to kick off the annual Fulton County Fair, weren't we?" he said, proceeding with the usual pleasantries. There were murmurs and assenting smiles from the crowd, even though most of them were probably wilting from the heat. It was a beautiful, sunshiny day, but as was typical for June in Atlanta, Georgia, it was also hot and sticky. He reasoned that the sooner he got the judging over with, the happier everyone would be.

"I was delighted to be asked to judge the Most Fragrant Rose Contest this year," he went on. "It's my first attempt at this sort of thing, and I'm very honored." Following some scattered applause, he said, "Now, let's get on with it, shall we?"

With that, Phillip commenced the judging. All the roses were large and lovely, and he made sure he complimented each of the nervous contestants on their entries as he sniffed his way down the table. However, not one of the flowers was more remarkable than the other when it came to fragrance. He was beginning to wonder how he was ever going to pick a winner—eeny, meeny, miney, mo, perhaps?—when he came to the last rose.

Phillip was astounded. The rose was the size of a cantaloupe, and appeared just as heavy. It was deep crimson and had huge, dewy petals that unfolded in perfect symmetry. He'd never seen such a lush, beautiful, extremely large rose in his life!

Blinking with amazement, he lifted his head and stared at the cultivators of such a gigantic specimen. Three pairs of twinkling blue eyes, set in plump, rosy faces, stared back at him. The Farley sisters, of whom the other women were, as it turned out, so justifiably jealous, looked like three slightly varying versions of Mrs. Claus as she was usually depicted on TV and Christmas cards.

They were all three as round as beach balls, with white hair that fluffed around their heads like halos of spun sugar. And perched on each of their noses was a pair of small, square, reading glasses. They were all wearing flowered dresses and had roses—of a much more moderate size than their contest entry—perched over their left ears. On each ample bosom was a stick-on name tag. Their names were Dahlia, Daisy, and—incredibly—Daffodil.

"Ladies, I'm very impressed," he murmured. "I've never seen such a large, beautiful rose."

"Wait till you smell it," Dahlia said eagerly. "I do believe it is our most fragrant variety of rose ever!"

Phillip bent near the rose and breathed deeply. A heady, musky, utterly divine fragrance immediately filled his head. In fact, he felt a bit dizzy. He braced himself against the table and stood up, his senses reeling.

"Oh, dear," he heard one of the Farley sisters whisper. "I think he took too big a whiff. We should have warned him. I hope he doesn't pass out."

Presently Phillip's head cleared and he looked with amazement at the Farley sisters again. "How did you do this? How did you concentrate so much fragrance in one single flower? Granted, it's a big flower, but in all my experience I've never been so bowled over by a scent."

The ladies beamed. "It's a secret, Mr. Fairchild," the one named Daffodil coyly informed him.

He smiled teasingly. "Or is it magic?"

"Oh no," Daisy disclaimed with a decided shake of her head. "It's not magic. It's *fertilizer!*"

A NEWS REPORTER appeared out of nowhere and cameras flashed as, from the midst of the crowd, Rorie watched Philip Fairchild hand over the winning blue ribbons, one for each of her godmothers. Expecting the Farley sisters to win again, the coordinators of the horticultural show had been prepared with three first-place ribbons for each contestant. Anyone who frequented the county fair knew what to expect, but apparently Phillip Fairchild didn't, and was just as astounded as everyone else was when they first encountered the results of her godmothers' incredible green thumbs.

Rorie folded her arms and narrowed her eyes, taking a good look at the man whose handsome mug was constantly smiling at her from the Atlanta *Sun*'s society pages. From Charity benefits, to theater openings, to the annual Swan House Ball, Phillip Fairchild was always in attendance. And for each event, he had a different beautiful woman on his arm. He seemed to change women like most people changed socks, but, with his devastating good looks, Rorie was sure he never had any trouble finding replacements for yesterday's discarded dates.

He was even more handsome in person, and Rorie couldn't shake the feeling that somehow, somewhere, they'd met before.... But that was a ridiculous idea. They definitely didn't move in the same social circles. After all, she was a pauper compared to the Perfume Prince.

He might have only been given the title by the media, but Phillip Fairchild really did look like a prince. He was tall—at least six foot two—with glossy black hair, chiseled cheeks, and striking gray eyes. Even today, in the sweltering heat, he looked as cool and confident as any royal potentate Rorie could imagine. As she'd watched him step out of his air-conditioned Mercedes a few minutes ago, he'd made one concession to the heat by taking off the jacket of his navy blue suit. But even in his crisp white shirtsleeves and red patterned tie, he looked regal as all get-out.

Too bad his behavior didn't match up with his looks,

Rorie thought grimly. According to Kim, a childhood friend from her old neighborhood, Phillip Fairchild was a user. After years of their not seeing each other, Rorie had recently met Kim again during a photo shoot for a mail-order clothing catalogue she advertised in. Kim, all grown up now and a gorgeous redhead, was working as one of the models.

Delighted to see each other, they'd become reacquainted over the course of the three-day shoot and Kim had confided in Rorie about her romance with Phillip. It seemed that Kim had had the dubious honor of having more than just a flash-in-the-pan relationship with the Perfume Prince. And it had been heartbreaking.

Kim said that Phillip didn't care about the people he bulldozed over in order to achieve success, but just ruthlessly went after and got whatever he wanted. Then when he was through with you, it was *"Adios, amigo."* He might ooze charm like an éclair oozed whipped cream, but apparently the Prince was no prince.

Rorie knew the media could be fickle and unfair, and she'd been noncommittal about all the rumors the press and the scandal sheets dug up or made up about Phillip Fairchild. But Kim's testimonial made it pretty hard for Rorie not to believe he was as bad as they sometimes made him out to be.

The crowd was breaking up, the disappointed contestants dispersing, but her godmothers were still deep in animated conversation with Phillip Fairchild. Rorie had a bad feeling she knew exactly what they were talking about. She sighed deeply and set out to rescue her godmothers from the notorious prince.

"Does your fertilizer work like this on all your plants?" Phillip inquired.

"We occasionally change an ingredient or two to adapt our basic formula to specific plants," Daffodil said. "But, yes, all the plants in our garden and in our yard are very large and productive."

"Miss Farley, do you suppose—"

"Call me Daffy," Daffodil interrupted with a demure smile.

"Yes, call us all by our first names," Daisy insisted. "Since we are all Miss Farleys, it could become a bit confusing if we stuck strictly to the formalities."

Phillip smiled. "Then you ladies must call me Phillip."

The Farley sisters tittered. "All right...*Phillip*," Daffy said with a blush. "Now, what was it you were about to say?"

"I was only going to ask if I might come by your house sometime to see your garden. Today, perhaps?"

The Farley sisters' faces immediately registered anxiety and doubt, and a voice from behind Phillip said, "That would be impossible."

Phillip turned around and locked gazes with a young woman...a beautiful young woman with long blond hair and eyes the color of sapphires. For an instant, he thought he might have met her before. There was something familiar about her.... But he dismissed the idea and continued to look at her with open admiration.

He judged her to be in her midtwenties. She was tall, slim, and very shapely in her cropped denim shirt and white tailored shorts. Phillip was a leg man, and one swift, surreptitious glance at this young woman's legs wasn't a bit disappointing...not even to the eyes of a connoisseur. However, the look in *her* eyes was about as welcoming as a quarantine sign.

"I'm sorry," he began politely. "Are you part of

the, er, Farley family?'' As he suspected that the elderly sisters with the flowery names were eccentric spinsters, he was wondering how the beautiful, leggy blonde could possibly fit into the picture.

"Yes, I'm their goddaughter," she answered, lifting her chin in an assertive pose. "We aren't related, but we're definitely family."

"Pleased to meet you," Phillip said, extending his hand. "I'm Phillip Fairchild."

"I know," the young woman answered, eyeing his hand for a moment, then hesitantly giving him hers. Her handshake was limp and grudging.

Hmm, thought Phillip. *This one doesn't like me.* He hoped she wouldn't interfere with the deal he had in mind.

Flashing what he hoped was a disarming smile, he said, "Then you have the advantage on me. I didn't catch *your* name."

"I'm Rorie McBride."

"Rorie?"

"Short for Aurora."

He raised a brow. "You mean, like the Roman goddess of dawn, or the northern lights?"

She wrinkled her nose. "My parents were hopeless romantics." *But you're not*, Phillip thought. *You're all business, and you've decided that I'm as bad as the press makes me out to be.*

When she'd mentioned her parents, she'd used the past tense, as if they were deceased. He wondered if the Farley sisters stood in place of Rorie's parents. A swift glance at her bare ring finger told him she probably wasn't married. Perhaps she lived with her godmothers and even handled their finances. If that was the case, he'd have to win her over to his way of thinking, too.

"As you heard, I was just talking to your godmothers about coming to see their garden," he said. "I'm fascinated by their skill at growing such huge, beautiful plants."

"Everyone is," Rorie said dampeningly. "But if you're also interested in the fertilizer they use for growing the plants, you're wasting your time, Mr. Fairchild."

"Call him Phillip, Rorie," Dahlia advised her, leaning near. "He doesn't like the formalities any more than we do, dear."

When Phillip found his voice, he said, "You shoot from the hip, don't you?" *And what lovely hips they are.*

"I believe in being up-front and honest, Mr. Fairchild. And if, as I said, you're hoping to buy my godmothers' fertilizer formula, you might as well forget it. The formula stays in the family."

As Phillip studied Rorie's serious expression, he wondered if her protectiveness toward the formula was completely unselfish. Maybe she was planning to sell it after her godmothers had passed on, so that she could pocket all the money. But somehow he didn't believe that. No one with a beautiful, romantic name like Aurora could be that mercenary. There had to be other reasons for her hesitancy.

"Is it so hard to believe that I just want to see their plants?" he asked with a wry smile.

She raised a skeptical brow.

He tried again. "Can I come by if I promise not to mention fertilizer?"

Something glimmered in her eyes that looked suspiciously like mischief. After a short pause, during which he could almost hear the wheels in her brain spinning, she said, "Sure, Mr. Fairchild, you can come by."

Surprised, he asked, "Today?"

She shrugged. "Anytime."

"Thanks, I will," he said doubtfully. Phillip should have felt triumphant, but instead he felt wary. Her capitulation was too quick and easy.

"It was nice meeting you, Mr. Fairchild," Rorie said with a definite note of finality in her voice, as if she never expected to see him again.

"Yes, it was delightful meeting you, Phillip," Dahlia said with much more sincerity and warmth, picking up the winning rose. The other sisters chorused her sentiments and threw him tender farewell glances over their shoulders as they walked away. It didn't appear as though the Farley sisters expected to see him again, either.

Phillip said goodbye and watched as the beautiful blonde and her three godmothers headed toward a white minivan in the parking lot. His jaw hardened with determination. Despite what they apparently thought, and despite the fact that Rorie McBride hadn't bothered to give him their address, he was definitely going to see them again. After all, there was nothing he liked better than a challenge.

BUCKLED INTO their seats in the minivan, with their blue ribbons piled in the back along with their various winning plants, Rorie's godmothers gently scolded her.

"How could you be so cruel, dearest?" Daisy inquired fretfully. "Taunting that poor man to come to the house like that.... You *know* what will happen."

"He's not the type that takes 'no' for an answer, Daisy," Rorie answered, guiding the minivan out of the park grounds and onto a busy street. "He's determined to get your fertilizer formula, and he's just going to have to learn the hard way that it's not going to happen."

"But inviting him to come without so much as a warning is positively mean!" Daffy declared. "We didn't raise you since you were five years old to be *mean*, Aurora Dawn!"

"Yes, and he's so nice and *so* handsome," Dahlia added worriedly. "I just hope he's smart enough to turn back before he gets hurt."

"He's handsome all right, and very charming," Rorie admitted. "He had you three wrapped around his aristocratic little finger."

She smiled ruefully at her godmothers in the rear-view mirror. "But, for heaven's sake, don't worry about him. Phillip Fairchild is smart enough to know when to cut his losses and take the safer option. I'm sure he won't get hurt."

Rorie could tell by her godmothers' expressions that they were not convinced that Phillip Fairchild would escape unharmed from the daunting task of making it to their front door. And the truth was, she wasn't so sure, either. But why should that bother her? He was a big boy. He certainly *ought* to be able to take care of himself. And it wasn't as if he'd had *her* wrapped around his little finger. In fact, there was no man on earth whose little finger Rorie had less inclination to be wrapped around than Phillip Fairchild's...no matter how darned sexy it was.

It was strange, though, how she still had a nagging

feeling that they'd met somewhere before. Somewhere near water...

DELPHINIA FARLEY Cadbury Bolregard Devine, dressed in her signature black, eyed her reflection in the mirror of her powder compact as she sat in the back seat of her Rolls-Royce, applying another layer of bloodred lipstick and waiting for her chauffeur cum spy to return from his latest assignment. She decided that despite the appalling amount of sunlight that still managed to seep through her tinted windows, she didn't look too bad for a woman on the shady side of sixty.

True, three face-lifts, an eye tuck, cheek implants, a nose job, and daily moisturizing massages had helped her retain her youthful beauty, but what did it matter how she stayed attractive? The pain of the surgeries and the money spent had been well worth it, because, after all, her looks had snagged her three husbands...so far...and lots of lovely alimony.

Trouble was, Delphinia mused broodingly, there was never enough money to support her lavish, but well-deserved life-style. That's why she needed to get her hands on her sisters' fertilizer formula. She'd made inquiries and she knew she could get a large chunk of cash for it on the international market, but, backed by that orphaned goddaughter of theirs, her loony-tune sisters had persisted in refusing to sell the formula to her. Family or not, she was beginning to think she'd have to resort to drastic measures against the old bats.

As for Aurora, or "Briar Rose," which was the sickeningly sweet, oddball nickname her sisters had given their goddaughter—who had been living with them ever since her parents were killed in a car accident twenty years ago—Delphinia was not afraid to cross swords with her. In fact, she would relish it. The girl was just too loyal and upstanding to be tolerated.

Instead of leaving after graduating from college with a degree in fashion design, Aurora had stayed at the house to keep an eye on her eccentric godmothers and to help support their social-security incomes with that mail-order business of hers. If not for Aurora, Delphinia was sure she could have tricked her sisters into giving her the formula long ago.

Smacking her collagen-injected, newly glossed lips together, and snapping shut her compact, Delphinia looked up when she heard the car door open. Her diminutive, balding, sprucely uniformed chauffeur slid into his seat.

"It's about time you got back, Simon," Delphinia complained. "It's hot in here, and I detest the very sight of all these common people skulking about with their cotton candy and stuffed toys."

"I left the air-conditioning on, madam," Simon said meekly, glancing timidly at her reflection in the rearview mirror. "And, begging your pardon, madam, but it would be very hard to escape seeing cotton candy and stuffed toys at a county fair."

"Never mind," Delphinia snapped, pulling a long, slim cigarette from a silver-plated case. "Just tell me what you saw and heard."

"You were right, madam, about Mr. Fairchild asking the Miss Farleys about the fertilizer."

"Of course I was right," Delphinia drawled, leaning forward so that Simon could light her cigarette. "He's a businessman. One look at their monstrous rose and he'd be a fool not to try to wangle a deal with them for their fertilizer formula," she said around her capped teeth as she drew the smoke into her mouth and throat.

"Phillip Fairchild is no fool. I assume he was unsuccessful? Everyone is, though I must admit I was more worried about him than all the others. The man's charm is legendary."

Simon nodded obsequiously as he stashed away the cigarette lighter in his jacket pocket. Delphinia noticed that his manner was more nervous than usual. Growing suspicious, she demanded, "They *did* refuse him, didn't they, Simon?"

Simon grimaced and his left eye twitched uncontrollably. "I don't know, madam. As the crowd dispersed, I had no one to hide behind, and I was afraid they'd see me. I didn't hear the last part of their conversation."

"Gawd," Delphinia moaned, dropping her head in her hands. "Can't you do anything right, Simon? Now I must visit them and ferret out the facts myself. I can't have a man like Phillip Fairchild disrupting my plans! But how I *detest* visiting that house! If only someone would poison that beast of theirs..!"

"We tried that, madam," Simon reminded her, flinching at the memory. "I nearly lost my hand."

"It wasn't poison. It was only a sedative," Delphinia reminded him impatiently. "I only wanted to dope him up so he'd let us through. I could swear he was *sneering* at our hot dog, Simon.... Now that you've memorized the route through the yard to the front door, he's the only thing keeping us from searching the house when they're gone." She sighed deeply. "But never mind that now. Was the girl there when Fairchild asked about the fertilizer? Was she swooning over the Perfume Prince...as they all do?"

Simon considered this and brightened. "Well, no,

madam. She wasn't swooning at all. In fact, she looked downright flinty-eyed.''

Delphinia gave a scornful snort, smiled grimly, and took another drag on her cigarette. ''The stupid girl. Prim virgins are so tiresome. She's probably been locked away in that old house with my crazy sisters for so long, toiling away on that spinning wheel and knitting one-of-a-kind sweaters for that puny business of hers, she doesn't recognize a prime specimen of a man when she sees one and can't respond like a *real* woman.''

Simon had no comment, and Delphinia's eyes narrowed as she contemplated what a prime specimen Phillip Fairchild really was. Perhaps he was too young for her, but she might be tempted to persuade him to overlook the discrepancy in their ages if the right opportunity arose. However, at the moment she was much more concerned with fertilizer than with romance. Her eyes narrowed speculatively.

''Even if they said no, I don't believe Fairchild will give up right away. And he may even have been attracted to Aurora.... Some men like that sort of insipid, *natural* look.'' She shuddered.

''He might even consider her lack of response a challenge,'' she continued. ''Any means he might use to insinuate himself into my sisters' good graces make for a risky situation, Simon, for there's nothing those silly twits want more than for their precious Briar Rose to snag a prince. So, regardless of what transpired during their conversation, we must pay a visit to my sisters and keep a close eye on Phillip Fairchild, as well. If anyone's going to get that formula, it's going to be me!''

''Yes, madam,'' Simon agreed automatically. After

a short pause, he added, "Do you wish to go home now?"

Delphinia leaned back against the soft leather seat and chewed the inside of her mouth, her cigarette hanging languidly from her fingers. "Yes. Take me home, Simon. We'll visit my sisters tonight after dinner. That should be soon enough. Besides, you know how I must fortify myself before a visit to *that house.*"

"Yes, madam," Simon replied as he turned the key in the ignition and the Rolls began to purr. "Then I suppose we had better stop at the liquor store. I believe we're rather low on your favorite brand of vodka."

Delphinia shrugged. "It's your job to know, Simon. Drive on."

PHILLIP LOOKED up at the tip of a Victorian-style witch's-hat turret that could just barely be seen behind enormous, moss-draped oak trees, a bemused smile on his lips. The street number was nowhere in sight, so it was impossible to check it against the address he'd found in the phone book, but he knew without a doubt that this was the Farley house. No one else could grow plants so large they actually hid the house from view.

Even for this older, rather genteel neighborhood full of Georgian-style houses and rambling Victorian mansions, their yard appeared very deep. And between the gate of the wrought-iron fence that surrounded the property and the front of the house, there appeared to be a virtual jungle of vegetation. Phillip was sure that somewhere in that shadowy tangle of trees, shrubs, vines and giant flowers, was a walkway leading to the door. He considered it a challenge to find it.

Then, just as he was about to open the gate, he no-

ticed a handwritten sign tacked to a tree. It read Beware
Of Dragon.

He immediately decided it must be a whimsical sign,
penned by the eccentric Farley sisters when they were
in a humorous mood. Chuckling to himself and clutching his bag of bribes, Phillip opened the gate and let
himself in.

Chapter Two

Fifteen minutes later, Phillip was hot, sweaty and exasperated...but not about to give up. The yard was a maze. He had finally found a walkway hidden in the shrubbery, but the red-brick path went off in several different directions...all seeming to lead nowhere! Surrounded as he was by thick vegetation, he couldn't seem to get his bearings. He didn't know whether he was facing north, south, east, or west! But who would have thought he'd need a compass to get to someone's front door?

He stopped, set down his glossy paper bag with the Fair Lady Perfumes logo emblazoned on the front, snatched a handkerchief from his jacket pocket and wiped his forehead. He peered up at the sky through the dense overhanging branches of a eucalyptus tree and noticed a glimmer of pink. The sun had gone down below the tree line, so it was impossible to calculate directions by its position in the sky.

Soon it would be pitch-black in the jungle the Farley sisters called their yard. If he didn't find his way out soon, he'd not only need a compass, but a flashlight, too!

He could only imagine how dangerous it would be

to venture along these paths after dark. The walkway was so thickly crisscrossed with vines, trailing both high and low, he'd had to pay close attention even in broad daylight to keep from tripping and falling flat on his face—or hanging himself. He supposed the Farley sisters never had pizza delivered. The poor schmuck would never make it to the front door!

But, despite his exasperation, Phillip couldn't help but he impressed. He'd never in his life seen such a variety of plants, flowering shrubs, and tall, thick-trunked trees. Everything was enormous. There were daylilies, gardenias, honeysuckle…and even orchids! There were peach, palm, pomegranate, and lime trees. Even chamomile grew in thick, green clusters between the cracks of the walkway. But, most of all, there was prickly bush after bush of roses in every imaginable color.

To make matters even more difficult, because the air was so thick with the scent of sweet flowers and the pungent smell of damp, dark soil, Phillip couldn't take a breath without feeling a bit dizzy. There was also the constant, lulling buzz of bees and other blissful insects that made their home in the Farley wonderland. The overall effect numbed a person's faculties.

But with such proof of the Farley sisters' skill, Phillip was more determined than ever to strike a deal with them. Obviously their fertilizer formula was pure magic. With such magic to use in his own hothouses, where fragrances were nurtured and later distilled, the potential for incredible perfumes and even more incredible profits was enormous.

Not that he cared that much about the money. He had plenty of that already. But the idea of improving an already superior product was exciting and challenging.

Now, if only he could find his way to the Farley door before the sun went down. It would be damned embarrassing to have to call for help. But at least that sign about the dragon was just a joke. He'd had concerns at first that the Farley sisters might have a large gila monster on the premises, or a dog that *looked* like a dragon. Thank goodness his concerns had been completely—

Uh-oh. What was that? Phillip had been congratulating himself too soon. He heard a noise behind him that sounded suspiciously like a growl. A very deep-throated, menacing growl. Slowly, carefully, he turned around to face…the dragon.

Phillip blinked several times. He thought some hallucinogenic pollen must have drifted into his ear and somehow embedded itself in his brain. The creature standing before him was, by all appearances, a shaggy sheepdog, but it was as big as a pony. And its teeth… That was how the dog got the name Dragon, he supposed. His teeth were sharply pointed and enormous. And with his lips curled back, Dragon was displaying an impressive mouthful of gleaming ivories.

"A less determined man would turn back at this point," Phillip mused aloud, standing stock-still.

Dragon snarled.

Phillip addressed the dog. "But if I did turn back, which way would I go? I have no idea where the gate is, and I might trip on these damned vines and break my neck if I let you chase me in the right direction. And if I so much as twitch a muscle, you *will* chase me, won't you, Dragon?"

Dragon took a step forward, foamy drool dripping from his bared teeth.

"Of course you will," Phillip said dryly. "So maybe I won't twitch a muscle. The thing is, since you only popped up now, after I've been wandering in this wilderness for twenty minutes, I figure I must be close to the house. Too close to turn back. Too close to give up." Phillip stared into Dragon's black eyes, which were half-hidden behind a fringe of hair. "I'm not budging, Dragon," he informed him. "So you might as well make friends with me and guide me to your front door."

RORIE WAS AMAZED, irritated…and reluctantly impressed. She had been watching Phillip Fairchild for the past ten minutes as he appeared and disappeared in the maze of vegetation that made up their front yard. She had a bird's-eye view from her lofty office window, which was situated in the turret of the house, facing the street. She had been sitting at her desk, putting some final touches on her latest design for a sweater. Then, rising to stretch her legs, she'd gone to the window and discovered they had a visitor.

After a few false turns, the Perfume Prince had made definite progress and was now only about fifteen feet from the front door. It was at this point that Dragon usually made his appearance, not having bothered to rouse himself at the sound of the gate creaking open, because visitors seldom made it very far before turning back. The ones that did make it as far as Phillip Fairchild had, however, took one look at Dragon and ran as though the hounds of hell were nipping at their heels. Rorie smiled to herself. Now *that* certainly was an apt metaphor.

But Phillip wasn't running. In fact, he didn't even look frightened at the sight of a slathering, three-hundred-pound dog with bared teeth. Such brave—or foolhardy—behavior was unusual. And intriguing.

Dragon must have thought so, too, because suddenly he was no longer growling and baring his teeth. He was still all systems on alert, his tail bristling and sticking straight out, but his ears had flattened and he was cautiously approaching his quarry. Wisely, Phillip did not move.

Dragon slowly circled Phillip, sniffing and examining his shoes, pant legs, and shiny paper bag. Finally, he stood in front of Phillip again and looked at him. Man and dog locked gazes. A tense moment passed, then Phillip extended his right hand, palm up.

Rorie held her breath. This was the crucial moment. She didn't like Phillip, but she didn't enjoy seeing a man get his fingers snapped off, either.

But Dragon did not snap off any of Phillip's fingers...not even his aristocratic pinky. Dragon sniffed his hand, looked at Phillip one more time, then began to wag his tail in a very friendly fashion. The next thing Rorie knew, the man was actually scratching Dragon behind the ears. Dragon got an ecstatic, dopey look on his face, and his tail wagged faster and faster. The legendary Fairchild charm had evidently struck again.

"Great," Rorie grumbled to herself, hastily turning away from the window and heading for the door. "Now I'm going to have to keep him from charming my godmothers in the same way!" Or was that even possible?

When she was halfway down the stairs, she heard the doorbell chime. She made it into the parlor just in time to see her godmothers crowded around the open front door. She decided to remain in the parlor and, willing herself to be as composed as possible, she sat down on the sofa and waited.

PHILLIP FELT sheepish. He'd said hello, but all three Farley sisters seemed unable to utter a greeting in reply. They simply stared wide-eyed at him over the rims of their reading glasses, with their mouths hanging open. Occasionally their gazes drifted to Dragon, who had sat down on his considerable backside next to Phillip and was looking quite tame and content.

Finally Daffy said wonderingly, "You...you rang the doorbell."

Phillip cocked a brow. "Should I have knocked instead?"

"You don't understand," Daisy said in a breathy whisper. "We haven't heard the doorbell ring in years! No one ever rings it!"

"Everyone either gets lost, or they can't get past Dragon," Dahlia explained.

"What, this old softy?" Phillip crooned, ruffling Dragon's fur. Even sitting down, the dog was nearly as tall as Phillip's shoulder. "He and I are the best of friends." Dragon's tongue lolled from his mouth and he panted happily.

"So it seems," Daffy quavered.

Phillip observed the three sisters exchange significant looks. He wasn't sure what those looks meant, but he had a feeling he'd done something they considered quite remarkable. He hoped that meant he'd have some influence over them when he pitched his deal.

"It's hot out here, ladies," he said ruefully. "I've come to see your garden, but I'd really enjoy a glass of iced tea first."

The Farley sisters seemed suddenly to remember their manners and they practically tripped over one another as they moved aside to let him in, each of them babbling apologies in a slightly different pitch. It was kind of like listening to a gaggle of geese, but Phillip found their chatter rather soothing. The house he'd grown up in was customarily as quiet as a tomb.

As he was ushered into the parlor, with Dragon fast on his heels, Phillip looked around at the quaint surroundings. The house was chock-full of old-fashioned charm. There were roses on everything…embroidered on pillows, footstools and table scarves, showcased in the wallpaper design, in pictures, and in vases that rested on almost every available flat surface.

In a corner of the room was a rickety old fan, barely moving the humid air. And on the flowered sofa, with her feet firmly planted on the flowered rug, sat Aurora McBride.

Although he had fully expected to find that Ms. McBride lived with her godmothers, it was still a bit of a shock seeing her. Because she was the only object around that wasn't covered with roses or flowers of some kind—not to mention the fact that she was a beautiful woman—Phillip thought his eyes should have fastened on her the minute he'd entered the room. But somehow he'd missed her. Maybe that was because she was sitting as still and quiet as a mouse.

Dressed in a white cotton shirt tucked into a pair of jeans, with her long blond hair pulled into a sleek ponytail, she looked demure and sexy at the same time. Her eyes shone intensely blue as they met his appreciative gaze, but he suspected that she was not looking at him with the same interest he felt for her. As she had earlier that day, she looked very wary…and stubborn as hell.

"Hello, Rorie," Phillip said, smiling.

"Hello, Mr. Fairchild," Rorie answered with a sardonic edge to her voice. "I see you took me up on my invitation to come see my godmothers' garden."

Phillip raised a brow. "Didn't you expect me to?"

"I didn't expect to see you so soon."

"I don't think you expected to see me at all."

They locked gazes. Friction filled the air as they each took the measure of the other. Rorie was the first to look away. "I don't know what you're talking about, Mr. Fairchild," she said coolly.

"Your godmothers seemed very surprised to see me, too," he said, taking a step closer and swinging his bag onto a nearby table. "I gather not many people make it to your front door. The, er, complex landscaping of your yard, and your formidable watchdragon, must be very effective in keeping unwelcome visitors away."

"Not always," she said with a frosty look.

"Oh, that reminds me…" Dahlia began distractedly. She looked anxiously back and forth between Rorie and Phillip as they coolly regarded each other, then she hurried out of the room. "The iced tea!"

"Won't you sit down, Phillip?" Daffy invited.

"Yes, *do* sit down," Daisy added, gesturing to a flower-sprigged wingchair near where Rorie sat on one of the two sofas in the room. "If you sit there, the fan will blow right on your face."

"Sounds good to me," Phillip admitted, smiling at Daisy and Daffy as he sat down. "I appreciate your hospitality." He slid a glance toward Rorie. "It's always nice to feel welcome."

Insufferable jerk, thought Rorie, sitting with her arms crossed over her chest as she watched Phillip Fairchild work his wiles on her godmothers. He was dressed in the same blue suit he'd worn earlier that day, but, while he'd appeared cool as a cucumber at the county fair, he did look a little hot and uncomfortable now. The light sheen of perspiration on his upper lip and the flush on his cheeks, however, only made him appear more human. Sexy, in fact. Damn the man.... No wonder the godmothers were all atwitter over him. And that was even before he'd opened his mouth and started sweet-talking them.

While Daisy and Daffy blushed and giggled like schoolgirls, Phillip expressed his admiration of their charming house, the beautiful needlework everywhere, the fabulous yard out front, and even the friendly disposition of their dog...who was stretched adoringly at his feet.

They lapped up his compliments like hungry kittens, and, with such encouragement, Rorie wasn't surprised that he continued to flatter them till Dahlia came in with a tray of iced tea. Then he repeated to her everything he'd said to her sisters.

Beaming, Dahlia handed him an iced tea and said, "I'm glad you like our plants, Phillip. It's just too bad you came to see us so late in the day. It's already growing dark outside, and there's not enough light to show you our garden in the back. If you were impressed with our front yard, you'll be delighted with the back. That's where we've really put extra effort into making our plants large and productive."

Phillip looked incredulous. "You mean you've got even bigger plants in the back?"

The sisters exchanged pleased looks. "Well, yes," Dahlia said shyly. "We only use our special fertilizer in the back. Our plants are already so tall in the front that we can't see the road except from Aurora's office in the turret.''

Phillip wanted to ask more questions, but he'd promised not to mention fertilizer during his visit, and Rorie looked as if she was daring him to break that promise. He didn't dare. He figured he'd bide his time for now and drink his tea, then proceed to the bribe portion of his program.

Finally he set down his empty glass, reached for his bag, and placed it on the floor in front of him. He smiled at the Farley sisters, who were lined up on a sofa just across from him. He tried to ignore Rorie, who sat alone on the other sofa, to his left. Her disapproving expression—and all the rest of her—were a bit too distracting.

"I have to admit, ladies, that I had an ulterior motive for coming out here tonight,'' he began.

Here comes the pitch, thought Rorie. But what was in the bag? Tied bundles of money?

"I did want to see your garden, but I also wanted to—'' he reached inside the bag and pulled out an elegantly shaped bottle of perfume ''—give each of you a gift.''

Rorie instantly recognized a Fair Lady brand of perfume. The various bottle designs were exquisite and always stood out in department-store displays. She had to admit she really liked the Fair Lady fragrances and frequently longed to buy a bottle of her favorite, Tears of Joy, but it was way too expensive for her. Why had she thought Phillip would be so crass as to try to bribe them with cash? He was much more subtle. He understood women well enough to know they'd be far more likely to be impressed by a personal gift, especially one as provocative as expensive perfume.

"I chose a different fragrance for each of you. I tried to pick the one that most suited your individual chemistries."

Rorie was skeptical. Since they'd only had a ten-minute conversation with him on the fairgrounds that morning, what could Phillip Fairchild possibly know about their *chemistries?* However, he *was* already quite adept at telling her godmothers apart, which some people never managed to do. She must admit, that showed *some* discernment. But chemistries?

The godmothers oohed and aahed as Phillip handed each of them a bottle. Incredibly, the choices he'd made for the godmothers had floral bases comprised of their favourite flowers. Since he couldn't possibly have accurately guessed what each of their favorite flowers were, and since most people, after seeing their decor, would have thought they were all three partial to roses, his choices really were very impressive.

Then he handed her a large bottle of Tears of Joy.

Astounded, Rorie automatically took the bottle out of his hands and stared at it. "How did you know...?"

"Spicy and mysterious," he said. "That's you."

As if hypnotized, Rorie stared into his gorgeous gray eyes for a long moment before she came to her senses. She gave him back the perfume and said firmly, "I can't accept this, Mr. Fairchild. And I can't help but wonder why you're giving us perfume in the first place. And don't try to tell me it's part of the prize for winning the Most Fragrant Rose Contest. But even if it were, *I* certainly wasn't one of the winners, and *I* couldn't possibly accept a gift from you."

Phillip looked ruefully resigned. "All right, I won't try to tell you it's part of the prize for winning the contest. I admit the perfume was my idea. You've explained why you won't accept the perfume, Rorie, but I hope you will allow your godmothers to make up their own minds about my gifts.''

"You mean your *bribes*. Remember, Mr. Fairchild, you promised not to mention fertilizer while you were here."

"Aurora Dawn!" exclaimed Dahlia, clutching her bottle of perfume to her chest. "Don't be so rude, dear. I don't mind if Phillip mentions fertilizer. In fact, we might as well have the conversation and get it over with."

"Dahlia," Rorie began with a sigh of exasperation, "what's the use? Since you don't intend to sell Mr. Fairchild the formula, talking about it will only give him false hope."

"Ah, but we *are* thinking about selling it to him, Rorie," Daisy piped up.

Rorie blinked. "When did you decide this?" she inquired incredulously.

"Just now, when Phillip came to the door," Daffy answered. "That was the decisive moment, wasn't it, sisters? It certainly was for *me*." She turned to Dahlia and Daisy for confirmation and the other two sisters nodded complacently.

Alarmed, Rorie rose to her feet and began to pace the floor in front of the sofa where her godmothers were seated. "My dear godmothers, what can you be thinking? This is not a decision you can make on the spur of the moment, or based on some...some *whim!* You haven't even talked this over among yourselves, and you certainly haven't discussed the matter with *me!* You know the fertilizer formula ought not to be sold to anyone. And especially not to...to..."

Rorie turned and gestured toward Phillip, who

quickly wiped the exultant smile off his face when he
realized she was looking at him.

He's gloating! Rorie fumed to herself. *And by the
look of his smug mug, he thinks he's already won!
Well, I have news for him!*

"Mr. Fairchild, would you mind leaving me alone
with my godmothers so we can speak privately?"
Rorie expressed herself in terms of a polite request, but
she was actually ordering Phillip out of the room...and
he knew it.

He gave her a look of grudging respect and stood
up. "Where shall I wait? In the kitchen? Or do you
have a dungeon where you'd rather I went and, er,
stretched my legs?"

"The kitchen would be fine," Rorie answered
tersely, ignoring his joke. "It's at the end of the hall."

Rorie tried to ignore the stirring of female awareness
she felt as she watched Phillip rise in a graceful, leisurely fashion and saunter out of the room. He had a
sexy self-confidence that made a woman feel...well,
like a woman.

Impatient with herself, Rorie swung around and
faced her godmothers. They were still staring at the
door through which Phillip had just exited.

"Godmothers!" she exclaimed. "Don't you see
what's happening? You're letting that man's good
looks and flattery sway you. After all the offers you've
received—and very wisely refused—for that fertilizer
formula, how can you possibly make a split-second decision like this and sell it to Phillip Fairchild...of all
people!"

"You don't like him, do you, Aurora Dawn?"
Dahlia said with a contemplative frown. "That's very
strange. I never thought it would happen this way."

She turned to her sisters. "Don't you think it odd that she doesn't like him?"

"Why should it be so remarkable that I don't like him?" Rorie reasoned. "For heaven's sake, what's so special about him?"

"He's *the one,* Aurora," Daisy said, as if the answer was self-evident.

"Yes, he's *the one,*" Daffy repeated dreamily.

"What *are* you talking about?" Rorie pleaded, exasperated. "He's the one...*what?*"

Dahlia slid an expressive glance toward her sisters as if to say, *I'll handle this,* then said to Rorie, "He's the one we've been waiting for."

"The one you've been waiting for?" Rorie repeated, mystified.

"Yes," Dahlia continued. "The one who deserves to possess that which is most precious to us. Our—" she darted a glance toward her sisters "—fertilizer formula."

Rorie threw her hands in the air. "You trust him?"

Dahlia smiled broadly. "Implicitly."

"But you don't even know him," Rorie protested. "And I thought we agreed not to sell the formula to anyone. You know how dangerous it could be in the wrong hands."

"Yes, if a drug lord got hold of it, for instance," Daisy acknowledged with a nod, "he could grow huge crops of drug-bearing plants."

"Exactly," Rorie agreed emphatically. "Or he'd blow his head off trying. You know how combustible the fertilizer is. It has to be carefully handled. Even the three of you have had an accident or two with the stuff. Do you want your *darling* Phillip to blow his head off?"

"It isn't combustible till the final ingredient is added," Daffy pointed out. "And if one is wise, one does not add the final ingredient till the last possible moment." She looked sly. "Besides, I'm quite sure a man like Philip can handle a little explosive material...aren't you, girls?" She raised her brows at her sisters and they giggled appreciatively.

"And what about that final ingredient?" Rorie persisted, trying to ignore her godmothers' schoolgirlish behavior. "You've never told me what it is. Are you sure it's perfectly legal? Because if it isn't, and you've got rows of it growing out back in that jungle of a garden, you three sweet old things could find yourselves behind bars!"

The godmothers exchanged glances and broke into giggles again. "Oh, don't worry about *that*, Aurora," Daisy assured her. "The final ingredient won't land us in the slammer. It's not illegal or anything. It's just...well, *special*, and not accessible to the general public."

Rorie sat down and rubbed her temples. She could feel a headache coming on. "I still don't understand why you've suddenly decided to sell the formula to Phillip Fairchild. He's done nothing to prove himself worthy of receiving anything...*special*. I hear he's a user and a womanizer. I don't understand how you can trust him."

"He passed a very important test when he made it to our front door, Aurora," Dahlia explained, patting Rorie's knee affectionately. "He proved that he possesses all the necessary traits for handling fertilizer. He's patient, persistent, and sensitive."

"Sensitive?" Rorie repeated doubtfully.

"He recognized Dragon's sweet nature behind his

huge size and that frightening growl of his, didn't he? You must admit, Aurora dear, that only a sensitive man would have been able to look past all those teeth and make friends with our formidable watchdog."

"Or his greed made him take a foolish risk," Rorie grumbled. She dropped her head in her hands and stared gloomily at the carpet.

After a pause, during which Rorie was aware of her godmothers whispering to one another, Dahlia said, "Aurora, dearest, look at us, please."

Rorie looked up into the clear and untroubled eyes of her godmothers.

"If it will make you feel better about it, dear," Dahlia continued, "we'll give Phillip three more tests before we hand over the formula."

"Three more tests? What kinds of tests?"

"Tests that will further demonstrate whether or not Phillip has the necessary traits for handling women, er, I mean *fertilizer.* You know...patience, persistence and sensitivity."

Rorie looked suspiciously at Dahlia, wondering why she'd mixed up the words "women" and "fertilizer." Then she dismissed the blunder, acknowledging to herself that her godmothers' behavior had been stranger than usual since Phillip came on the scene.

Rorie considered the test idea and brightened. She couldn't imagine an in-control kind of guy like Phillip submitting himself to the whims of her godmothers just for the privilege of buying a fertilizer formula; although he certainly did seem interested and had been quite determined so far. And if he did agree to the tests, it was very likely he'd show his true colors before he was halfway through the first test. Then he'd be outta there!

The bottom line in this whole mess, of course, was that the formula belonged to her godmothers and it was theirs to do with as they pleased. In the end, Rorie could only give advice and leave the final decision up to them.

"Very well," she said, cautiously hopeful. "I'll invite Mr. Fairchild to come back into the parlor, you can tell him about your tests, and then we'll ask him what he wants to do."

PHILLIP HAD BEEN gazing out a back window at what looked to him like a South American forest! He wouldn't have believed it, but by the glow of a porch light, he could see that the backyard was even more lush, more fantastically green, and had more huge plants in it than the front yard!

He smiled to himself, amazed at his incredible good luck in discovering these quirky sisters with their magical green thumbs, and the even more magical fertilizer they'd developed in their "enchanted" greenhouse, as the two jealous ladies at the fair had called it. And for some reason Phillip couldn't quite fathom, they'd decided to sell *him* the fertilizer, when they'd adamantly refused to sell it to anyone else.

Phillip frowned. But...why? Why him? He wasn't vain and foolish enough to think that their quick decision had anything to do with his charm or his perfume. He'd only hoped to make small inroads into their confidence and friendship with such obvious ploys. No, there was something else behind the Farley sisters' reasoning. But what?

"Mr. Fairchild?"

Phillip turned and saw Rorie standing at the door. The lighting from the hallway behind her made a halo around her head. With her blond hair pulled straight back into a ponytail, accentuating her delicate bone structure and the creaminess of her complexion, he was struck again by the perfect beauty of her face. And the patent distrust in her eyes.

"Why don't you call me Phillip? Your godmothers do."

"My godmothers make friends easily," she replied stiffly. "I don't."

"What about male friends?" he couldn't resist asking.

"You must have noticed, Mr. Fairchild, how hard it is to get to my front door," she answered with sweet sarcasm. "The men aren't exactly beating it down."

"Maybe it isn't the jungle out front that's keeping the men away. Maybe they sense an invisible barricade."

"You're way out of line, Mr. Fairchild," Rorie snapped. "I just came in here to tell you that my godmothers are ready to talk to you now." She turned to lead the way, but he took two quick steps and caught her arm.

A jolt of awareness shot through him at the touch of her skin against his. Confused, his gaze sought hers. She looked just as shocked, just as troubled.

For a moment, neither of them moved or spoke a word. A dizzying sense of déjà vu swept over him. Rolling water, the sound of seagulls cawing, the rush and swirl of the tide, the sand beneath his bare feet, the salty breeze... Then it was gone.

"What do you want, Mr. Fairchild?" Rorie asked him in a cool voice, shrugging free of his grasp. She tried to act unaffected by it, but Phillip could tell something had happened to her, too, when he'd touched her.

He swallowed hard and composed himself. "I only wanted to make it clear to you, Rorie, that I have no intention of offering your godmothers anything but the most generous of deals."

"Money isn't everything," she said stiffly.

"But it sure as hell comes in handy now and then," he retorted. "This is a big house. It would cost a lot to put in air-conditioning, but I'm sure your godmothers would be far more comfortable in the summer with it installed. Social security doesn't go very far these days."

"I have an income, too," she informed him.

"What do you do?" He was really interested, and maybe it showed, because instead of telling him it was none of his business, she answered him in a civil voice.

"I have a small business."

He raised a brow. "We have something in common then. As you know, I'm in business, too."

"I hardly think our situations are similar," she said repressively. "I design and make wool sweaters. People get a basic idea of what I can do from an advertisement I run in several catalogues specializing in handmade clothing, but every sweater is personalized. It's slow and painstaking, but very rewarding. And each sweater goes for a bundle."

"You do all the work?"

"No, I have a few part-timers who do most of the knitting."

"It sounds seasonal, though. And that brings me back to the money issue. In exchange for their fertilizer formula, your godmothers would be financially comfortable for the rest of their lives. No...comfortable is too inadequate a word. They'd be rich." He paused and looked at her consideringly, then said something he knew would get her hackles up again. "Then you could quit worrying about them and get on with your own life."

"You're treading on thin ice again, Mr. Fairchild," she cautioned him in a cold voice. "*My* life is *my* business. As for the money issue, I never thought you'd try to swindle my godmothers. I wouldn't allow that to happen."

"Then why are you so suspicious of me?" he couldn't help asking. "Why do you dislike me so much?"

She met his questioning gaze with a veiled expression. "My godmothers must do what they think best, but you just don't seem like the kind of man I'd trust with *my* fertilizer formula."

And with that enigmatic statement, she turned to go, and Phillip had no choice but to follow.

Chapter Three

"That's all I have to do?" Phillip couldn't believe it. The three tests the Farley sisters were asking him to do seemed simple as pie. Except, perhaps, for the last one.

"I don't understand what you're up to, godmothers," Rorie fumed. "It seems to me that you've made it *impossible* for Mr. Fairchild to pass all three tests. You must know that he'll never convince me to go out on a date with him. *Never!*"

"If you think it's impossible for Phillip to win the right to buy the fertilizer formula, Aurora, then you ought to be happy," Dahlia calmly replied. "I don't know why you're in such a huff. You wouldn't have liked it if I'd made the tests easy, now would you?"

Rorie crossed her arms and scowled down at her godmothers, who were sitting like a regimented row of tulips on one of the sofas. "You should have left me completely out of it. I don't want to be one of Mr. Fairchild's tests. He'll only annoy me."

"Apparently I already annoy you," Phillip said dryly, enjoying the flush of anger on her cheeks and the way her beautiful blue eyes sparkled. "So what's the difference?"

"I don't want to be pegged by the paparazzi as one of your...*women*. I don't want my photo showing up on some gossip sheet."

"We can go somewhere private," he suggested innocently.

"Not likely!"

He shrugged. "Do you have any objection to the first two tests?"

"Only that they're too easy. Helping my godmothers in the garden for a day, and giving Dragon his semi-annual bath and taking him to the groomers to get his hair clipped, does not seem difficult enough for what's at stake."

"But you must admit that the last test, getting you to go out with me for an evening *and* bringing you back happy, is so hard it makes up for the first two."

"None of the three tests are easy," Daisy said, nodding sagely. "You just wait and see, Phillip. Besides, we picked these particular tests because in order to successfully complete them you must demonstrate patience, persistence and sensitivity. All important traits when—"

"Handling combustible fertilizer," Phillip finished for her. He grinned. "Yes, I know. They're important traits when dealing with women, too."

Rorie fixed her angry gaze on Phillip. "Now that he sees how futile his efforts would be to succeed at all three tests, Daisy, maybe Mr. Fairchild has changed his mind. Maybe he doesn't want the fertilizer formula that badly," she said with a toss of her head, the movement making her ponytail swing against her shoulder. Phillip fought the urge to reach out and give that silky-looking ponytail a tug, drawing Rorie close enough to kiss.

"Are you kidding?" he said. "I like a challenge."

And he wasn't just talking about winning the fertilizer formula. He was developing a strong interest in a certain female who designed sweaters. Was it just because she didn't like him? he wondered. Did he find her desirable because she presented a challenge? "Lack of persistence and patience has never been a shortcoming of mine," he finished.

"But what about sensitivity?" she inquired archly. "From what I've heard—" Rorie quickly clamped her lips together and looked away.

"What have you heard?" Phillip asked, arching an eyebrow. When she did not respond, he said, "So that's why you've taken such an instant dislike to me. You were prejudiced against me from the start. Someone's told you something about me—about something I've done—that you don't approve of."

He waited, but Rorie still did not answer. "Well, whatever it is," he continued, "it could be true, or it could be a complete lie. When you're in the limelight, even on a small scale, people like to talk about you. And the juicier the story the better. Then the press takes the rumors and flies with them. It sells papers. Tell me, Rorie," he urged. "Tell me what you've heard so I can either deny it or admit to it. If we clear the air, maybe we can start over and actually become friends."

"Now *that* would be lovely!" Daffy exclaimed, beaming at them both.

Rorie looked at Phillip suspiciously. He'd sounded sincere enough, and it was certainly true that people liked to talk about public figures and celebrities and sometimes made up stories about them. And the press, of course, couldn't always be believed.

But what reason did she have to doubt Kim? As if she'd badly needed a confidante, Kim had talked and talked during that three-day photo shoot, and Rorie had been a sympathetic listener…just like when they were kids. But because Kim hadn't given her permission to speak to anyone about her affair with Phillip, Rorie couldn't confront Phillip with what she knew.

Besides, his sincere act was probably just that, an act…and part of his strategy to get her to agree to go out with him so he could pass the third test.

"It's not important, Mr. Fairchild," she said.

"It is to me," Phillip retorted, and for a minute Rorie was tempted to believe him. The expression in his eyes seemed to confirm his tense interest in the topic. He looked almost…well, *hurt*. A doubt flickered in Rorie's mind. It wasn't like her to make hasty decisions about people. What if Kim had simply been mistaken about Phillip's feelings? What if—

The phone rang and the spell was broken. Thankful for being rescued from the famous Fairchild charm, Rorie hurried to pick up the receiver. But when she heard the voice on the other end, she was sorry she'd answered the phone at all. She spoke briefly and hung up.

"That was Delphinia," she said, her voice flat and gloomy. "She was calling from her cellular phone. She's outside right now and is waiting for someone to come out and escort her through the 'dreadful weeds.'"

Phillip watched the effect Rorie's announcement had on all the occupants of the room. At the mention of the name Delphinia, Dragon's ears had picked up. Now he was baring his teeth and snarling at the door, turning his head toward the Farley sisters from time to time as if begging them to let him out.

But the Farley sisters were too busy whispering among themselves to pay any attention to Dragon.

They didn't seem exactly frightened by the arrival of this person, but they were definitely agitated.

"Good God, who is this Delphinia?" Phillip asked Rorie.

"She's their youngest sister," Rorie answered, her eyes fixed thoughtfully on her godmothers.

"Ah, I should have known. The name is a dead give-away, isn't it? But why's everyone in a tizzy?" When Rorie did not answer, Phillip asked, "Is she your godmother, too?"

That question brought a response. Rorie's lips curled with grim amusement. "Oh, no. I'm sure Delphinia is no one's godmother. Now, please excuse me, I have to lock Dragon in the basement." She gave Phillip another rueful smile. "You see, Mr. Fairchild, be advised…we do have a dungeon."

Phillip stood back and watched as everyone prepared for the arrival of Delphinia. The Farley sisters stopped whispering among themselves and started setting out ashtrays—at least a dozen of them—on every available surface. And Rorie lured Dragon away from the door with a fat, foot-long sausage that had such a strong odor, Phillip could smell it clear across the room. Apparently Dragon couldn't be bribed with the usual puny hot dog.

Once the dog was safely jailed, Daffy admitted with a sigh to it being her turn to escort Delphinia through the yard, and she staunchly marched out the front door, clutching a flashlight, to do the dreaded deed.

Phillip couldn't wait to meet another Farley. He wondered if this one was as talented and as quirky as her sisters.

When Delphinia slunk into the room, Phillip was immediately convinced that the youngest Farley sister had inherited the family quirkness, all right…but in a scary sort of way. She was nothing like Dahlia, Daisy, and Daffy. Nothing at all.

Delphinia was tall and thin as a rail. And the black, sleeveless sheath, black hose, and black, sharp-toed, high heels she wore only accentuated her gauntness.

Her dyed hair was as black as her dress and was pulled into a sleek chignon. Dangling jet earrings hung from her long ears, and bracelets circled her emaciated arms.

Her face was…well, that part of her was hard to describe. It was obvious to Phillip that she'd had far too many cosmetic surgeries. Her paper-thin skin had been pulled so tightly behind her ears, she had the perpetual expression of someone sitting in the back of an open speedboat going one hundred miles an hour. Her cheeks were painfully prominent, her lips were artificially full, and her eyes were heavily made up with black liner and purple eye shadow.

If Phillip hadn't known it was June, he'd have sworn it was Halloween and someone had hired Morticia Addams to do a children's party.

She even had a lackey. A small man in a chauffeur's uniform followed Delphinia through the door. His ferretlike eyes darted about the room, then suddenly lighted on Phillip and widened with astonishment.

When she saw Phillip standing by the window with his arms crossed casually over his chest, Delphinia's reaction was identical to her servant's. Her expression changed from pinched disdain to an unflattering display of eye-bulging, jaw-dropping shock.

"You see, Delphinia," Daffy informed her with a self-righteous sniff, "I'm *not* losing my mind. We *do* have a visitor."

While everyone stared, Delphinia struggled to compose herself. Finally conjuring up a smile and an air of nonchalance, she took several long, floating steps across the room and extended her hand.

"How do you do?" Delphinia breathed throatily. "I'm Delphinia Devine. I believe we've met before, Mr. Fairchild."

Phillip stared down at Delphinia's hand and felt an instant aversion to taking it. The fingers were long and skinny, the nails impossibly elongated and painted bloodred...just like her lips.

Aware of Rorie's watchful gaze, Phillip forced himself to take Delphinia's hand. Her skin was cold and dry, and he barely repressed a shudder. "You say we've met before? I'm sorry. I don't recall..."

A piqued expression flitted briefly over Delphinia's face, but she soon recovered and drawled, "Perhaps you don't recall because when we were first introduced, I was known as Lady Bolregard. Sir William Bolregard was my second husband. It was at the opening of an African craft show at the High Museum of Art."

"Ah, yes. The High Museum of Art," Phillip murmured noncommittally. He couldn't for the life of him figure out why he *couldn't* remember such an over-the-top character as Delphinia Devine.

"I had no idea you were acquainted with my sisters," she continued, still holding fast to his hand. "They get out so infrequently and no one *ever* comes *here*. How did you manage to get through the weeds, pray tell? Did you bring a machete with you? Or perhaps you had a guide." She glanced in Aurora's direction and smiled cunningly.

"We met Phillip at the fair this morning," Dahlia said, stepping up to Delphinia and gently grasping her arm. "Please sit down, Delphinia, and we'll all have a nice chat."

Phillip was extremely grateful to Dahlia for diverting her baby sister. And he was very glad to get his hand back. He had begun to feel cornered.

Delphinia gave Dahlia a sneering smile and allowed herself to be guided to the sofa. After arranging herself in an elegant pose on the cushions, she snapped her fingers and her chauffeur hurried to her side, drew a silver cigarette holder from his inside jacket pocket, and flipped it open. Delphinia dug out a cigarette with her long nails and tucked it between her lips, drawing deeply as her servant lit it for her.

While Delphinia settled herself, the other three sisters chose seats on the adjacent sofa. Rorie continued to stand near the door, silent and sober-faced, leaning against the wall. She did not seem eager to be very close to Delphinia, and Phillip couldn't blame her. The woman gave him the creeps in a big way.

But since it would seem impolite if he continued to hover in the distance, he took his seat again near Delphinia. He had just sat down when a wonderful thought occurred to him. Since this was a family gathering, maybe he should leave!

He cleared his throat and leaned forward. "I feel as though I'm intruding," he began, smiling at Dahlia, Daisy, and Daffy. "We've settled our business, ladies, so maybe I should leave you to visit with your sister."

"Nonsense," Delphinia rasped, rising to her feet and pacing the rug in front of the sofas. She held her cigarette loosely between her fingers, tapping ashes in the general direction of the several ashtrays that were strewn about, but scattering most of them on the rug. "You're not intruding in the least," she insisted with a bright, menacing smile. "Besides, I'm incredibly curious as to what 'business' you have with my sweet, homebody sisters." She stopped pacing and stared down at Phillip, her eyes glittering.

By the way the Farley sisters were exchanging looks of dread, Phillip knew he'd probably been unwise in mentioning the fact that he'd conducted business with them. But what concern was that of Delphinia's? From the brusque and impersonal way she'd treated her sisters in the last few minutes, Phillip found it hard to believe that Delphinia was concerned about their welfare. She was probably just being nosy, and that was not reason enough, in his opinion, to demand private information.

Goaded, Phillip answered with a charming smile, "Sorry, Ms. Devine. I never discuss my business except with parties concerned in that business."

Delphinia's extravagantly arched, kohl-black brows lifted and her lips thinned to a grim line.

"Your sisters may feel free to explain the business that transpired between us, but that's their decision," he added with a good-natured shrug. "I really ought to be leav—"

"I don't mind telling you what's going on, Delphinia," Dahlia spoke up, jutting out her round chin and looking brave. "You're not going to like it, but you might as well hear it now."

Phillip was confused. Maybe Delphinia's curiosity about their business deal was more than mere nosiness. Was it possible that Delphinia wanted the fertilizer formula, too?

Phillip looked across the room at Rorie, and the expression on her face told all. Foul stuff was about to hit the fan.

"We're considering selling Phillip the fertilizer formula," Dahlia began, picking nervously at her flowery bodice. She darted a furtive glance at Delphinia, whose face seemed to have frozen into a hard, cold mask. She hurried on, "I know you've wanted to buy the formula for a long time, Delphinia, but you must understand that this decision has no bearing on our feelings for you. We will always, er, *love* you as our sister, but we've always felt very strongly that our fertilizer formula should only go to someone who has the, um, particular traits we feel are necessary for the successful management of such a unique, er, product."

Dahlia's explanation quavered to a halt. She peered anxiously at Delphinia and asked, "Are you very angry with us, dearest?"

The room was deathly still as everyone waited for the expected outburst. The only sounds were the creak and whir of the old fan, and Dragon's snarl and wheeze and an occasional loud thump as he nudged against the basement door.

Phillip was wondering if he'd made an implacable enemy for the rest of his life when Delphinia's tight-as-a-drum face stretched into a very scary smile.

"Nonsense, Dahlia," she said smoothly. "Why would I be angry? The formula was yours to do with as you pleased. But what do you mean you're 'considering' giving it to him? Are there conditions he must meet first?"

Visibly relieved by Delphinia's surprisingly calm reaction, Dahlia cheerfully explained their idea of testing Phillip to make sure he was the right person to whom they should sell the fertilizer. With that same fixed smile on her lips, Delphinia patiently listened to every detail. When Dahlia was through explaining everything, Delphinia remarked that the tests were "a quaint idea," then changed the subject.

Ten strained minutes later, after smoking several cigarettes and distributing ashes everywhere as she paced and posed, Delphinia left. On her way out, as Dahlia once more apologized for not selling the fertilizer formula to her, she said, "Don't say another word about it, Dahlia. After all, it wasn't that important to me. It's not as if I need the money." Then she laughed. Or maybe it was more of a cackle. Whatever it was, it gave Phillip the heebie-jeebies.

RORIE FIGURED that if Dragon and Delphinia hadn't scared Phillip away from their family for good, maybe there *was* something special about him. Or something terribly *wrong* with him....

"We'll see you bright and early tomorrow morning," Dahlia said as she and Daisy and Daffy crowded around Phillip at the door. Even Dragon, released from the basement, stood in the semicircle and looked as if he, too, was sorry Phillip was leaving.

"Bright and early," Phillip agreed.

"Be sure to wear your grubbies," Daisy added. "We get down and dirty in the garden, you know."

Phillip grinned, flashing those perfect white teeth of his and catching Rorie's eye over Daisy's shoulder. "I'm looking forward to it."

"Well, get a good night's sleep," Daffy advised. "It's already way past our bedtime." She yawned and delicately patted her mouth. "Aurora will guide you to the gate. Good night, Phillip!"

While Rorie had wanted to show him the door several times, she had never volunteered to guide Phillip to the gate. But the godmothers evidently had other ideas. Giving her no opportunity to argue, they instantly scurried away, waggling their plump fingers at Phillip as they climbed the stairs to their bedrooms.

Sighing resignedly, Rorie trudged into the parlor and found the flashlight Daffy had used to guide Delphinia through the yard. She picked it up off a table, turned around and bumped right into Phillip Fairchild's hard chest.

They both mumbled apologies and scooted away from each other.

"I didn't know you followed me—"

"I just wanted to tell you—"

Rorie could feel herself blushing. She averted her eyes and tucked a stray wisp of hair behind her ear. She didn't know why, but the accidental collision of her body against Phillip's had sent shock waves to every nerve in her system. *Pleasant* shock waves. She chalked it up to an instinctive biological reaction, because she definitely didn't like him as a person.

"You were saying?" he prompted politely.

Rorie looked up and was flustered when she realized how close to each other they were still standing. She took a step backward and only managed to stumble on one of her godmothers' old-fashioned claw-footed table legs. She wobbled and Phillip steadied her by grabbing her shoulders. The strength of his fingers as they pressed into her skin was disturbingly arousing.

"Are you okay?" he asked, a hint of laughter in his voice.

Rorie forced herself to look up at him one more time. "Of course I'm okay," she said, realizing she sounded defensive but unable to help herself. "You…you can let go of me now."

Those cool gray eyes of his looked different up

close. Or maybe it was the dim lighting of the parlor that made them appear suddenly warmer, darker. Kind of like a stormy sea.

The sea... Earlier, in the kitchen, when he'd caught her arm, she'd thought of the sea. She'd heard the waves lapping at the shore. She'd heard seagulls cawing, and felt sand beneath her bare feet. It was like a fuzzy, but very pleasant dream. But why on earth would Phillip Fairchild make her think of the sea?

As they continued to stare into each other's eyes, Phillip's hands slowly slid down Rorie's arms to her elbows...and then he released her. Despite her dislike of the man, Rorie felt strangely bereft when they were no longer physically connected. She fought the urge to touch him.

He smiled apologetically. "I'm sorry you have to guide me to the gate. I know you don't want to, but I'm afraid that if I try to find my way alone, I'll be wandering in that jungle all night."

"Well, you are supposed to be here bright and early tomorrow," she replied, forcing a breezy tone as she slipped past him and walked determinedly to the door. "You wouldn't have far to travel in the morning if you spent the night in the yard."

"That gives me an idea," she heard him say from close behind her, his deep voice sending unexpected chills down her spine. "Maybe I should just sack out on the couch?"

An image of Phillip in his skivvies, stretched out on the couch, flashed into her mind. Her breath caught and she swung around, saying emphatically, "Not a chance!" Then, by the amused look in his eyes, she realized he'd only been kidding.

Embarrassed and blushing again, she turned her back

to him and opened the door. Turning on the flashlight, she moved quickly down the walkway through the thick shrubbery and trees, following the convoluted trail to the gate.

Phillip wished Rorie wouldn't walk so fast. He decided that the Farleys' front yard could be quite romantic if a person was allowed to stroll down the walkway instead of speeding down it like a runaway train.

Moonlight filtered through the trees and fell on Rorie's hair and shoulders. For a hardened bachelor, Phillip found the swing of her demure ponytail surprisingly arousing.

The air was moist and warm. The crickets were singing. The sweet scent of flowers was intoxicating. Dizzying. The setting was perfect. So was the girl. But the perfect girl in the perfect setting apparently would rather kiss a frog than kiss the Perfume Prince.

How was he ever going to get her to go out with him? he wondered. It would be a challenge…but definitely one he was going to enjoy.

And not just because he wanted to pass the test and earn the rights to the fertilizer formula. He was interested in the woman, too.

FROM THE SMOKE-FILLED back seat of her Rolls-Royce, Delphinia watched Phillip and Rorie as they stood and exchanged brief words at the gate. But when Rorie disappeared into that horrid maze of weeds her sisters called a front yard, Phillip Fairchild gazed after her like a lovesick fool.

"It's as bad as I feared, Simon," Delphinia whispered hoarsely. "He likes her. As he has a dreadful reputation with women, the infatuation may not last for long, but for now…he definitely likes her."

"So it seems, madam," Simon agreed.

"And that means those stupid sisters of mine like *him*," Delphinia sneered. "Even if he doesn't pass their imbecilic tests, we've got trouble on our hands. As long as he shows a romantic interest in their sweet Briar Rose, they'll find a reason to keep him around, and eventually he'll trick them into giving him the formula."

"Then you perceive it as hopeless, madam?" Simon suggested.

"No, you moron," she snarled. "That formula is mine, do you hear me? Mine!"

"Yes, madam," Simon said, his voice barely above a whisper.

There was a long pause as Delphinia broodingly watched Phillip step into his white Mercedes and drive away. Then she barked, "Aren't you going to ask me what I propose to do to foil Fairchild's conniving plot?"

"Er…what do you propose to do, madam?" Simon obediently inquired.

"It's very simple, Simon. I plan to be twice as conniving as he is," she answered with a self-satisfied smirk. She took a long draw on her cigarette, then, along with the smoke, she breathed out the ominous words, "Phillip Fairchild has no idea what he's up against."

"No, madam," Simon agreed solemnly. "No idea whatsoever."

Chapter Four

Rorie had been trying unsuccessfully for over an hour to work on a new sweater design. She'd finally given up and had decided to do some spinning instead. But for the last ten minutes, she'd simply stood by the spinning wheel, absentmindedly trailing her fingers over the smooth wood. A small, rueful smile tilted her lips. She wondered what Phillip Fairchild would think if he knew she actually spun the wool for the sweaters she designed and marketed.

He'd probably think she was nuts, she decided. With today's technology, nobody needed to go to so much trouble for a single piece of clothing. But it would take a much more sensitive man than Phillip Fairchild to appreciate her feelings about actually creating something entirely from scratch. It was an art. Besides, spinning was such a soothing, rhythmic activity. She did some of her best thinking while she was spinning.

And this morning, while she waited for the phone to ring, expecting Phillip to call from his cellular to ask for an escort to the front door, she definitely needed to do some thinking. She needed to ask herself why she'd tossed and turned all night, and, during her brief fits of slumber, why she'd dreamed about Phillip.

In her dream, she and Phillip had been at the beach, feeding seagulls, running through the shallow surf, laughing...kissing. Rorie pressed her cool hands against her warm cheeks. Oh, those kisses...

When the doorbell chimed, Rorie nearly jumped out of her skin. She hurried to the window and looked straight down at the top of Phillip's head, the dark hair gleaming in the bright morning sunshine. Sitting next to him, of course, was Dragon.

"All right, Fairchild, I'm impressed," she mumbled to herself as she turned and left the room. "You're smart. You found your way to the front door. But that doesn't make up for being a first-class cad."

Since Rorie's godmothers were outside in the back-yard already, she had no choice but to answer the door. But, as she quickly descended the stairs, she wondered about her choice of clothing that morning. What had possessed her to put on a skirt and blouse, and to wear her hair down?

In the entry hall, Rorie had to stop for a minute before opening the door. Pressing her palm flat against her midsection, she forced herself to take a couple of deep, calming breaths.

"What's the matter with me?" she whispered to her-self. "After all, he's just a pretty face."

Finally she opened the door, and admitted to herself that Phillip Fairchild was more than a pretty face. He also had a body to die for. Standing in a relaxed pose, with one hand resting on Dragon's furry neck, and with a small package tucked under the opposite arm, he flashed a dazzling smile.

"Hi," he said, but Rorie could only gulp nervously. Phillip was devastating in a suit, but in jean shorts, a tucked-in T-shirt and a pair of athletic shoes, he had the earthy sexiness of the boy next door—the kind of guy that as a young girl you had a killer crush on; the older brother of your best friend who took off his shirt to mow the lawn, then sweated till his chest glistened; the forbidden fruit of your wonder years.

Rorie's gaze wandered uncontrollably over Phillip's taut physique, taking in the broad shoulders, the smooth contours of his chest, the trim waist and narrow hips, and the muscular legs.

Oh, my...

"Is this bright and early enough?" Phillip inquired, jarring Rorie out of her reverie.

She felt herself blush as she looked into Phillip's teasing gray eyes. Caught lusting after her enemy in the fertilizer war, Rorie was furious with herself. Pushing out her chin in a belligerent pose, she retorted, "My godmothers have been working outside for nearly two hours already."

Phillip raised a brow and crooked his elbow to glance at his watch. Rorie couldn't help but admire his tan, smoothly muscled arm, lightly dusted with dark hair. "It's only eight o'clock. Besides, I have to drive thirty minutes to get here, you know."

"Save your explanations, Mr. Fairchild," Rorie advised him. "It's my godmothers you need to impress, not me."

"I gather you think it would be a pretty hopeless endeavor to try to impress you, anyway," he said wryly.

"That's right. And you'd be saving yourself a lot of time and trouble if you'd come to the same conclusion. Why work so hard at the first two tests, then fail miserably at the third? You know you'll never get me to go out with you."

"I choose to be more optimistic than that," he replied cheerfully. "Dragon didn't like me at first, and now we're best friends." He ruffled Dragon's hair and got an adoring look in return. "He was even waiting for me at the gate this morning. I was wondering if I'd be able to find my way alone, but as it turns out, I had nothing to worry about. It was as though he was expecting me."

Rorie frowned at Dragon, suppressing the urge to call the dog a traitor, but the pet that was previously devoted to her seemed oblivious to her disapproval. He was too busy being devoted to his new idol, the Perfume Prince.

"This package came for Dahlia," Phillip said, holding out the small brown box he'd had tucked against his side.

Rorie took the box and frowned down at it. "For Dahlia? How'd you get it?"

"A delivery van pulled up just as I got out of my car. The guy asked me if I was going inside, and when I said yes, he shoved it at me."

"There's no return address," she mused, examining the package. "But it must be some seeds she ordered, or something to do with gardening. She's always trying new plants and garden tools. But the guy usually leaves our packages by the mailbox, and he's never come this early before."

"If you want, I'll take the package out to her," he suggested pointedly. "You're not trying to sabotage my chances on the first test by keeping me standing at the door all morning, are you? That wouldn't be fair, Rorie."

"Certainly not," she replied coolly, setting the box on a nearby table and stepping aside so Phillip could pass through. "I don't need to resort to sabotage. I'm sure you'll blow this gig all by yourself, Fairchild."

Phillip caught a whiff of Rorie's perfume as he passed by. Having purposely left behind the bottle she'd refused to accept as a gift yesterday, he was hoping she'd be wearing Tears of Joy. She wasn't. But he couldn't help but feel she was not as completely repulsed by him as she pretended to be. After all, she'd certainly put on an outfit that morning that was pleasing to the male eye. He'd like to think he had something to do with her choice of attire since he was probably the only man that had been in the house in years... except for Delphinia's chauffeur, of course. But that twitchy little lackey didn't count.

As Phillip followed her down the hall and through the kitchen, the gauzy, pastel-floral skirt she wore swayed back and forth. It was long and full, floating several inches past her knee, which only made the view of her trim, bare calves and ankles all the more provocative. She wore sandals, and her toenails were painted a pale pink. The peasant blouse she wore was a thin white cotton, the wide, dipping neckline showing off her pretty shoulders.

If pressed to explain her ultrafeminine outfit, Rorie could certainly claim that the materials were cool and comfortable and very appropriate for the exceptionally hot day that had been forecast that morning on the news. But Phillip couldn't help but hope that she—perhaps unconsciously—had dressed to be alluring. After all, if she was trying to defeat the heat, why was she wearing that glorious hair of hers down?

Stepping outside through the open back door, Phillip was struck anew by the incredible lushness of the vegetation that grew on the Farley property. In the morning sunshine, it almost hurt his eyes to look at the bright greens and various vibrant colors of the flowers that blossomed everywhere. He cupped his hand over his brow and squinted.

"You should have brought sunglasses," Rorie remarked unsympathetically, guiding him down a narrow path through towering sunflowers.

"I was in such a hurry this morning, I guess I left them at home," he admitted.

"Well, they won't do you much good there, will they?"

"Frankly, it never occurred to me that I'd need them for gardening, anyway." Then an alarming thought occurred to Phillip. "I should have brought bug repellent, shouldn't I? I've noticed that you have lots of bugs." And bees. Damn. He was allergic to beestings.

"Like you said, we've got lots of bugs. And, like everything else on the premises, they grow pretty darn big." She smiled smugly over her shoulder at him, apparently hoping for a nervous reaction. He had no intention of obliging her.

"I'm not worried," Phillip assured her, although that was a flat lie. Ants and mosquitoes didn't worry him...but bees did. The few times he'd been stung by bees had been very painful, unpleasant experiences. Fortunately the allergic reaction to the sting was always localized. He wasn't one of those unlucky people who swelled up like a Macy's Parade balloon or quit breathing and keeled over in a dead faint.

"Well, there really isn't any reason to be worried, anyway," she finally admitted with a rueful smile. "The bugs in my godmothers' garden are too fat and happy to bother anyone, even an outsider like you...more's the pity."

Phillip grinned and shook his head. She was a hard little cookie all right, but he had a sneaking suspicion that, like an Oreo, she had a soft, sweet center.

Finally, the path opened up to a small square of corn on one side and tomatoes on the other. It was only early June, but there were already fat, ripening tomatoes on the vines, and the cornstalks were four feet high.

Bending over the rich soil beneath the corn stalks were the Farley sisters, wearing baggy, flower-sprigged pedal pushers and cotton blouses. They also wore high-top sneakers and hats with tinted visors to block out some of the sun...or to make a fashion statement, he wasn't sure which.

"Phillip!" exclaimed Daisy, who was the first to spot him. "I'm so glad you're here!"

Daffy and Dahlia shouted similar greetings and the three sisters crowded around their favored visitor, unintentionally forcing Rorie to step back for fear of getting trounced on. Even Dragon, who had followed them from the house, warily retreated several feet away from Prince Phillip and his court.

Rorie folded her arms and watched for a minute, then began walking back to the house. She called softly to Dragon to follow her, but he only gave her a brief, distracted look before turning his worshipful gaze back to Phillip. With a resigned shake of her head and a grim smile, Rorie continued on by herself.

When a pause in the conversation finally allowed Phillip to look around for Rorie, he was disappointed to find that she'd left without a parting word...or even an insult. Dahlia seemed uncannily aware of his thoughts, because she leaned close and whispered, "Don't worry. She'll be back. She makes our lunch and eats with us in the gazebo."

Phillip tried to look only politely interested in this information, but he suspected that Dahlia—who seemed the sharpest of the three sisters—knew his interest in Rorie was much more than merely polite.

"So, what do you want me to do first?" he inquired enthusiastically, rubbing his hands together as if he'd waited all his life to get dirt under his manicured nails.

"Today we'll mostly do weeding. First we'll finish the corn patch, then we'll—" Dahlia stopped abruptly and frowned up at Phillip. "Didn't you bring a hat and sunglasses? How about sunscreen?"

Phillip chuckled and waved his hand dismissively. "I've already got a tan, Dahlia. I won't burn. I play golf and tennis several times a week, and I never wear a hat."

"It's going to be very hot today, Phillip, and this kind of strenuous work can really be exhausting if you're not used to it."

Phillip thought Dahlia was exaggerating. How could gardening possibly be as strenuous as tennis and golf? And if three old ladies could tolerate the work and the heat, certainly a thirty-three-year-old man in perfect health could, too.

"I think I'll be all right, Dahlia," Phillip said, trying not to sound condescending. But by her shrewd look, he wasn't sure he'd succeeded. "Now, let's get started, shall we, ladies?"

AT EXACTLY twelve noon, Rorie walked down the sunflower path toting a large basket filled with food. Tucked under her arm was the small box that had been delivered for Dahlia. She also carried an enormous thermos full of iced tea.

She'd had to force herself to stay away from the

backyard all morning, trying to keep busy in the house, but dying of curiosity about how Phillip was doing at his first test. She couldn't even spin to while away the dragging hours, because it was too hot in the turret to tolerate being in there for any reason...and it was getting hotter by the moment.

They *could* use air-conditioning, she conceded, remembering Phillip's remark from last night. But *she* was actually the one that suffered from the heat, not her godmothers. They had some kind of genetic tolerance for it. Like the flowers they planted and nurtured, the sunshine gave them life and vitality.

Rorie walked past the corn and tomato patches and several other neat squares of flourishing plants, then moved further on through a meandering garden of perennial flowers and shade trees. This was her favorite part of the yard. It seemed like an enchanted forest from a fairy tale...so lush and fragrant and cool. The birds loved it there, too, and since she always brought bread to feed them, they had already begun to flock around her as she made her way along the cobbled walkway.

At the very end of the deep yard was the gazebo—the coolest spot on the property. She and her godmothers ate a quiet, pleasant lunch there quite frequently in the warm months of the year. Then, afterward, the godmothers went back to their gardening and Rorie went back to her work in the turret.

Only today they'd have an extra guest...a man who was used to charming women over wine and dinner. Was he being charming now, she wondered? So charming that he'd convinced her godmothers that the three tests were unnecessary?

Her anxiety rising like a geyser, Rorie quickened her

step. She rounded a shrub and stopped in her tracks, staring at the sight of a half-naked man sitting on the steps of the gazebo, soaking his head with a garden hose and looking as exhausted as if he'd just finished climbing Mount Everest. Dragon sat next to him, occasionally lapping at the stream of water coming from the hose whenever Phillip pointed it his way.

Evidently hearing her footsteps, Phillip looked up and smiled sheepishly. His wet hair hung over his forehead in plump, shiny waves. Rorie tried hard not to stare at his chest, but it was almost impossible. His chest was so very…nice.

"Hi," he said. "I hope you've got food in that basket."

Rorie couldn't help but smirk. "Done in?"

His eyes glinted. "Only temporarily. I always recover quickly."

Her smirk quavered a little at the corners. She looked away. "Where are my godmothers?"

"Your indefatigable godmothers are finishing weeding the cantaloupe patch. Those damned weeds have roots that—"

"Reach to China?" Rorie finished for him. "I know. The fertilizer is good for the regular plants *and* the weeds."

"I'll have to figure out a way to change that before I start marketing the stuff," he mused, shutting the valve off and throwing the hose aside, then gazing thoughtfully into space.

"Pretty sure of yourself, aren't you?" Rorie snapped, annoyed by his unshakable confidence. "You look like you've just run a marathon. What makes you think you're even going to pass the first test?"

"Your godmothers didn't say I had to be as good as

they are at this," he informed her, an irritable edge creeping into his voice. "They only said I had to stick it out for a day. And, for crying out loud, Rorie, cut me a little slack, will you? It's damn hot. And your godmothers were right when they said gardening was strenuous. I'll never doubt another thing they tell me."

Rorie did not reply. She lifted her nose and walked past him into the gazebo, shook out a flowered table-cloth, placed it precisely on the round picnic table, then began to set out bright yellow paper plates. As she worked, she was all too aware of Phillip Fairchild's watchful eye. If he put his shirt back on, it might be possible to ignore him. But with it off...

Phillip enjoyed watching Rorie. It was obvious that his intense scrutiny made her nervous...and he enjoyed that, too. He could sit here for hours, just watching her. Only trouble was, he was sure there'd come a time when just looking at her wouldn't be enough.

"Feeling better, Phillip?" chirped Dahlia as she came briskly around the shrub with her two sisters right behind her. None of them looked the least bit tired or hot.

"Yes, much better," he told her, rising to his feet and sliding a meaningful glance Rorie's way. "And once I eat a little something, I'm sure I'll be as good as new."

"You did wonderfully, Phillip," Daisy assured him, washing her hands with water from the house. "Especially for a first-timer at this sort of work."

"Yes, it's so nice to have a big, strong man around to help out," Daffy added with an approving smile as she took her turn with the hose. Her gaze drifted to Rorie, who was silently arranging food on the table. "Did you get some spinning done, dear?" she called.

"Spinning?" Phillip repeated, looking curiously at Rorie.

Rorie threw Daffy what Phillip could only construe as a warning glance and said nothing. By Daffy's confused and troubled look, Phillip could tell that she'd brought up a topic that Rorie did not want openly discussed. At least, she didn't want it discussed around *him*.

Hmmm, he thought. *Spinning? As on a spinning wheel?*

"I hope you packed plenty of food, Aurora, dear," Dahlia commented brightly, seeming determined to change the subject. She climbed the steps of the gazebo and stood beside Rorie. "I'm sure Phillip has worked up quite an appetite."

"I always bring plenty of food," Rorie mumbled in a grudging tone, her fall of hair nearly hiding her face from view. "I also brought a package that was delivered for you this morning, Dahlia. Why don't you open it while I pour the iced tea?"

Dahlia picked up the small package that Rorie had set in the middle of the table and looked it over. "I wonder what it is? I sent for some peony seeds, but that was just three days ago. I'm not expecting anything else. And, look, the package appears to have been damaged!"

Phillip, along with everyone else, peered over Dahlia's shoulder. Even Dragon nudged his large body close to sniff at the three pencil-point-size holes in the bottom of the package.

"Well, open it, sister," Daisy advised. "That's the only way you're going to find out what it is."

Dahlia shrugged and tore off the brown paper, cut the mailing tape with her fingernail, then removed the lid of the cardboard box. She immediately jumped back with a loud gasp when three large bees flew out and began to buzz wildly around the gazebo.

"Oh, my goodness!" squealed Daisy, ducking a dive-bombing bee. "Who would have sent you *those?*"

"They're not our kind of bees, are they, Dahlia?" Daffy exclaimed, taking off one of her shoes and holding it like a weapon.

"No, I believe they're those nasty African bees," Dahlia confirmed. "They're stingers!"

This was not good news for Phillip, who was standing at the edge of the gazebo next to Rorie. They both remained perfectly still as the bees continued to dip and dive around them. Having been boxed up for several hours, the bees were evidently pretty mad. Phillip knew that African bees weren't exactly known for being good-natured, anyway, and they would just become further agitated if they swatted at them. And with the house so far away, making a run for it didn't seem like a good idea, either.

Phillip figured their only chance to avoid being attacked was to stand still and hope the bees would eventually be lured away by the incredible flowers just a puddle jump away.

Trouble was, Dragon seemed challenged by the bees and was chasing and snapping at them, obviously making them angrier than ever. Phillip knew it would be fruitless to attempt to constrain the huge dog and would, at the same time, make him a moving target himself.

"Sit, Dragon!" he ordered.

"Yes, Dragon, *sit*," Dahlia hissed between her teeth.

Dragon finally obeyed, plopping himself down right

next to Phillip. This would have been a fine plan if
only Dragon had remained motionless. Two bees had
buzzed off, but one bee remained...a bee that seemed
especially ticked off at Dragon for his inhospitable con-
duct. Phillip felt droplets of nervous sweat collect on
his upper lip as the buzzing insect continued to circle
and swoop around him and his canine companion.

"Just remain as you are," Dahlia quietly advised
them all, but with an especially expressive look at Phillip. "Movement will just draw the bees' attention. It's
their nature, you know, to attack."

Phillip wanted to say that he was pretty sure he and
his hairy friend had already drawn the bees' attention,
but he refrained from even that small amount of movement.

His restraint was all for nothing, however, because
Dragon, goaded beyond endurance, suddenly went into
a barking frenzy. One of the bees, too, had apparently
had enough and dove in for the attack. But instead of
attacking Dragon, the agitated insect headed straight
for Phillip...who was perhaps an easier, less hairy target...and stung him right through his jean shorts on the
right buttock.

It happened so fast, Phillip had no time to react. All
he knew was that suddenly his butt was on fire. "I
don't believe this," he muttered in numb resignation.

"Oh no, Phillip, you haven't been stung, have you?"
Dahlia cried, as she and Daisy and Daffy rushed over.

"Do you even have to ask, Dahlia?" Rorie inquired.
"Just look at his face."

Yes, the fact that he'd been stung was evident in
Phillip's expression. Rorie could tell he was trying hard
not to show it, but from the sudden waxiness of his

complexion and by the way he was clenching his jaw, she knew he was in considerable pain.

"You aren't going to faint, are you?" Dahlia quavered, grabbing his arm.

"No, I won't faint."

"How do you know?"

"I've been stung before."

"But I'll bet you've never been stung by an *African* bee," Daisy interjected ominously. "You look very ill, Phillip."

"I'm allergic to beestings, but the reaction is localized. Hives, swelling, *pain.*"

"Still, you'd better sit down and put your head between your knees."

"I assure you, Dahlia," Phillip said through clenched teeth, "I don't feel the slightest urge to faint. Besides, I *can't* sit down. I think the stinger's still in there."

"We'd better get you to the house," Dahlia said fretfully, tugging at his arm. She turned and peered into his face. "Or would you rather go to the hospital?"

"No. Absolutely not," Phillip said firmly. "The paparazzi would be on me like ticks on a dog. By tomorrow morning my rear end would be on the front page of every rag around."

Rorie knew it was quite painful to be stung by a bee, and she was very much in sympathy with Phillip…but she was having a hard time holding back the giggles. Her mouth kept wanting to turn up at the corners. Her godmothers crowded around Phillip as they returned to the house, but she hung back, afraid someone would see her smiling.

But someone did. And that someone was Phillip.

"You think it's pretty funny, don't you?" he said

wryly, peering at her over his shoulder as he walked stiffly and slowly back to the house.

She widened her eyes and bit her lip, trying to compose herself. "Oh, not at all, Phillip," she lied, gulping down a laugh.

Then he surprised her by smiling sheepishly and saying, "Well, *I* do. This is the most ridiculous situation I've ever been in. You have my permission to laugh, Rorie. It would probably make us *all* feel better to let loose with a good laugh."

And they did. Even Phillip laughed. It was partly just a release of tension, because no one was really happy about Phillip's predicament—not even Rorie— but the idea of the Perfume Prince being unceremoniously stung on the buttocks *was* kind of comical.

Wiping her brimming eyes as they entered the house, Rorie had to admit that she admired a man who could laugh at himself. Especially when he was in pain. But she didn't want to admire Phillip, so the idea that she possibly *could* admire him sobered her up pretty fast.

"Let's put you in here, Phillip," Dahlia said, still holding on to his arm as if he might keel over any minute as she led him down the hall to their downstairs guest bedroom. Daisy and Daffy followed closely behind, but Rorie hung back again, worried now about how they were going to take care of their patient.

If he was going to go into shock, he would have done so by now, so she was comfortable with Phillip's decision not to go to the hospital, and completely understood him not wanting his mishap reported in the gossip sheets. An antihistamine would make the swelling go down, but the stinger still needed to be removed and the wound doctored. Who was going to do *that?*

"Take off your shorts and lie down on your stomach

on the bed,'' Rorie could hear Dahlia instructing Phillip, and Rorie's own stomach did a flip-flop. It was disturbing enough having a *half*-naked Phillip around. Now he was going to be completely naked.

Dahlia closed the door and she and Daisy and Daffy came down the hall, all of them wearing serious faces. Rorie followed them into the kitchen and they huddled together for a little conference.

"I suggest we draw straws,'' Dahlia said.

"You mean to see who has to remove the stinger?'' Rorie inquired.

Dahlia smiled. "No, my dear. To see who *gets* to remove the stinger.''

"Dahlia!'' Rorie exclaimed, surprised by the sly glint in her godmother's eye.

"Aurora, dear,'' Dahlia said demurely, "I may be old, but I'm not dead!''

Chapter Five

Loaded down with the necessary supplies to tend to a beesting, Rorie stood outside the closed door of the guest bedroom with the distinct impression she'd been tricked. She glanced down the hall and met the innocent gazes of her godmothers, who were encouraging her with coaxing little movements of their hands.

Rorie sighed resignedly and nudged aside Dragon, who had been sitting by the door with a woeful expression on his shaggy face ever since Phillip had been brought inside. She turned the knob and opened the door a couple of inches. "Are you decent?" she called through the crack.

A muffled voice replied, "That depends.... Is that a morals question?"

"Very funny, Fairchild," Rorie replied drolly. "Just tell me, are you covered or not?"

"Are you coming in?"

She gave a huff of exasperation. "If you give me the right answer to my question, I'll come inside the room. I repeat, are you covered or not?"

There was a pause. "Well, I want you to come in, so what's the right answer? Do you *want* me to be covered?"

"Listen, Fairchild," Rorie said sternly, throwing her amused godmothers a beleaguered look. "If you can kid around like that, you're obviously not in much pain. So maybe I'll just take my antihistamine and my tweezers and find some other injured party to nurse back to health."

"Hey, I'll be good," he promised. "I never could resist a woman with tweezers."

"Okay," she said, trying very hard to be patient. "I'll ask you one more time. Are you covered?"

"As much as I can bear to be," he said. "It's hot in here and parts of me itch like hell."

Rorie figured that was the most satisfactory answer she was going to get, so she cautiously opened the door a few more inches and peered around it into the dim room. Phillip lay on his stomach, a thin sheet pulled up to the dip of his lower back, and one long, bare leg crooked at the knee and sticking out of the sheet on the side nearest the edge of the bed. His head rested on a pillow, and his hair was drying into an attractive tumble of waves. He looked like a model posing for a beefcake calendar.

When Phillip flashed a lazy grin, Rorie's heart started hammering and her throat went dry. How on earth had she gotten herself into such a predicament?

"'Come in,' said the spider to the fly," Phillip taunted her.

"Will you please can the immature comments, Fairchild?" Rorie said tartly as she came into the room with Dragon right behind her. She made sure she left the door wide open behind her, then flicked on the overhead light. "Don't you know it's bad policy to irritate your nurse? Didn't you see *One Flew Over the Cuckoo's Nest*?"

"Why *are* you my nurse?" Phillip inquired, his brows drawing together. "Not that I'm complaining, but I would have thought you'd be the last one to volunteer."

Avoiding looking at her patient, Rorie set her supplies down on the nightstand and began to unscrew the bottle of liquid antihistamine. "You're right about that. I *would* be the last one to volunteer."

"Then how…"

"We drew straws." She poured him a tablespoon of the purple liquid.

He grinned. "And you won?"

"I lost!" she shook her head disbelievingly. "Somehow or other, I lost. Now shut up and take your medicine."

He eyed the spoon. "I don't know if I can swallow lying down like this."

"Then sit up," she said briskly.

"I can't sit up. Remember, the stinger's still lodged in my behind? I'd have to *stand* up."

"That won't be necessary," she said quickly. She was scared to death he'd lose his sheet in the process. "I'm sure you can manage to swallow this lying down."

"If you say so, Nurse Ratched," he said with feigned meekness. "But you'll have to come down to my level."

"Heaven forbid *that* should ever happen," she retorted dryly, leaning down to spoon the medicine carefully into Phillip's open mouth. Their faces were close together and their gazes met over the spoon. His eyes danced with mischief. She glared back at him.

After she'd straightened up and was replacing the cap on the antihistamine bottle, he said, "I wish you'd tell me why you dislike me so much. I know it's got to be because someone has told you something negative, or you've heard something through the grapevine. Why don't you just spill it, Rorie?''

"I don't know what you're talking about, Fairchild," she said coolly, picking up the tweezers.

"Yes, you do. You just won't—''

"If you know what's good for you, you won't continue to annoy me with this topic." She pinched the tweezers together several times and raised her brows in a warning gesture. "My hands are not very steady when I'm annoyed.''

"Fine," he said with a shrug. "Be that way.''

Rorie was about to say something back, but she realized that their conversation had deteriorated into an adolescent-sounding squabble. Instead, she pulled a chair near the bed and sat down.

"Wouldn't it be easier if you sat on the bed?" Phillip suggested, peering over his broad, tanned shoulder.

He was right, but Rorie didn't want to admit it. She didn't want to sit on the same bed that Phillip lay on completely naked. It was bad enough having to look at him, she didn't want to take the chance of actually brushing up against his bare, muscular thigh...or any other part of his body, for that matter.

"I think I can manage this way," she muttered, leaning over the bed. "But it will be easier if you tuck your leg under the sheet and lie perfectly flat on the bed.''

He obliged, and Rorie let out a sigh of relief to see that gorgeous leg disappear from view. But the worst was still to come. She swallowed nervously as her gaze shifted to the hard mound under the sheet that was Phillip Fairchild's fanny.

"Which...er...side is the sting on?" she inquired.

"All you have to do is pull down the sheet and you'll see for yourself," Phillip drawled. "It's bound to be as red as a beet by now."

"I only want to expose the injured side, Fairchild," Rorie explained testily. "I'm trying to save you a little embarrassment."

"I think you're trying to save *yourself* a little embarrassment," Phillip replied. "It's the right...er... cheek that was stung."

Rorie nodded and grimly set about her task. She decided that if doctors and nurses could be objective about this sort of thing, so could she. Pretending to be as cool as a cucumber, but feeling even warmer than the hot day outside could be blamed for, Rorie pulled down the sheet on the right side and exposed the injured area.

Suddenly it was easy for Rorie to forget for a while about her own embarrassment and her own attraction to Phillip's very sexy, very naked body. She was filled with sympathy! The poor man must be in terrible pain. The whole area around the sting was blotchy with hives.

Forgetting how much she disliked Phillip Fairchild, she quickly and carefully removed the stinger, then patted the tender area with a cotton ball soaked in alcohol. She knew that when the antihistamine kicked in, the hives and the itching would improve, but for now he was just going to have to tough it out.

"Thanks," he said, as she covered him again and stood up, carefully avoiding his eyes. "How soon do you think I can put my pants on?"

She frowned. "Comfortably?"

"Well, reasonably comfortable would be nice."

"I'd say you should probably stay where you are the

rest of the afternoon. Anyway, that hefty dose of antihistamine I gave you will make you sleepy. Why don't you take a nap?''

"No chance, Rorie. I'm not forfeiting this test just because I've got a sore rear.'' He pushed up on an elbow and glowered at her. "You didn't plan this, did you?''

"Do you honestly think I'd put my godmothers in danger by releasing killer bees in their garden?'' she asked angrily.

"No, I'm not accusing you of that,'' he clarified. "But it just seems darn convenient that I'm laid up like this.''

"Well, if you think you've been sabotaged, Fairchild, maybe while you're lying there with nothing to do, you should mentally review your list of enemies.''

"What makes you think I've got a *list* of enemies, for crying out loud!''

"Well, *we* sure don't.''

"I don't know about that. Have you considered that it might be those jealous women at the fair who sent Dahlia the bees?''

Rorie grudgingly admitted he had a point. Frustration that had built up over several years of competing against the Farley sisters in the horticultural show might have made some poor, sun-dazed gardener snap.

"I don't know who sent the bees,'' she said. "But if you're looking for someone to blame for your predicament, blame that person, not me.''

He looked at her consideringly for a moment, then covered his mouth as he yawned. "Are you sure you had to give me such a big dose of antihistamine?''

"I'm sure,'' she answered. "In fact, when that one

wears off, you'll need some more. Now I'll just leave you so you can get some—"

"I'm not resting, Rorie," Phillip said stubbornly, scooting on his side toward the edge of the bed. "If I have to drink an entire pot of coffee to keep me awake, I'm going to finish out this day with your godmothers in the garden. I refuse to lose the chance to buy the fertilizer formula just because some dumb bee—"

"You haven't lost your chance, Phillip," came Dahlia's voice from the door. Dragon, who had been watching his idol undergo minor surgery from just inside the door, moved aside as Dahlia came to stand at the foot of the bed. "You did enough work this morning to prove you've got pluck. The girls and I are in complete agreement that you passed our first test with flying colors."

"Shouldn't he at least have to work in the garden a half day tomorrow?" Rorie objected. With only one more test to pass before the test that personally involved her, Rorie was beginning to feel panicky. Of course, he'd never succeed in convincing her to go out on a date with him, but she wasn't looking forward to the tricks he'd employ to try to change her mind.

"No, I think he's done enough," Dahlia said with a satisfied nod as she beamed at Phillip.

And Rorie couldn't argue. This wasn't her test, nor was it her fertilizer formula.

"Thanks, Dahlia," Phillip said sleepily. "I'm getting off pretty easy, but I'm too tired to argue with you. I think I'll take Rorie's suggestion and have a nap."

"That's a good idea, Phillip," Dahlia agreed, flicking off the light switch. "Sleep tight!"

As Dragon settled on the floor at the foot of the bed,

Rorie opened a window and followed Dahlia out of the room, pulling the door nearly shut behind her. If she left it open a couple of inches, the air might circulate a little.

In the hall, Dahlia touched Rorie's arm and whispered, "Why don't you get the kitchen fan and set it up in there? I'm sure it would make him more comfortable."

Rorie wondered peevishly how it had become her lot in life to make Phillip Fairchild comfortable, but she nodded and smiled anyway and went into the kitchen to get the fan. Her godmothers couldn't help it if they were too softhearted for their own good, and had been taken in by Phillip's calculated charm.

She unplugged the fan and picked it up off the counter, then carried it to the guest bedroom. En route, she noticed that her godmothers had disappeared. She supposed they'd gone back to the gazebo to finish their lunch and would then return to the garden to finish their weeding.

She pushed open the door of the guest bedroom and peeked around the corner. Since she expected Phillip to be asleep, she hadn't called out first to make sure he was decent. And, as luck would have it, he wasn't. But was that *bad* luck or *good* luck? Who could say...when the sight before her was as pleasing to the eye as any fine work of art she'd ever had the privilege to gaze upon?

As if in a daze, Rorie stepped into the room and stared. The bee-stung half of Phillip's bottom was covered, but that was about it. The leg that had been sticking out before, was sticking out again. Rorie couldn't resist taking a leisurely perusal of Phillip that started at his bared left foot, traveled up his long, muscled leg, curved around his taut bottom, dipped into his slim waist, and lingered on his broad shoulders and back with a sigh of admiration. And to add to his allure, covering Phillip's sun-kissed skin was a sexy sheen of light perspiration.

Dragon lifted his head and cocked it to the side, looking at Rorie as if she were crazy. But maybe she *was* crazy, because she just kept standing in the middle of the room, clutching the fan to her chest and ogling Phillip. Since he appeared to be fast asleep, it was an irresistible opportunity to ogle without getting caught. But when Rorie began to fantasize about touching his smooth, brown skin, and even slipping under the sheet with him, she knew it was time to set up the fan and get the heck out of there.

Putting the fan on a small table and pulling it to within a few feet of the bed, Rorie plugged it in and turned the speed control to medium-low. She watched as the air breezed over Phillip's face and ruffled his hair.

She seemed in danger of falling into another trance, when suddenly Phillip's eyes opened. "Thanks, Rorie," he said with a wink and a sly grin. "That feels great. But, while I appreciate your concern, you don't have to stand around all day and watch me. Don't worry, I'm not going to croak."

Rorie had never been so mortified in her life! She was sure she must have turned bright red as she realized that Phillip had been awake all along—and had been perfectly aware of her presence in the room! And with a huge ego like his, she was sure he'd jumped to the conclusion that she had been ogling him...admiring him...*lusting* after him!

And the most mortifying fact of all, thought Rorie

as she hurried out of the room, was that he was absolutely right!

AS THE HOT AFTERNOON wore on, Rorie paced restlessly through the house. Georgia had plenty of hot days, but this one was a scorcher, and while Rorie generally could push herself to work no matter how hot it got, today was turning out to be very nonproductive. The only thing she'd actually accomplished was washing and drying Phillip's T-shirt after Daffy brought it in with the picnic basket and empty tea thermos.

Despite the heat, at five o'clock Phillip was still sleeping. Rorie had checked on him frequently during the course of the day, feeling it her duty to make sure the venom of an African bee didn't have a delayed and potentially harmful effect on him, although, given what she'd read about African bees, that was far from likely. But she could just imagine the publicity they'd have to endure if the Perfume Prince was found dead—and naked!—in their guest bedroom. But, she told herself, that was the *only* reason she worried about him.

Since the godmothers liked to eat dinner early, Rorie headed for the kitchen to see what she could rustle up that wouldn't require much cooking. Without the fan to help cool off the kitchen, on such a hot day it would be crazy to turn the stove on for more than a few minutes. Maybe they could have a salad.

Walking quickly down the hall, Rorie collided with Phillip as he came around the corner from the guest bedroom. Just like the last time they'd bumped into each other, Rorie was stunned by the strong physical reaction she experienced as their bodies made contact. And to make matters even worse this time, as Phillip automatically caught her arms to steady her, he lost his grip on the sheet he'd wrapped around his waist and it dropped to the floor.

"Don't look down," Phillip said with a sheepish smile, his hold on her arms increasing. "I think I just lost my toga."

"Wh-what are you doing walking around the house in...in just a sheet, anyway, Fairchild?" Rorie asked breathlessly. She hated to admit it, but she was extremely tempted to look down.

"I was going to ask you if I could use your shower. There wasn't any point in putting on my pants just to take them off again. Besides, I'm not sure I'm ready to put on anything more confining than a sheet for at least a few more hours."

Rorie stared into Phillip's gray eyes, seemingly immobilized. She wasn't sure why she didn't turn away and head straight back to the parlor, allowing him the privacy he needed to bend down and retrieve his sheet. But he wasn't moving, either. His grip on her arms was just as firm, his gaze just as steady as hers.

He smelled good. It wasn't a just-showered smell, but a manly scent, with a mix of fern and flowers from gardening with her godmothers and the faint, salty tang of clean sweat.

His hair was wild from being wet, then drying haphazardly on a pillow. She could tell his hair was naturally curly and that he probably had to work at getting it into the sleeker style he usually wore.

Suddenly the vision of a young boy with dark, curly hair blowing in the wind flashed into her mind. The boy was laughing. He was carrying a bucket. He was collecting something.... Shells?

"Well, Daffy, I'm sure there's plenty of endive for the salad. But did you get enough—"

Rorie heard Dahlia's voice first, then she saw her over Phillip's bare shoulder. She and Daffy and Daisy were standing just inside the back door, holding baskets of produce they'd picked from the garden. She had a straight line of vision from where she stood in the hall to where they stood in the kitchen. And there was only one obstacle between them…Phillip. Luckily he was facing away from her godmothers, but the fact that he was as naked as a jaybird was still patently obvious. That she, their goddaughter, was basically standing in his arms was obvious, too.

It was no wonder they seemed to have turned into statues and simply stared at her and Phillip with their mouths open.

Phillip snatched a glance over his shoulder, muttered an expletive under his breath, quickly scooped up his sheet and made a beeline for the guest bedroom.

"Dahlia, Daffy, Daisy…" Rorie began faintly. She gestured helplessly down the hall. "That was not what it looked like."

Dahlia blinked several times. "Phillip wasn't naked?" she said wonderingly. "But I could have sworn—"

"Oh, yes, he *was* naked," Rorie admitted with a desperate edge to her voice. "But there's a perfectly good explanation for it."

"My dear, there always is," Dahlia agreed with a sage nod of her head. "But I had no idea you'd warm up to each other so fast. Goodness, if I'd only known that all you needed was a little push in the right—"

"Dahlia, I don't know what you're talking about," Rorie interrupted sternly. "Phillip has been asleep all day. I was headed for the kitchen to find something for dinner when he came barreling around the corner in nothing but a sheet. He simply wanted to ask permission to use our shower. We collided, and then..."

As her godmothers waited expectantly, Rorie wondered how to continue. And then *what?* And then she got lost in his eyes? And then she took in the manly scent of him and decided she liked it? And then she admired his curly hair and compared it to a vision she'd been having a lot lately about some boy on a beach somewhere?

"And then *you* came in," she finished lamely.

"It seems you left something out," Daisy suggested. "Somewhere in there Phillip must have, er, *accidentally* dropped his sheet. Perhaps when you collided?"

"Yes, Daisy, you're right," Rorie answered with a nervous smile. "Thank you for pointing that out."

"Well, it's always best to get one's story straight, you know," Daisy replied complacently. "Details are good, too."

Rorie puzzled over this comment for a minute, but suddenly Daffy piped up, saying, "We're having salad for dinner, Aurora. It's too hot to cook. Do you think Phillip likes salad?"

And the godmothers were suddenly bustling around the kitchen as if nothing out of the ordinary had occurred. Surprised but grateful for this nonchalant attitude toward an event that would have horrified most sweet old ladies, Rorie tried to take their behavior as an example and act as normal as possible, too. Only she really *was* putting on an act. She'd seen much too much of Phillip for one day, and she was definitely feeling the strain. She might never feel "normal" again.

PHILLIP WAS in a quandary. He'd had a shower and the cool water had been incredibly refreshing. But his butt still hurt. The swelling had gone down a bit, but he'd tried twice to put on his shorts and had barely been able to endure the rubbing of the rough fabric against the inflamed area. And there was no way he could sit down.

How on earth was he going to drive home? After seeing him standing in the buff, with their precious goddaughter seemingly in his embrace, he hardly expected the Farley sisters to invite him to spend the night.

There was still an explanation to be made about that little debacle.... He hadn't liked leaving Rorie to stutter through an explanation of her own, but circumstances being what they were, he'd thought it best to spare the poor ladies' blushes.

Dragon, who had for some reason decided to be Phillip's bosom buddy, was lying in the gentle breeze of the fan and watching him pace the floor. He looked sympathetic. "You understand, don't you, Dragon?" Phillip said with a sigh and a smile. And Dragon wagged his tail with lethargic goodwill.

There was a knock at the door and Dahlia's voice called out, "Phillip?"

Phillip went to the door, opened it a crack and peered around at Dahlia. "I'm so sorry, Dahlia," he began immediately. "I know what that looked like out there, but I was just—"

"I know," Dahlia interrupted with a smile. "Aurora explained. Nothing more need be said. I've just come to tell you that dinner is ready."

Phillip blinked. "I'm invited to dinner?"

"Well, of course. You missed lunch and I'm sure you're ravenous by now. You didn't think we'd let you starve, did you?''

"You're very kind," Phillip began, wondering how he could phrase it delicately, yet make Dahlia understand that his behind was still on fire. "But there's a little problem."

She cocked her head to the side, and he could almost swear there was a twinkle of mischief in her eyes. "Oh?" she said.

"Yes, you see I'm not exactly dressed for dinner," he informed her in a mortified voice.

"We're very casual here, Phillip," she replied demurely.

"No, I'm serious. I'm not *dressed* for dinner."

Her eyes flitted over the part of his chest that could be seen through the narrow crack in the door. "You're wearing your shirt. Aurora laundered it for you, you know."

"Yes, and I appreciate that," Phillip assured her. "But my shorts—"

"Absolutely kill you when you put them on over your sore fanny."

Phillip sighed. "Exactly. And even without my pants on, it's really impossible to sit down."

"Then eat standing up. That beesting didn't affect your appetite, did it?"

"No, but—"

"But you don't see how you can come to dinner without your pants on?"

Phillip grinned. "Right again."

"Well, you can't hide away in that stuffy bedroom all night, Phillip. We don't mind if you eat in a sheet. Heavens, we're not a bunch of uptight old fogies."

"But what about Rorie? *She* might object."

"I don't think she'll object if you make quite sure the sheet doesn't fall down again. There's a sewing basket on the shelf in the closet, Phillip. Get some big safety pins out of it and pin the sheet securely. We'll be waiting for you in the kitchen."

And without another word, Dahlia left, leaving Phillip no choice but to do as he was told. He found the sewing basket and pinned the sheet, then put on his socks and athletic shoes. Standing in front of a full-length mirror that had been secured to the back of the door, he couldn't help but laugh at his appearance.

"Well, *you* certainly look ridiculous," he chided his reflection, ruefully shaking his head. "The way things are going, how are you ever going to convince Rorie to go out with a dork like *you?*"

But he *was* going to convince her, he promised himself. For more reasons than one.

"HIS CAR IS STILL there, madam," Simon informed his employer, as he rounded the corner and stealthily parked the Rolls-Royce under some trees about a block from the Farley house.

"Yes, I can see that, you idiot," Delphinia snapped. "What time is it?"

"It's almost seven-thirty, madam."

"Surely they wouldn't still be working in the garden," Delphinia mused.

"I daresay they quit working in the garden a couple of hours ago, madam," Simon ventured to suggest.

A muscle in Delphinia's jaw ticked. "Yes, and Fairchild should have left by now."

"Perhaps he stayed for dinner, madam."

"Even so, as my sisters eat quite early and are generally in bed by eight or nine, the fact that he is still there does not bode well," she muttered grimly. "It does not appear that the bees caused much trouble, either."

"Begging your pardon, madam, but didn't you think it was a long shot, anyway? We had no idea where the bees would be released or whether or not they'd go after the intended target of Mr. Fairchild."

"At such short notice, it was the only thing I could think of to do," Delphinia replied sulkily. "When you read that tabloid story about Fairchild and discovered that he was allergic to beestings, the African bees seemed the best and only plan of attack for the situation. My sisters' bees are too lazy to sting anyone!"

She sighed heavily. "With all of them sequestered in that overgrown yard, and guarded by Dragon, it is difficult to get *at* them! But tomorrow Fairchild must leave the premises to take that beast of a dog to the groomers." She tapped her chin and furrowed her brow in a contemplative frown. "Yes, tomorrow it will be much easier to cause mischief."

"But what will you do, madam?" Simon inquired, still looking rigidly forward. "Have you come up with something, er, *better* than the bees?"

"We don't know that the bees were such a bad idea, Simon," Delphinia snarled. "In fact, we have no proof either way. If only we could see what they're doing, hear what they're saying...." She narrowed her eyes, thinking hard. Then it hit her.

"Aha!" Delphinia shouted, making Simon flinch. "That's it, Simon. I'm surprised *you* didn't think of it! There *is* something we can do that will enable us to at least hear what they're saying. We can bug the house!"

"But, madam, we'd have to go inside the house to plant the bugs," Simon protested weakly. "Are you sure you want to go back again...so soon? And I'm not sure I remember where we stashed the bugging equipment after we used it on your last husband. And, as you may recall, Mr. Devine crushed one of the receiving devices under the heel of his shoe. What if we should need a replacement part to get things up and running? At this hour, all the stores will be closed. Besides, I thought you wanted me to search for more information about Mr. Fairchild in the old news stories we've gathered? When will I have time to do everything?''

Delphinia leaned back in the seat and crossed her legs. ''You'll find time,'' she said. ''Even if you must stay up all night. As for going back inside that house, as long as there's still plenty of vodka on hand to prepare myself for the encounter, I'm willing to make the sacrifice. We'll go first thing tomorrow morning, which means you must—by hook or crook—have the equipment ready by then, Simon. Do you understand?''

''Yes, madam,'' he said gloomily. ''But as I've got such a lot to do, madam, do you suppose we could head for home now?''

''Not yet,'' Delphinia replied, reaching for her cigarette case. ''We'll sit here for an hour or two and see if he leaves. Light me, Simon, will you?'' She leaned forward, her cigarette at the ready.

Simon sighed and reached for his lighter. ''Certainly, madam. Whatever you say.''

Chapter Six

"Standing up or sitting down, that was the best peach pie I've ever tasted," Phillip said as he patted his flat-as-a-washboard stomach, crossed his feet at the ankles and leaned back against the kitchen counter. Rorie glared at their sheet-draped dinner guest and wished he'd go home. It was late by her godmothers' standards. But, despite the hour, they'd lingered at the dinner table much longer than usual. She'd never seen them so talkative and vivacious.

The one thing she couldn't get them to talk about, however, was the bees and where they might have come from. But once Phillip was gone, perhaps her godmothers would be less distracted...she knew she certainly would be!

"We're so glad you like the pie, Phillip," Daffy said with a pleased smile. "I made the crust, you know. I'm the best at it. Dahlia peels and cuts up the peaches, and Daisy mixes everything, but *I* make the crust...which, as you know, is the most important part of the pie."

"Posh," Daisy said, waving her hand at her sister. "Everyone knows it's the amount of sugar and such that's put in the mix that makes a pie good or bad."

"I beg to differ," Dahlia interjected, pouring herself

more coffee, then standing up to refill Phillip's cup, too. "It's the peaches that make the pie so good, and none of us can take credit for that."

"You all deserve a share of the credit," Phillip said diplomatically. "After all, it's probably the fertilizer that makes the peaches grow so big and juicy, and you all had a part in creating the formula, didn't you?"

The godmothers slid glances at one another and Dahlia answered, "Yes, we all helped create the formula. But if it weren't for the secret ingredient, which we chanced upon quite accidentally, I'm not sure the fertilizer would be half as effective as it is."

"How long have you known about this…er…secret ingredient?" Phillip inquired, taking a sip of coffee.

Dahlia's gaze wandered to Dragon, who was, as usual, prostrated at Phillip's feet. "Hmm. Let's see now. It's been ten years since we got— Yes. It was ten years ago that we first discovered the secret ingredient."

"That's all?" Phillip was incredulous. "Those trees in the front got that big that fast?"

"They were pretty big to begin with," Rorie said impatiently, pushing away her own untouched pie and standing up. If her godmothers didn't get this peep-show-in-a-sheet on the road, she would just have to take matters into her own hands.

"I know you must hate to eat and run, Fairchild, but we'll understand if you want to go home now. It's been a long day." *For all of us,* she added to herself.

"Goodness, Aurora Dawn, where are your manners?" Dahlia admonished her with a frown. "One doesn't rush away one's guests! Besides, Phillip is spending the night."

"He is?"

"I am?"

Rorie threw Phillip a horrified glance. Phillip smiled back.

"Well, I thought that was understood," Dahlia said, beginning to stack the dishes. As if cued by their older sister, Daffy and Daisy got busy, too, filling the sink with sudsy water and sponging off the kitchen surfaces.

"After all, Phillip can't stand to wear his pants," Dahlia continued. "How do you expect him to drive all that way home without his pants on? And I just bet you've got leather seats in that nice car of yours, don't you, Phillip?"

Phillip chuckled. "Yes, I do, Dahlia."

Dahlia widened her eyes expressively. "Well, and we all know that the combination of bare skin and leather does *not* make for comfortable sitting."

"And what if he were pulled over by one of those tough motorcycle cops, Aurora?" Daisy added, peering over her shoulder as she washed dishes. "How would he explain himself?"

"I'm not suggesting that Phillip drive home without his pants on," Rorie exclaimed, totally exasperated. "He can wear his boxers...or the sheet, for all I care!"

"But just imagine what your neighbors would think if I walked from your house to the car dressed so, um, casually," Phillip said, his eyes twinkling.

"No one will see you," Rorie answered irritably. "As you know, no one can see into our yard, and you're probably parked right in front of the gate. Besides, it will be dark soon."

"But there's still a chance he'd be seen," Dahlia said. "However, that's not *really* the point. The point is, it still hurts him to sit down Aurora. Do you want him to be in pain all that time when he really doesn't need to be?''

All three of Rorie's godmothers turned and gave her The Look. It was the look all mothers used when trying to convey a sense of guilt to their children. It was working. Yes, despite Phillip's smug smile, it was working.

"Fine," Rorie said, defeated. "Fairchild can spend the night. What difference does it make to me?''

BUT IT MADE a lot of difference to Rorie. That night, long after she speculated that everyone else was fast asleep, she lay awake in her bed, staring at the ceiling. Just knowing *he* was in the house was extremely unsettling.

She knew what kind of guy Phillip was, so why did she still let him get to her? Rorie wondered. But she knew why. It was that blasted charm of his. He had lots of it...pure, unadulterated, one-hundred-proof charm. She supposed his charm—that seeming sincerity, that open boyishness—was what had made Kim fall in love with him, and why she'd continued to go out with him even after he'd started treating her like dirt. Rorie couldn't even imagine staying in a relationship like that...no matter how good-looking, rich or charming a man was.

Rorie got out of bed and paced the floor. She paused at the window and looked out at trees and shrubs drenched in moonlight. The crickets were singing. The air was heavy with scent and still warm and sultry from the day's heat. Like never before, she felt a yearning to be held and kissed. She'd dated a bit over the years, but she'd never met a man who made her blood rush through her veins like Phillip did.

But Rorie was no fool. She knew what was going on. She knew she was simply sexually attracted to him. And she knew the attraction would go away as soon as *he* went away. Surely she could withstand his charm for another day or two.

Besides, she thought, staring up at the stars above the treetops, she knew there was someone special out there for her. Someone who was meant for her. She would be patient...and wait.

Having talked herself into a little peace of mind, Rorie picked up a large candle from the dresser, lit the wick with a match, then left the room, carefully guarding the flame with a cupped hand. She walked quietly down the wide hall, past her godmothers' bedrooms, to the narrow staircase that led to the turret. If she couldn't sleep, she could spin. And maybe she'd spin herself a dream or two....

PHILLIP COULDN'T sleep. He knew he could logically attribute his restlessness to the very long nap he'd had that day, and the awkwardness of sleeping on his stomach when he was used to sleeping on his side, but he was honest enough to admit to himself that the main thing keeping him awake was...Aurora Dawn McBride.

Why did she dislike him so much? And why did he still like her despite her dislike of him?

And why had he suddenly started dreaming about beaches?

Dressed in his boxer shorts, Phillip left the stuffy bedroom and, by the illumination of a small night-light in the hall, he found his way to the kitchen. He opened a cupboard, grabbed a large glass, filled it at the tap with cold water, and started to gulp it down. What he probably needed was a cold shower, he acknowledged to himself. Having warm thoughts about a woman on such a hot night made it doubly hard to sleep.

You're behaving like a lovesick jackass, Phillip told himself, finishing off the water with a satisfied gasp and wiping his mouth with the back of his hand. *Keep your mind off the girl and on the fertilizer.*

But as he headed back down the hall to the guest bedroom, Phillip paused at the bottom of the stairs and looked up. Did he imagine it, or had he really seen the flicker of a candle and the wisp of a white nightgown?

Phillip didn't believe in ghosts, but the idea of one of the Farley sisters wandering around with a candle was a potentially scarier thought, anyway. Suppose one of them was sleepwalking? They might accidentally burn down the house.

Phillip hurried back to the guest bedroom, pulled on his T-shirt and grabbed his sheet. If the person with the candle happened to be awake, he didn't want to be caught again even partially undressed. Although it *had* been rather nice that afternoon finding himself in the buff with Rorie practically in his arms.

Phillip quietly climbed the stairs, grateful that his constant companion of late, Dragon, was sleeping outside on the front porch and wouldn't thud around and wake everyone up. This was the first time he'd been upstairs, and he noticed that there were five doors leading off the spacious hall. One was a bathroom with a night-light beaming from its open door, and he assumed the other four doors were bedrooms.

Three of the doors were shut, but the first one on the left, was wide open. Phillip peeped inside and decided it had to be Rorie's room, because its decor was light and airy and devoid of flowers of any kind. The bed was empty.

So, Rorie is the mysterious candle bearer, he concluded, highly intrigued. And for some reason she'd gone up to her turret office in the middle of the night. He smiled and turned toward another set of stairs at the far end of the hall. He paused and considered, chewing his lip, then decided that he couldn't resist. He had to follow her up there and ask her why she couldn't sleep, either.

Wrapping the sheet around his waist and tying it in a haphazard knot, he walked softly down the hall to the narrow spiral stairs that led to the turret, grateful that two small windows supplied enough moonlight to see by. As he ascended, he heard a soft whirring sound. At first he thought it must be a fan, but all the fans he'd had experience with in the Farley household made creaking, clicking noises. No, this was something different.

He stepped onto the small landing, then into an octagonal room that was bathed in moonlight and candlelight. He blinked at first, not sure whether he was seeing something real or a fantasy.

Rorie was sitting at a spinning wheel, dressed in a white nightgown with a demure neckline and tiny capped sleeves. The soft-looking cotton material was bunched above her knees, apparently to accommodate the movement of her legs as her feet pressed rhythmically at the treadle that made the wheel turn. Her hair fell over her shoulders like spun gold.

Spun gold. Hell, had he somehow stepped into a fairy tale?

As he watched, mesmerized, Rorie seemed totally unaware of his presence. Her hands were expertly guiding and adjusting the feeding of wool fleece from a cigar-sized roll into the spindle of the spinning wheel. Her eyes were half-closed, her expression was dreamy. It appeared as though she could do what she was doing in her sleep. Maybe she *was* asleep.

A sharp intake of breath and the clatter of Rorie's chair falling backward as she stumbled to her feet, her hand on her heart, her blue eyes wide and glinting with fear in the candlelight, testified to the fact that she was *not* asleep.

"Wh—what are you *doing* up here?"

"Rorie, I'm sorry I frightened you—" he began, advancing toward her with one hand extended.

"Stay where you are, Fairchild!" she hissed. "Aren't I even safe from you up here?"

Phillip frowned and his arm fell to his side. "What do you mean, 'safe'?"

She seemed to recollect herself. "That didn't come out right. I...I was just so surprised to see you. It must be—"

"Two o'clock," he supplied for her, eyeing her keenly. She was practically pressed against the opposite wall. "You can relax now. It's just me...not a burglar or anyone sinister. And I'm perfectly decent." He spread his arms. "See? Shirt, sheet and boxers, all securely in place."

Rorie's gaze trailed over him and he thought he saw her shiver. It bothered him to think she might be afraid of him for some reason, but maybe she wasn't over the shock of his unexpected appearance.

"I'm really sorry I frightened you," he repeated.

Rorie finally seemed to loosen up a bit. She stepped away from the wall, picked up her chair, and sat down again by the spinning wheel. She grabbed the roll of

wool she'd been drafting and said in a decidedly un-
friendly voice, "What do you want?"

"I couldn't sleep. I got a drink of water from the
kitchen and was headed back to my room—"

"It's not *your* room, Fairchild," Rorie reminded
him, fixing him with a cold stare.

"The *guest* room, then," Phillip amended carefully.
"But as I walked down the hall, I glanced up the stairs
and thought I saw candlelight and a white gown. I was
afraid something or someone might need my attention,
so I—"

"We've survived all this time perfectly well without
your attention, Fairchild," Rorie said with an indignant
sniff. "You should have stayed downstairs. My godmothers certainly didn't give you permission to roam
the house."

Phillip shook his head. "You are determined to hate
me, aren't you? What did I ever do to you, Rorie?"

"It's not what you did to *me*—" she began, then
stopped, her hair falling over her face, hiding her expression.

He lowered his brows and crossed his arms. "Then
it's something I did to someone else. Tell me, Rorie.
Tell me, so I can clear up this misunderstanding between us. I'd like us to be friends."

Rorie lifted her head and stared at Phillip. Even if it
had been possible—which it wasn't—to clear up the
misunderstanding between them, Rorie preferred not
to. She didn't want to be friends with Phillip. She
didn't even want him in the house. He was far too
attractive to have around. Seeing him now in the moonlight, the flickering of the candle reflecting in his gray
eyes, made goose bumps erupt all over her body. She

wasn't afraid of him; she was afraid of herself and the way she felt when he was near.

"I'm not in the mood to talk, Fairchild," she muttered. "I'm trying to get some work done."

"In the middle of the night?"

"It was too hot during the day, and you were kind of a distraction with your beesting and all—"

"You couldn't sleep, either, huh?"

Their gazes locked. He seemed to be daring her to deny it. When she didn't, he smiled ruefully and his gaze shifted to the spinning wheel.

"So you really do make your designer sweaters totally from scratch. Don't tell me you raise the sheep and shear them, too?"

Rorie sighed. She should have expected this sort of levity from him. She knew he wouldn't understand her spinning.

"I'm just teasing," he said, seeming to sense her thoughts. "I'm amazed that you can do this. It takes talent. It's a wonderful craft. No, actually it's an art, isn't it?"

Her head reared up and she glared suspiciously at him. "Don't patronize me, Fairchild."

"I'm serious," he assured her. "I'm genuinely impressed. I know a little about the process, you know. My grandmother used to spin."

"You're kidding," she said drily. "You're just trying to get on my good side so I'll go out with you and help you win your precious fertilizer formula."

"You need proof, I see." He moved forward and was soon standing over her and the spinning wheel. He was so close she could feel the warmth radiating from him and smell the soap from his shower. It felt like all her nerves had suddenly caught on fire.

"This is called the mother-of-all," he said, pointing to the spindle apparatus. "If I didn't know anything about spinning, how would I know something like that?"

He was right. She looked at him doubtfully, wondering if there really was a human being under that smooth facade.

"She used to let me help her card the wool and roll it into—What did she call those things? *Rolags*, I think. I got pretty good at it. Do you need some help? My grandmother said I was the best helper a spinner could ask for."

He smiled engagingly, and Rorie was betrayed into a responding smile, although it was a rueful one. "Grandmothers are notorious for lying to their grandchildren to make them happy. She probably *liked* you, Fairchild."

"Believe it or not, lots of people like me, Rorie."

"You mean, besides your grandmother and maybe your parents?" she suggested.

His eyes glinted with mocking amusement. "A few. As for my parents, maybe they only felt a certain obligation to like me...seeing as how I'm their only child."

She smirked. "I could have guessed that."

"Because you think I'm spoiled and self-centered? Aren't you an only child, too?"

"My parents didn't have much of a chance to increase the size of the family before they were killed in a car accident," she said quietly.

Phillip could have kicked himself. "I'm sorry. I didn't mean to bring up sad memories."

"No, it's all right. Despite a shaky start, I've had a pretty idyllic childhood. I've got three mothers instead of just one, and while they're not typical, they're never boring.''

"I'll say. And Delphinia slinking in and out of the house has probably kept things interesting over the years. I don't understand how she can even be related to your godmothers. She's nothing like them.''

"Well, she's actually only a half sister. She was born when Daffy, who's the youngest, was twelve years old. Their father remarried, briefly. When he died, he left the house equally to all four daughters. But the only time Delphinia comes around is when she wants something. Lately, because she's got a bee in her bonnet about buying the fertilizer formula, she's been coming around a lot.''

"Speaking of bees, you don't think she sent that box of stingers, do you?''

"No, I really don't. I don't believe Delphinia would purposely endanger her own sisters.''

"I suppose your godmothers think just like you do?''

"Delphinia was raised in a different house by a different mother...'' Rorie paused and smiled ruefully. "I suppose that's why she's so...different.''

"To say the least,'' Phillip murmured.

"But she's still family and my godmothers try to give her the benefit of the doubt.''

Rorie suddenly realized that she was having a friendly conversation with Phillip Fairchild, and it made her really nervous. She bent her head again and toyed with the rolag of wool, wishing he wouldn't stand so close.

"Do you always work by candlelight?'' he asked, suddenly changing the subject.

"Just when I'm in the mood,'' she replied evasively,

then hoped he hadn't taken that comment the wrong way. "How about you?" she joked weakly.

"I do my best work by candlelight."

Rorie could feel herself blushing.

"Sorry. I couldn't resist that. It was a perfect setup." Phillip gave a slightly apologetic smile and turned away, moving to the window. Rorie's eyes were drawn to his broad back. Despite the fact that he was garbed in a sheet, he still moved with the elegance and self-confidence she'd found sexy from the beginning.

"My office is in the center of downtown Atlanta. It's a little higher than your office, but you've definitely got the better view."

"Are you sure?" Rorie said dryly. "Aren't the Fair Lady offices in the Grand? And somewhere I read that you also live in the building, in a condominium on the fifty-third floor, at the very top." Actually, Kim had told her that little tidbit about Phillip, but she couldn't reveal her source.

He did not turn around, but simply inclined his head to the side as if admitting reluctantly to such an exclusive address.

"It must be a nice place to work...and to live. I'm surprised you could tear yourself away. How does the office keep chugging along without you? Don't you have to be there every day?" she ventured.

"I told them I was taking the week off. When you're the boss, you can get away with playing hooky now and then."

"But this is business," Rorie reminded him.

Phillip turned. It started out that way, he thought to himself. He stared at her for a long, tension-filled moment. She stared back. Her eyes were luminous in the soft lighting, and for an instant he entertained the idea that maybe she didn't dislike him as much as she wanted him to think she did.

And maybe a kiss wouldn't be entirely unwelcome....

"You've got a full day ahead of you tomorrow, Fairchild," she said in a firm voice, rising suddenly, snatching up the candle, and padding to the door in her bare feet.

Disappointed, and chiding himself for entertaining unfounded hopes, Phillip followed her to the top of the stairs. She turned, her profile outlined against the golden glow of the candlelight, to say, "You may think you've got Dragon wrapped around your little finger, but he hates baths. You're going to need all your strength to get that dog to cooperate tomorrow," she warned him. It'll be one time the famous Fairchild charm won't do you any good."

"No, it will be just *another* time my so-called famous Fairchild charm didn't do me any good," he murmured in a low voice.

"What was that?" she asked him as she floated down the stairs.

"Nothing," he muttered. "Nothing at all."

RORIE WATCHED Phillip descend the stairs and turn down the hall to the guest room, then she closed her bedroom door and collapsed against it with a heavy sigh of relief. "One more second alone with that man and I would definitely have made a fool of myself," she whispered out loud.

She pushed off from the door and walked slowly, with her arms wrapped around her waist, to the window. Yes, one more minute alone with Phillip Fairchild and she would have been unable to hide her desire for him. He'd looked so sexy in the softly lit room, his hair mussed from tossing and turning on the pillow, his shoulders so broad, the sheet so— She smiled. Yes, even in a sheet he was sexy. And for a minute there, she thought he just might have been considering kissing her....

Rorie shook her head as if trying to rid her brain of naive romantic notions. Yes, Phillip Fairchild probably was thinking about kissing her...just like he'd kissed a million other women over the years. And nothing about *her* lips would be any more special than the lips of all those other women. With this reality check to keep her from regretting the missed kiss, Rorie went back to bed.

Trouble was, the reality check didn't work. She tossed and turned, and dreamed fitfully of kisses and sandy beaches all night long.

Chapter Seven

After a few hours of fitful sleep, Phillip got up the following morning, showered, put on his shorts and T-shirt and ventured down the hall toward the kitchen. He could smell breakfast cooking and he couldn't wait to sink his teeth into whatever the Farley sisters placed in front of him. So far they'd proved to be as good at cooking as they were at gardening. But as eager as he was to eat, he was even more eager to see Rorie. Their candlelit encounter in the turret last night had made the idea of getting to know her even more intriguing.

However, while all three Farley sisters were present and accounted for when he entered the kitchen, Rorie wasn't.

"Phillip!" exclaimed Dahlia, turning from the stove where she was flipping pancakes on a griddle. "Good morning!" Daffy and Daisy, who were sitting at the table, chorused their sister's greeting.

"Good morning," Phillip replied, smiling.

"Have some juice," Daffy offered, bustling over with a large glass of orange juice. "It's freshly squeezed from our own fruit."

"Thanks, Daffy," Phillip said, taking the juice, "but

you didn't have to get up. This morning I can actually sit at the table like a civilized human being.''

"You can sit down?" Daisy exclaimed. "Well, that's certainly good news. Does that mean your, er, *beesting* is feeling better?''

"Yes, my *beesting* is much better today. The antihistamine did the trick, I guess. That, and Rorie's tender loving care,'' he added ruefully. The sisters chuckled. He sat down at the table and casually asked, "By the way, where is Nurse Ratched this morning?''

Dahlia brought a platter piled high with pancakes to the table. She frowned. "She's running errands. I don't know when she'll be back. I had no idea she planned to go out today.''

Dahlia sounded as disappointed as Phillip felt. Because it would bring him that much closer to obtaining the fertilizer formula, he ought to be excited about getting on to the next test, but not having Rorie around to tease and annoy him made the whole undertaking a lot less fun.

As he dug into a stack of fluffy pancakes and homemade blueberry syrup, he told himself that he needed to focus more on the real reason he was there. Thoughts of Rorie were sidetracking him.

During breakfast, Phillip praised the food and kept up a lively chatter with the Farley sisters, but he kept wondering when Rorie would be back. As he downed his third cup of coffee, the phone rang. Dahlia left the room to answer it and came back looking fretful.

"That was Delphinia,'' she revealed. "She's out front.''

"Again?" Daffy and Daisy both said with an unmistakable note of dread in their voices.

"You mustn't think we don't love our sister,''

Dahlia said quickly, turning to Phillip with an apologetic smile. "It's just that sometimes she's a bit of a—"

"Pain?" Phillip supplied with an understanding grin.

"Exactly." Dahlia smiled back. "We hardly ever see her, but lately she's been coming around more often. I thought after she found out we were going to sell the fertilizer formula to you, she'd quit coming so much. So, who knows, maybe she really does come by just to see us," she added, but she looked as unconvinced by such an idea as Phillip was.

"Or maybe she's checking to see how I did on my first test," Phillip suggested. "She doesn't strike me as the type who gives up easily."

"You're right," Dahlia agreed, her brows furrowing. "I was amazed when she took the news so well the other night."

"Delphinia's a strange one," Daisy said, clearing the dishes.

"Amen to that," Daffy agreed as she carried the milk to the refrigerator. "And it's your turn to guide Miss High and Mighty through the yard, Daisy."

Daisy made a face and carefully set some glasses in the sink before heading for the door. "I'm surprised they haven't memorized the route by now. They've come often enough lately."

"Put Dragon in the backyard first, won't you Daisy? And remember to lock the gate," Dahlia called after her. "We'll be in after we clean up the kitchen."

"You two go ahead," Phillip said. "I'll wash the dishes."

"Oh, but we couldn't ask you to—" Dahlia began, looking horrified.

"I insist," Phillip interrupted her, shooing them toward the door.

"But, but—" Dahlia stuttered.

"I'm a nineties kind of guy, ladies," he assured them, tongue in cheek. "You cooked, so I'll clean up."

Finally, still looking a bit distressed at the idea of the Perfume Prince scrubbing their pots and pans, Dahlia and Daisy were persuaded to leave the kitchen and Phillip closed the door behind them, breathing a sigh of relief. Phillip didn't mind doing the dishes, but he knew his generosity was largely motivated by an earnest desire to avoid Delphinia Devine.

After finishing the dishes, Phillip opened the kitchen door a crack to listen for voices. If he heard Delphinia's throaty drawl, he would stay hidden a while longer. But he heard nothing. Venturing out, he heard footsteps upstairs and distant voices…one of them unmistakably Delphinia's. He wondered what the heck they were all doing upstairs, but wasn't about to stick around to ask.

He was headed back to the kitchen when he heard a soft hiss coming from the parlor, like someone cursing under their breath. He turned back and looked around the corner of the arched entryway into the parlor and saw Simon on his hands and knees under an end table.

Phillip walked quietly into the room and stood over the diminutive chauffeur, his arms crossed. "Lose something?"

Simon was so startled, he bumped his head on the underside of the table. He muttered another soft oath, crawled out backwards and straightened up. Even with Simon standing his tallest, Phillip towered over him. His weasely little eyes rolled up to meet Phillip's, then darted nervously away.

"Good morning, Mr. Fairchild," he said. "I thought you were outside, er, washing the dog."

Phillip raised a brow. "Did you? Apparently I'm not as early a riser as you are, Simon, rarin' to go at the crack of dawn. I just got out of bed thirty minutes ago."

Simon's eyes bulged, then flitted over Phillip, from his still-wet-from-the-shower hair, to his bare feet. "You just got up? You...you mean you spent the night?"

"Yes, I spent the night. Did you lose something, Simon?"

"Lose something, sir?"

"You were on your hands and knees under the table, so I assumed—"

"Yes, sir. My...my contact, sir."

"Did you find it?"

"Yes. No. That is—"

'Maybe I could help you." Phillip scanned the rose-covered carpet.

"That's not necessary, sir," Simon quickly assured him. "They're disposable. I've got another one in the car."

Phillip nodded, his eyes narrowing as he closely observed Delphinia's twitchy hired help. "Well, that's good. We wouldn't want you driving home with just one good eye."

"Exactly, sir," Simon agreed with a strained smile.

Phillip thought Simon seemed even more nervous than usual. But if he wasn't looking for his contact, what was he doing under the table? He certainly wouldn't find the fertilizer formula there!

While he stood in the parlor and puzzled over Simon's behavior, Phillip heard the Farley sisters coming down the stairs. For a minute he considered trying to slip out of the room before Delphinia came in, but he knew it was hopeless. He was trapped. He'd have to tolerate being in the same room for a few minutes with the spider woman. She entered the parlor just ahead of her sisters.

"Simon, it's time to—" Delphinia broke off when she saw Phillip. Her look was one of chagrin, quickly covered by a hideous smile. She approached him with that contrived slink of hers, her hips seeming to reach their destination before the rest of her. As before, she was dressed in black—this time in a pair of pants with a wide flare at the ankles and an oversized top—and was waving a long cigarette.

"Phillip, what are you doing here so early? No, don't tell me—you didn't even go home last night, did you? Goodness, what will the neighbors think?" Her tone was light, but her eyes glittered strangely.

"You're right," Phillip answered politely, forcing a smile. "I spent the night because I was stung by a bee yesterday on a rather tender part of my anatomy...my posterior."

"Indeed?" Delphinia replied, her eyes wide with affected concern as she took a long drag on her cigarette. "How very...*uncomfortable.*"

"Exactly. I was too sore to sit down, and your sisters graciously invited me to sleep here so I wouldn't have to put up with the misery of driving all the way home sitting on my...er...injury."

She flashed a wincing smile. "My sisters are the very models of hospitality."

"*I* think so," Phillip said, glancing past Delphinia and giving Daisy, Daffy and Dahlia a warm smile. The sisters returned it.

Delphinia observed the affectionate exchange between Phillip and her sisters with absolutely no expression on her face. Then she announced, "Well, we had better be off, Simon. Goodbye, Phillip. Goodbye, er, the rest of you. We're driving to Savannah to spend the entire day at a wonderful spa I discovered down there. They have an herbal wrap that does absolutely marvelous things for the upper arms. You three ought to try it sometime. Ta-ta!"

She slinked for the door and Simon hastened ahead of her to open it. Daisy, the unlucky one with guide duty, hurried to catch up.

"That was very strange," Dahlia said as the door closed behind them. "She wanted to see Aurora's spinning wheel, and she insisted that we all three accompany her. She stood and fawned over it and stroked it as if she thought it was something special. I wonder what she's up to?"

Phillip looked keenly at Dahlia. "So you think she's up to something?"

"Unfortunately, yes."

"What exactly would she be up to?"

Dahlia looked troubled. "I wish I knew."

"Horned worms!"

Rorie set the bags of groceries on the table and turned around to see Dahlia poised at the back door wearing flower-sprigged gardening gloves, a large straw hat, and a look of rock-jawed determination. She was holding a gallon-sized glass jar.

"What are you talking about, Dahlia?"

"There are horned worms in the tomatoes," Dahlia explained agitatedly. "Daisy, Daffy and I are going to have to spend the entire day picking off the blasted

things, or they'll eat holes in every one of our tomatoes! That would mean no homemade salsa this win-
ter!''

"Oh, dear," Rorie said sympathetically. "When did
this happen? You didn't say anything about a worm
invasion yesterday."

"It happened overnight," Dahlia informed her
briskly. "It will take us all morning to round up the
little critters, and once we've got them in jars, we're
going to walk down to the park and let them loose."

Rorie nodded, used to her godmothers' tender treat-
ment of all creatures great and small. Then she got an
idea and, with an air of innocence, suggested, "Maybe
you should make Phillip help you herd the worms. He
actually still owes you a half day of work in the garden."

"Phillip's got his hands full with Dragon," Dahlia
told her. "And since I've got my hands full, too, do
me a favor and take the dog shampoo out to him, won't
you, dear? There's a new jug under the sink." Then
she turned and left.

Rorie looked frowningly after her godmother. She
had no desire to help Phillip in any way to pass his
tests. But, as they seldom asked for favors, she rarely
refused to do anything her godmothers asked her to do.
And since Phillip really couldn't be expected to know
where the dog shampoo was kept, Rorie felt it was only
fair that she take it to him.

After putting away the perishable groceries, Rorie
dragged out the large jug of dog shampoo from under
the sink and carried it outside. Dahlia hadn't told her
where Phillip was, but she figured he'd be on the east
side of the house where there was the most sunshine.
That's where she and her godmothers always bathed

Dragon, and she supposed they'd explained that to Phillip.

It was going to be another hot day and Rorie had dressed for the heat in a pair of white shorts, a pale yellow T-shirt and sandals. Resisting the urge to wear her hair down again, she'd pulled it back in a no-nonsense ponytail.

Sure enough, as Rorie walked around the side of the house, she saw Phillip filling up the swimming pool while Dragon sat on his haunches and watched soberly. As she approached, Phillip looked up and smiled as if he was genuinely delighted to see her.

Rorie steeled herself against his charm. The man had robbed her of a decent night's sleep, and she wasn't about to let that happen again. Or was she? Despite her good intentions, her heart was beating way too fast to fool herself into thinking she was immune to Phillip Fairchild.

"I thought you said he hated baths," Phillip said as Rorie placed the jug of shampoo at his feet.

"He does."

"Well, why isn't he running away?" He gestured toward Dragon. "He's just sitting there."

"If you were as big as Dragon, would you feel the need to run away? Believe me, if Dragon doesn't want to get in the water, he won't. You can't physically drag him in, you have to coax him."

"But when you said I'd need all my strength today, I figured you meant—"

"I meant you'd need all your strength once you started actually scrubbing him down. Dragon is a lot of dog. I figure that bathing him takes about as much effort as whitewashing a barn."

"No wonder your aunts made this one of the tests," he said.

"Yes, and no wonder we do it only twice a year."

"Why don't you let the groomers bathe him?"

"They flatly refuse, and they can't be bribed, either. We're just grateful they're willing to trim him. It takes them an hour to sweep up the hair." Rorie glanced down at the pool, which was about fifteen feet in diameter and a couple of feet deep, with an aluminum frame instead of a soft, inflatable rim. Phillip had filled it about half full.

"You know, I usually fill the pool up a couple of hours before I bathe Dragon, so the water will have time to warm in the sun. Dragon doesn't like cold baths."

Phillip released a huff of exasperation. "Why didn't someone tell me that?"

"My godmothers have a worm crisis, and you really didn't expect *me* to tell you, did you?"

Phillip turned off the hose valve and said, "Well, then, I'll just wait a couple of hours before I give him his bath."

Rorie glanced at her watch. "No time," she announced breezily. "The appointment at the groomers is in two hours. They won't trim him dirty, and he needs at least an hour in the sun to dry."

Phillip threw Rorie a scowling smile. "You're enjoying this, aren't you?"

"Immensely," she replied. "Well, I'll leave you to your task. Or should I say *test?* Good luck," she said in a saccharine tone. Then she turned to go.

"Wait, Rorie," Phillip called after her. "Won't you at least tell me how you coax him into the water?"

"With a large sausage," she answered over her

shoulder. "Hickory smoked, of course. It's the only kind he likes."

"You wouldn't happen to have—"

"Fresh out!"

"Fine," Phillip said grimly. "I'll get Dragon in the water without a bribe. I don't need your help *or* your sausage."

Rorie was just about to turn the corner of the house, but she couldn't resist looking back to see what Phillip was up to. Resting on one hip, with her arms crossed over her chest in a casual pose, she waited and watched.

Aware of his audience, Phillip threw her an I-can-do-this, just-watch-me look and stepped into the pool. Then he actually sat down in it! You could tell by his expression that the water was quite cold. Then, as she and Dragon watched, he took the jug of shampoo, dumped some into his palm and began to lather his arms and legs.

An incredulous laugh broke from Rorie's lips. "You're crazy, Fairchild." When she bathed Dragon, she wore rubber boots and a mackintosh. She certainly didn't get any wetter than necessary.

"Crazy like a fox," he retorted, dunking his head in the water and rubbing lather into his hair, too. "When he sees me doing this, he's going to want to do it, too."

Bemused, Rorie moved closer and closer, till she was standing over the pool. She couldn't believe what she was seeing! The Perfume Prince taking a bath in dog shampoo? What wouldn't the man do to get the results he wanted?

Apparently Dragon couldn't believe what he was seeing, either. He cautiously approached the pool and sniffed the soapy water, looking at Phillip with bright, beady eyes.

"Man, this is great, Dragon," Phillip lied to the dog. he splashed around and flipped a few beads of water on Dragon. "Don't you want to come in and have some fun, too?"

Dragon was obviously undecided. He began to pant and emit frustrated little whines. He knew he didn't like baths, but his new idol seemed to think they were great.

Finally Dragon could stand it no longer. With a yip that clearly said, "What the hell!" in dog language, Dragon suddenly bounded over the side and into the pool, splashing several gallons of water high into the air.

Since Rorie had never actually believed that Dragon could be tricked so quickly and easily, she wasn't at all expecting the tidal wave of sudsy water that hit her. With a squeal of surprise, she jumped back...about ten seconds too late.

Rorie looked down at her soaked clothes and felt her drenched ponytail slither around her neck and shoulders, then glared at Phillip. "Fairchild, I could cream you!"

Phillip stood up and wrapped his arm around Dragon's neck. "Sorry, Rorie. Looks like you got caught in friendly cross fire. But since you're already wet—" And before Rorie knew what was happening, Phillip grabbed her arm and gave it a firm yank. Tottering off balance, she stumbled over the rim of the pool and came down on her hands and knees in the cold, soapy water.

Rorie tossed back her wet hair and looked up at Phillip's gleeful expression with narrowed eyes. "All right, you asked for it,'' she warned him, then she sat back on her heels and began twirling her arms like a couple of paddlewheels.

"Water fight!" yelled Phillip, and all hell broke lose.

Mad at first, Rorie couldn't help but smile as she gave back as good as she got. Soon she was giggling, then she was laughing like a lunatic as she and Phillip scooped handfuls of water at each other, falling, lunging, chasing each other around the small pool.

Dragon, an excited onlooker, had removed himself as far as possible from the pandemonium while still remaining in the pool. As big as he was, staying out of the way was really impossible and he ended up as wet as they were. Barking wildly, he seemed to be rooting for Phillip.

Gasping for breath, Rorie slowed down for a minute and Phillip grabbed her waist from behind. He slipped on the slick bottom and fell backwards, taking Rorie with him. They landed with a splash, then just lay there breathing hard, wide smiles on their faces.

But as the seconds ticked by, Rorie became all too aware of the warm, muscular body that cushioned hers. His arms were still wrapped around her waist, her legs were tangled with his under the soapy water, and his chin rested on her shoulder. She could feel his breath on her neck, his fast heartbeat against her back. The smile slipped off her face and Rorie turned, braced her hands against his hard chest, and looked at Phillip with a quivering of uncertainty in her stomach.

His smile was gone, too. Up close, he was handsomer than ever. He hadn't been able to shave that morning, and the light stubble on his masculine jaw made him look morning-sexy. His eyes were clear and luminous in the sunlight, and the expression in them as he stared back at Rorie took her breath away. She could tell he wanted to kiss her...as much as she wanted him to.

Her gaze drifted to his lips. They were chiseled, sensuous, and—she couldn't doubt—extremely capable of doing the kind of kissing that made a girl's knees go weak.

She was leaning forward, her eyes were drifting shut...when a large, cold, rough tongue lapped up against her cheek with the force of a hard left hook.

Rorie's eyes flew open in time to witness Dragon giving Phillip the same sort of affectionate buss on the cheek he'd just given her.

"Hey, get lost, Dragon," Phillip growled, pushing the dog away. "Can't you see we're busy here?"

But Rorie was eternally grateful for the interruption. It was just the shock she needed to wake her up to exactly what was going on. And what was going on was a lot crazier than a water fight in a tub laced liberally with dog shampoo.

She pushed herself to her knees, caught hold of the rim of the pool, and stood up.

"Hey, where are you going?" Phillip called after her, as she marched determinedly toward the back of the house.

"To look for my marbles," she replied crossly. "I think I lost them awhile ago."

"Aurora Dawn, you're just scared," Phillip taunted. She glanced over her shoulder just before she turned the corner. Phillip was standing in the pool, hands on his hips, feet spread apart. His shirt clung to his sculpted chest and his hair hung over his forehead in plump, shiny waves. He was gorgeous. But he was dangerous, too, she reminded herself. Kim said he broke women's hearts on a regular basis, and Rorie was experiencing firsthand how easily that could be accomplished. Phillip was right about one thing...she *was* scared.

NEARLY TWO HOURS later, after a shower and some stern self-lecturing in the privacy of her bedroom, Rorie was trying unsuccessfully to read a magazine when someone knocked on her door.

"Rorie? It's me, honey." It was Dahlia.

"Yes?" Rorie was reluctant to open the door. On the other side was temptation, and her godmothers were the culprits who had invited that six-foot-two-inch tower of temptation into their previously safe-from-scoundrels' home.

"Briar Rose, I need to ask you a favor."

Briar Rose. Her godmothers rarely called her by that nickname. As a child, she'd begged them not to because it had embarrassed her. But sometimes, during moments of tenderness or illness, or if they wanted to butter her up for some reason, the name slipped out.

"What's the favor, Dahlia?" Rorie asked suspiciously. "If it has anything to do with Phillip Fairchild—"

"He doesn't know how to get to the groomers, Rorie. I wish you'd go with him so he doesn't get lost."

"Can't he follow directions?"

"You know how men are about that, dear, and the Critter Care beauty salon is rather hard to find if you're not familiar with that part of town. If he makes a couple of wrong turns, he'll be late and we'll lose our appointment. You know how hard it is for Lynette to fit Dragon into her busy schedule. She has to leave a big chunk of time open and hire extra help. We're lucky she's willing to do it at all. I don't think we ought to jeopardize our relationship with her by being late, do you?''

Rorie rolled her eyes and gave a mighty sigh. ''All right, Dahlia,'' she said with weary resignation. ''I'll do it for your sake and for Dragon's. But even if you pass Phillip on this test, there won't be another one, 'cause I will never go on a date with him. Never! Do you understand, Dahlia?''

''Yes, dear, I understand,'' Dahlia answered meekly. There was a pause, then she added, ''But dear...never say never.''

As Phillip waited out front by the minivan with Dragon on a leash at his side, he ruminated about how he'd spent a lot of his time at the Farley house in a sheet. After his water fight with Rorie and then Dragon's bath afterward, he'd had to hand over his shorts, T-shirt and boxers to Dahlia to be washed and dried before going to the groomers. She'd luckily taken time off from her anti-worm crusade to fix lunch for herself and Daffy and Daisy and had noticed his soaked-to-the-bone condition. When he asked her why Rorie hadn't made them lunch as usual, she'd answered that Rorie had for some reason shut herself up in her room.

It was then that Phillip realized he had a real dilemma on his hands. More than any other woman he'd ever met, he was intrigued by and attracted to Rorie. And, more than any other woman he'd ever met, she resisted the slightest advance he made as if he were Lucifer.

Other women sometimes played hard to get, but they were usually just playing. Rorie was dead serious. She wanted nothing to do with him. Judging by their near kiss in the pool, he was pretty sure she was attracted to him, too, but she was fighting the attraction...seemed almost frightened of giving in to it. Obviously, she had a good reason, a *real* reason for feeling the way she did. He was determined to find out what that reason was and fix it if he could.

"Okay, Fairchild, put Dragon in the back and let's go," Rorie said as she breezed through the gate and headed for the driver's side of the minivan.

She wouldn't even look at him, but Phillip made sure he got an eyeful of her. She'd changed into a sleeveless, romper-style shorts outfit. It was pale blue with white roses on it...of all things. Again she'd pulled her hair back in a ponytail and there wasn't a smidgen of makeup on her face. She looked like the girl next door, squeaky-clean and sexy as hell.

He quickly opened the sliding door in the back, undid Dragon's leash, then stepped aside so the dog could jump in. As he did, the van dropped by several inches. He noticed that someone had taken out the middle seat so Dragon would have room to sit down.

"I hope this car's got good struts," he remarked, slipping into the passenger's seat and putting on his seat belt. "Dragon must weigh a ton."

Rorie didn't answer; she just slipped on her sunglasses, started the car, checked her mirror, and pulled onto the street.

"So now you're not talking to me?" he said in an exasperated tone. "Damn it, Rorie, just tell me why you think I'm such a bastard. Don't I even have a right to defend myself?"

They drove on for a mile or two in silence. Frustrated, but trying to be patient, Phillip stared into the side mirror at the traffic. There was a rusty Volkswagen bus behind them with daisies painted around the headlights. It looked like a relic from the sixties.

He was beginning to think Rorie wasn't going to utter a single word during the entire trip when she suddenly said, "I can sum up my dislike of you in two words, Fairchild."

He turned to look at her. "Okay. Let's hear them."

She flitted him a cold glance, then said, "Kim Norville."

Phillip felt sick. "Don't tell me you know the lady?"

"We were friends when I was a child. I met her again during a photo shoot about six months ago. She modeled some of my sweaters for a catalogue. It was great to see her again, but she seemed unhappy about something. Then she started confiding in me about this bad-news romance she'd had with a man, and for three days she did nothing but talk about you, Fairchild. And from everything she told me—"

"You concluded that I was a monster," he finished for her.

"According to her, you lied to her, cheated on her, promised her things so she'd do whatever you wanted, then dumped her like yesterday's garbage. She cried a lot. I felt sorry for her."

"And you believed everything she said without question, I suppose?"

"Why should I doubt her? Like I said, we go way back. Besides, I had already heard stuff about you."

"You mean you read stuff about me in those scandal sheets, right?"

She ignored this interruption. "Everything she said seemed to make sense. And now I suppose you're going to tell me that everything she said was a lie?'' She turned and regarded him coolly, skeptically. ''Well?'' she prompted. ''Aren't you going to defend yourself? Isn't that what you said you wanted to do...explain?''

''I *will* explain,'' he answered, his gaze fixed again on the side mirror. They'd turned several corners, and still the Volkswagen bus was behind them, staying a discreet two or three car lengths back. ''But first I think you ought to know...we're being followed.''

Chapter Eight

"We're being *followed?* That's a pretty lame avoidance tactic, Fairchild."

"I'm serious, Rorie," Phillip told her. "There's a ratty-looking Volkswagen bus that's been on our tail ever since we left your neighborhood."

She sighed and shook her head, staring straight ahead at the road. "You've been reading too many Grisham novels. It must be purely coincidental that they've been behind us all this time. They're just headed in the same direction as we are. Maybe they're even going to the same groomers. Do you see a dog in the car?"

Phillip peered into the mirror, straining to see. "No, just two people. The driver is a short man with dark, shaggy hair and a mustache. He's wearing sunglasses and some kind of little cap. There's a woman sitting next to him, much taller than him, with long black hair. It looks like they're both wearing loud, flowered vests. Geez, if this were the sixties, I'd almost swear I was seeing Sonny and Cher!"

"But this is the nineties," Rorie said drily. "And, in case you haven't heard, Sonny and Cher broke up years ago. It was a good split though, 'cause she went on to win an Oscar and he became a Representative in the House.''

''All right, so don't take me seriously,'' Phillip said irritably. ''But I'm keeping an eye on them.''

''Whatever,'' Rorie said with a beleaguered sigh. ''We're almost there, anyway.''

A minute later, Rorie turned into the parking lot of a strip mall and pulled in front of a small glass-fronted building with a sign reading Critter Care above the door.

''Okay, don't get out till I see what the Volkswagen does,'' Phillip cautioned, still staring into the mirror at the traffic going by. Within seconds the bus sped past.

''So what are you going to come up with next to put off your explanation about Kim?'' Rorie asked him in a sarcastic tone. ''A UFO sighting?''

Phillip grimaced and got out of the car. He still had a bad feeling about that Volkswagen bus, but maybe he was just being paranoid. The African bees showing up at the Farley House still hadn't been explained, and he was feeling a little nervous about what might happen next. Was the bee incident an isolated incident, a prank by a disgruntled loser from the horticultural show at the fair, or did someone have other tricks up their sleeve?

''I brought a sausage in my purse to use as a bribe,'' Rorie revealed as she came around to the passenger side of the car. She pulled out the sausage and peeled off the plastic wrap.

Phillip raised his brows in surprise. ''Earlier you said you were out of sausage.''

''I lied.''

''So why are you helping me now? I thought you had to be coerced to drive me here.''

"I'm doing this for my godmothers," she explained, opening the sliding door of the minivan. "And for Dragon. If he doesn't get trimmed, he'll die from the heat this summer."

Recognizing where he was, Dragon had plastered himself against the driver's side of the minivan, but when he saw and smelled the sausage his ears pricked up and he came eagerly forward.

"Put the leash on," Rorie instructed. "It really doesn't do much good, because we probably couldn't stop him if he tried to run away, but Lynette insists that we use it."

"He won't try to run away, will he?"

"He never has before."

Satisfied, Phillip did as he was told and Rorie waggled the sausage in front of Dragon's nose. Salivating, the dog followed her out of the car and toward the building. Phillip hurried forward to open the door.

Everything seemed to be going smoothly, when suddenly the very same Volkswagen bus Phillip had been watching in the mirror came skidding into the parking lot from the back of the store and screeched to a halt. The back door flew open and about a dozen cats jumped out! Then, tires squealing, the bus did a tight U-turn and disappeared down a side street behind the store, leaving a trail of rubber behind it.

As the cats scattered wildly, Dragon's head seemed almost to spin on his neck as, panting and drooling, he tried to keep track of where they were all running off to. But several remained in the middle of the parking lot, spitting and hissing and swishing their tails.

This was too much temptation for any dog to resist, and despite the fact that Rorie was frantically waving the sausage in front of his nose and calling his name,

Dragon gave in to his primal urges, let loose with a soulful howl, and charged after the congregation of cats who still loitered, expressing their indignation, in the middle of the parking lot.

Phillip dug in his heels and held fast to the leash, but he was no match for a three-hundred-pound dog. Dragon actually dragged him several feet, wearing down the heels of his sneakers and leaving a rubber trail similar to the one left by the Volkswagen bus, before the leash snapped in two. Phillip fell backwards and landed hard on his sore bum on the hot asphalt of the parking lot.

"No, Dragon! Not the street!" Phillip heard Rorie yell just before she passed him at warp speed. She was running after the wildly barking dog, who was chasing several of the cats right into the path of busy oncoming traffic!

"Rorie! Stop!" Phillip called, struggling to his feet and racing after her. But Rorie seemed oblivious to everything except her pursuit of Dragon.

The cats were in the street now, with Dragon hot on their heels. It was chaos! Drivers slammed on their brakes and swerved around the bewildered and terrified cats and the humongous dog that was chasing them.

Rorie charged into the midst of the pandemonium, calling and scolding Dragon and waving the sausage, with Phillip about ten paces behind her, feeling frustrated as hell. He thought Rorie seemed to be trying to watch for traffic, but it became obvious that she wasn't doing a very good job when she sprinted right into the path of a Ford Explorer!

Too far away to push her or grab her, Phillip lunged into the air and caught Rorie around the waist, yanking her with him as he tumbled to safety on the soft shoulder of the road.

Lying on his back in the overgrown grass, with a few burrs making themselves known through the thin material of his T-shirt, Phillip breathed hard and clung to Rorie as if she might leap to her feet and endanger her life all over again. He heard car doors slamming and the scuffle of feet approaching.

"Are…are you all right, Rorie?" Phillip managed to say in between pants, speaking raggedly into her hair.

"I'm…I'm okay," she said shakily. "Are…are you?"

But before he could answer, several worried-looking people were suddenly standing over them and asking dozens of questions. Rorie and Phillip were helped to their feet and made to sit down on the side of the road. Phillip assured them that, except for a few superficial scrapes and bruises, they were fine, but they continued to hover. Traffic in the area had come to a virtual standstill and Phillip heard sirens approaching in the distance.

"Dragon! Where's Dragon?" Rorie exclaimed as soon as she got her wits about her.

"If you mean that huge dog that was chasing the cats," said the man who was driving the Explorer, "last I saw of him he was headed east."

Rorie turned woeful eyes to Phillip. "I should have been more careful."

Phillip put his arm around her shoulder and gave her a squeeze. "It wasn't your fault, Rorie. We were sabotaged."

"But who would do such a thing?"

"I have my suspicions," he answered grimly.

"You probably saved this young woman's life, you know," the man said, interrupting Phillip's angry thoughts. "I braked, but I was still going close to thirty miles an hour, fast enough to cause some very serious injuries. And you risked your own life doing it."

Phillip looked up in surprise. He hadn't thought of it that way at all. He glanced at Rorie and she looked just as surprised as he did.

"Yes," she said wonderingly. "You *did* save my life, didn't you? And you could have been hurt...or killed."

Phillip didn't answer. He didn't know what to say. All he knew was that he'd do it all over again, a thousand times, just to make sure Aurora Dawn McBride walked on the same earth and breathed the same air that he did.

AN HOUR AND A HALF later, after answering questions from the police and being quickly examined and treated for minor cuts by the paramedics, Rorie and Phillip got in the minivan and headed back to the house. Phillip drove and they both searched the streets as they went along, but there was no sign of a giant dog anywhere, or—for that matter—any people fleeing from a giant dog.

"At least no one was hurt, no cars were damaged, and none of the cats got squashed in the road," Rorie said, looking for something positive to say. "I saw the truck from the Humane Society picking them up. And, luckily for you, the media didn't show up, either."

"I don't think anyone recognized me in my grubbies," Phillip said. "But I have a feeling the word will get out and suddenly the rags will be singing my praises, calling me a hero. That'll be a change from my usual press."

Rorie stared at his grim profile. "What you did *was* heroic."

"I did what anyone would do under the circumstances. I didn't even think about it. You were going to get plowed down by a truck if I didn't move fast, so I moved fast. End of story."

Rorie didn't know what to think of the way Phillip was downplaying the fact that he'd saved her life. His matter-of-fact attitude left her feeling vaguely disappointed. But ever since the accident, he'd seemed distracted, absorbed in his own sober thoughts.

The thought that continually repeated itself in Rorie's brain was that Phillip Fairchild had probably saved her life. *He'd saved her life.* If not for him, she'd be in the hospital or at the morgue. For the past two days she'd given him nothing but grief, thought of him in the worst possible context. Then, disregarding his own safety, he'd performed an act of heroism for her sake.

Obviously, finding favor with her godmothers had had nothing to do with it. If anything, with her out of the way, his path would have been clearer for obtaining the fertilizer formula. His motives had to have been purely unselfish. He'd thought only of her.

It was depressing, but there was no way around it; Rorie had to start thinking of Phillip Fairchild as a decent human being. Talk about opening up a can of worms....

"What's the matter, Rorie?" Phillip said, suddenly coming out of his reverie and giving her a concerned look. "Thinking of Dragon?"

"That, too," Rorie mumbled.

"He's a smart dog," Phillip said. "I'll bet he finds his way home."

"He doesn't know his way around," Rorie said gloomily. We hardly ever take him out because his size terrifies people, and, as you know, it's impossible to hold on to his leash if he decides to chase a squirrel or a cat. I suppose there's a chance that Animal Control will pick him up, but you know how hard he can be to manage." She sighed. "If he doesn't come home one way or the other, my godmothers will be heartbroken."

He reached over and touched her shoulder. She turned and he smiled sympathetically. "You're attached to him, too. What about *your* heart?"

"It would be a lot more convenient to go through life without one," she said ruefully, trying to hide her distress behind a joke.

He gave her a look that clearly indicated he knew what she was doing, and said, "Yeah, it would be more convenient. But it'd be damned cold, too."

Rorie did not reply. The conversation was getting too serious for comfort. And she was feeling way too friendly toward Phillip. She reminded herself that he still hadn't explained away Kim's accusations. Maybe he couldn't.

"Why were you so vague when the police asked you for descriptions of the Volkswagen bus and the people in it?" she asked him, changing the subject. "I know you saw them clearly."

"I can't explain right now, but thanks for following my lead. I'll tell you my theory when I have more facts to back it up. But I don't think we're going to want the police involved."

Rorie nodded, too tired and too worried about

Dragon to try to decipher Phillip's answer. As with his explanation about Kim, it seemed she had no choice but to wait for this explanation, too.

Despite the fact that she was dreading telling her godmothers about Dragon running away, Rorie was relieved when the minivan finally turned down their street. She closed her eyes and leaned back against the headrest, mentally going over how she'd break the news to Dahlia, Daisy and Daffy.

"I don't believe it!"

Rorie's eyes popped open. She stared at Phillip, who had a huge smile on his face. "You don't believe what?"

Rorie turned as he pointed straight ahead through the front window. "There, by the gate. It's—"

"Dragon!" Rorie bounced in the seat. "He made it home!"

Phillip was barely able to get the van parked before Rorie jumped out and ran to Dragon, throwing her arms around his neck and simultaneously petting and scolding him. Dragon just sat there—probably too tired to do anything else—and looked as relieved and happy as they were. Obviously he'd been through a few fields on his way home, because he was covered with dust and burrs and dry grass.

Phillip shook his head and smiled. "So much for your bath, Dragon. You already need another one, but don't count on *me* to give it to you."

"We'd better get him inside," Rorie said, self-consciously blinking away the moisture in her eyes. "I'm sure he's thirsty."

They had been in the house for just a few minutes, still fussing over Dragon in the kitchen, when the godmothers showed up. Coming in through the back door, they stopped in their tracks when they saw that Phillip and Rorie had bandages on their knees and elbows and dirt on their clothes, and that Dragon looked like he'd just returned from visiting a family of dingoes in the Australian bush.

"Oh, dear," Dahlia said faintly. "What happened?"

Probably trying to downplay the danger of what had occurred, Rorie calmly explained about the cats, the traffic jam, the police, and the runaway dog. But her godmothers were too sharp to be fooled into thinking the incident was less serious than it was. All three collapsed into chairs and stared at Rorie.

"Briar Rose!" exclaimed Daffy. "You might have been killed!"

Phillip noticed that Rorie blushed and slid an embarrassed glance his way when Daffy called her "Briar Rose." He immediately thought the name fitted her perfectly. She was like a beautiful rose…with thorns. He was intrigued by the nickname and wondered how it had come about in the first place, but to spare Rorie's blushes he pretended not to be interested at all.

"And *you* saved her life, Phillip," Daisy added. "How can we ever thank you?"

A less scrupulous man might have taken advantage of the Farley sisters' gratitude and asked for the fertilizer formula then and there. Hell, even three days ago he might have used the opportunity to push his own agenda, Phillip admitted to himself. But now that he knew the Farley sisters—and their goddaughter—there was no way he would take advantage of them.

"Well, you might cut me a little slack on this last test," he suggested with a wry smile. "I obviously blew it. I managed to bathe Dragon, but he's already filthy again. And the trip to the groomers was a total fiasco. In fact, Lynette came out and told us you'd have to take your business elsewhere from now on.''

''Humph! Well, we'll just learn how to clip him ourselves, won't we, girls?'' Dahlia said indignantly. ''But finding a way to trim Dragon is the least of our troubles. The bee incident was trivial compared to this. Obviously, someone is intent on causing us a lot of trouble and grief, and we have to find out who it is and why they're doing it.''

''But how?'' was Daisy's very reasonable question.

''Let me see what I can find out,'' Phillip offered, meeting Dahlia's gaze and establishing an immediate understanding between them. He knew that Dahlia shared his suspicions about who the villain was in this little drama.

Dahlia nodded grimly. ''All right, Phillip, find out what you can. I know I can trust you to be…discreet. But take care, you understand? This person, or persons, might not have intended for things to happen exactly as they did today, but someone could have been seriously hurt.''

Phillip nodded soberly.

Minutes later, Rorie walked Phillip to his car.

''You and Dahlia think it's Delphinia, don't you?'' she asked him.

Phillip didn't reply.

''She's a strange person—cold and manipulative— and I've never liked her, but I never thought she would do anything to hurt her sisters. I don't understand how *anyone* could hurt such sweethearts.''

''In case you hadn't noticed, your godmothers haven't exactly been the prime target of these pranks,'' Phillip pointed out.

"Do you think Delphinia's trying to keep you from passing the tests and getting the fertilizer formula?"

"I'd rather not say just yet," Phillip said cautiously. He didn't really want Rorie involved.

"Once again I must wait till 'later' for an explanation, I see," she said with a sigh.

Phillip turned to her and said earnestly, "I promise I'll let you know what I find out as soon as I know more. I'll explain about Kim, too. But right now I think we could all use a little downtime."

Rorie shrugged. "Whatever you say, Fairchild." She turned to go, then turned back. She looked at the grass, the trees, the sky, at everything but him. "By the way…thanks."

"For what?"

"For saving my life."

He smiled. "You're welcome."

She met his gaze and held it for a moment, then smiled shyly. Abruptly she turned again and disappeared into the shrubs and foliage.

Phillip stood there for a moment, feeling conflicted and miserable. He didn't want to go home. Even though Delphinia was probably targeting only him, he didn't like leaving Rorie and her godmothers unprotected for even a moment. But maybe they were in *more* danger when he was around. Now *that* was a somber thought.

He tended to believe—as Dahlia had suggested in so many veiled words—that Delphinia hadn't meant the cat incident to endanger everyone's life, but her behavior was still terribly irresponsible and meanspirited. Even—dare he say it?—downright *wacko!*

How did one handle a wacko person? he wondered. Should he confront Delphinia, accuse her of her crimes and threaten her with a harassment suit? It was a tempting idea but, unfortunately, so far he didn't have any rock-solid proof that would stand up in court. Besides, getting the authorities involved would cause the Farley sisters distress and embarrassment. And maybe they'd want to deal with their sister on a more private and personal level.

So, as an alternative plan, should he give up the fertilizer formula so Delphinia would have no reason to play her malevolent little tricks?

But Phillip knew that giving up and moving on wasn't the answer, either. With or without competition, Delphinia would still want the fertilizer formula. The Farley sisters had made it clear that they didn't want to sell the formula to their half sister—and Phillip was beginning to think they had good reason not to—but that wouldn't stop Delphinia. Her recent behavior smacked of desperation. What would she do next?

No, there was no way he was going to bow out now. But, while he still wanted the formula, his main reason for sticking around had changed. He was determined to stop Delphinia from bullying her sisters or harming them in any way. He wasn't going to let her bully or harm Rorie, either.

Briar Rose. He smiled. What an apt name for Rorie.

Now, what was that saying about when you save someone's life you're responsible for it from then on? The idea had interesting possibilities....

"HE'S DRIVING away, madam."

Delphinia's plump lips, coated with white, frosted lipstick, curled in a contemptuous smirk. "Finally. At least he isn't spending the night again. And perhaps he isn't coming back at all. He must have failed miserably at the second test. Too bad we couldn't stick around to watch the outcome of our little plan." She snickered. "That beast of a dog must have gone completely berserk when he saw all those cats!" She pulled down the visor and looked into the mirror attached to the underside, checking to make sure her false eyelashes were still securely in place.

"Yes, madam."

Satisfied with her lashes, Delphinia turned up the visor. "We know, at least, that he ran away, but I must confess I'm amazed that he had the brains to find his way home." She stuck a long nail under the edge of her wig and scratched. "Speaking of home, Simon, it's time we got back and listened to our surveillance tapes to see if my sisters and *Briar Rose* and the *Prince* have said anything remotely interesting...hopefully, something we can use against them. Besides, this damned wig is getting hot and itchy."

"Yes, madam." Simon turned on the ignition and the Volkswagen's engine sputtered to life. He did a U-turn in the wide residential street and headed east toward the exclusive neighborhood of Buckhead.

Jiggling and jolting along, and wincing every time Simon ground the gears, Delphinia missed the comfort of her Rolls with a passion, though the Volkswagen had been a necessary part of their disguise.

She glanced over at Simon, who made a perfect Sonny to her Cher. It had actually been rather fun finding the sixties-style clothing at the Goodwill. Besides, she thought smugly, with *her* figure she was made to wear hip-huggers.

Gloating over a job well done, Delphinia leaned back and lit a cigarette. "Turn on the radio, Simon," she said. "Find me an oldies station. I'm in the mood for some rock music."

"Yes, madam."

Simon steered with one hand, searching the radio dial and shifting with the other, while Delphinia lazily viewed the passing scenery through the window. Suddenly, she sat up and slapped Simon's hand. "Leave it there, Simon. It's a news broadcast and I thought I heard something about—"

"Cats. About a dozen cats were released from a van in front of Critter Care, a pet-grooming business on Kennesaw. Phillip Fairchild, a local celebrity, reputed ladies' man, and C.E.O. of Fair Lady Perfumes, was entering the establishment with a woman when the dog Fairchild was holding by a leash broke away and chased the cats into oncoming traffic."

Simon looked at Delphinia, an expression of shock and alarm on his face. "I thought the cats would run around to the back of the building. I never thought they'd dash into the street!"

"Shut up, Simon!" Delphinia hissed.

"The woman, identified as Aurora McBride, followed the dog—an exceptionally large, indeterminate breed—into the street, apparently trying to lure him away from danger with a sausage."

"Oh, Lord," moaned Simon, pulling to the side of the road and killing the engine. He took off his hat and wig and wiped his brow with a shaky hand.

"Shh!"

"Several cars were forced to brake as the animals and Ms. McBride remained on the road. At one point it looked like Ms. McBride was going to be hit by a Ford Explorer going about thirty miles an hour, when Fairchild raced into the path of the oncoming vehicle and carried Ms. McBride to safety."

"Thank God!" Simon whispered fervently.

"Except for a few minor scrapes and bruises, Fairchild and McBride escaped the chaotic scene without serious injury. Fortunately none of the animals or other passengers in the cars involved in the incident were harmed, either. Police Chief Malcolm Davis says Fairchild's quick response to Ms. McBride's dangerous situation was heroic."

"Damn him!" Delphinia growled. "He *would* come off a hero!"

"As to the perpetrators of this irresponsible prank, which according to Chief Davis, could have had a much more disastrous outcome, no arrests have been made. The only witnesses to the actual dumping of the cats were Fairchild and McBride, and neither of them can give detailed descriptions of the vehicle or the drivers. Police call the incident a malicious act by immature pranksters, but Phillip Fairchild—ladies' man extraordinaire and Perfume Prince—is also being called a hero. In other news—"

"Turn it off!" Delphinia snapped, giving the dashboard a furious whack with her fist. "A hero! A *hero!*"

Simon turned off the radio and stared horrified at Delphinia. "Madam, don't you realize that we might have caused someone an injury? That Aurora might even have been killed?"

"But no one was hurt, you foolish little man!" she snarled. "And now things are more desperate than ever. My sisters will be so grateful to Fairchild, they'll hand over the formula without even requiring him to finish the tests!"

"We don't know that, madam," Simon reasoned, fearfully observing Delphinia's growing agitation. "Don't...don't despair just yet. Let us go home first and listen to the tapes. No doubt your sisters will have discussed the incident among themselves. We can know within minutes how things stand and whether or not we have something to worry about."

Delphinia calmed down a little. Though such was seldom the case, she realized that Simon was probably right. It was too soon to panic.

"Very well, Simon, drive on," she presently ordered. "We'll listen to the tapes."

STRIDING INTO his bedroom after a long, hot shower, a towel draped loosely around his waist and hanging low on his hips, Phillip picked up his cordless phone and punched in a series of numbers.

As he waited for an answer, he moved to the window and looked out over downtown Atlanta. He had a great view all right, but he still preferred the verdant scenery visible from Rorie's office window. Or was that just because Rorie had been viewing it with him?

"Fair Lady Perfumes. Mr. Fairchild's office."

"Zach?" Phillip ran a hand through his wet hair.

"Mr. Fairchild? I heard on the radio about you saving that woman's life!"

Phillip pinched the bridge of his nose with his thumb and forefinger and bowed his head. "Don't tell me it's on the news?"

"Yep." Zach paused. "Is that bad?"

"Let's just say I hate publicity. Unless it's for a charitable event or good cause, I hate all kinds of publicity."

"Er...sorry, Mr. Fairchild."

"That's okay, Zach. Say, listen, I have something I need you to do."

"Yes, sir?"

"I need you to get as much information as possible on a woman named Delphinia Devine." He spelled it for him.

"Strange name, sir."

"Strange woman," he answered drily. "Hire an investigator, if necessary. Whatever. Just find out whatever you can about her. I'll call you tomorrow afternoon to see what you've come up with." Phillip figured that his best defense against Delphinia was to know as much about her as possible. It seemed to be the only thing he could do at this point. That, and waiting for her next move and hoping to trip her up somehow.

"All right, sir. Anything else?"

"No, Zach. Everything going okay at the office?"

"A few things have come up...but they'll hold till you're back. Are you enjoying your days off, sir?"

Phillip laughed. "That's debatable, Zach. Talk to you tomorrow." He hung up the phone, walked to the closet, dropped his towel and slipped into a robe. He stretched out on the bed and crossed his arms behind his head.

Staring at the ceiling, he asked himself, *Am I having a good time?* Or was he falling in love? Could the two things possibly be synonymous? Because he'd never been in love before, he didn't know.

Would Rorie understand about Kim? Would she believe his side of the story?

Briar Rose. What a fitting nickname for a woman with a sharp tongue and the softest skin he'd ever touched.

Briar Rose. Would he be able to talk such a prickly beauty into going out with him tomorrow?

He drifted off to sleep, dreaming of beaches and sand pails and seagulls, and of a little girl with long blond hair and eyes the color of sapphires....

Chapter Nine

Rorie stood in her office, a skein of pale yellow yarn in her hand, staring out the window at another bright and beautiful day. Three new orders for sweaters had come in the mail that morning, but she couldn't seem to focus on the task of collecting the different colored yarns, matching them with the right pattern, and deciding on the right worker to do the knitting. She couldn't seem to focus on anything or anyone but...*him.*

Damn you, Phillip Fairchild, she grumbled to herself. *Why did you have to come into our quiet lives and disrupt everything?*

Impatient with herself, Rorie moved away from the window and rummaged through her shelves full of yarn. But she found herself frequently glancing at the clock on her desk. It was eleven o'clock already. Eleven o'clock and nothing done.

And no Phillip, she added sullenly.

"Don't worry, dear, he'll be here soon."

Rorie turned to see Dahlia standing at the door, a knowing and sympathetic smile slightly curving her lips. Aware that it was a childish reaction, but unable to help herself, Rorie gave a haughty little sniff and replied, "*Who* will be here soon, Dahlia?"

Undaunted, Dahlia replied with a twinkle in her eye, "Why your prince, of course."

"Phillip Fairchild is no prince."

"He saved your life, dear."

"Yes, but he also ruined the life of a friend of mine from the old neighborhood."

Dahlia's wispy white eyebrows lifted. "Ah, so that's why you don't like him. What did he do? Break her heart?"

"Yes, and he did it in a cruel and selfish fashion."

"Have you asked him about this friend?"

"Yes, yesterday."

"I'm sure he had a perfectly good explanation."

"That remains to be seen. He says he has an explanation, but I haven't heard it yet."

"Well, you must admit, yesterday was a rather hectic day for everyone."

"Yes, and today is a busy day for me," she said briskly, still aimlessly rummaging through the yarn. "I received three new orders in the mail today and—"

"But you *will* take the time to listen to Phillip's explanation, won't you? It's only fair. And he's planning to ask you out, you know. It's the last test."

"Don't get your hopes up, Dahlia," Rorie cautioned. "I haven't changed my mind. I'll listen to him—if he ever shows up—but he'll never convince me to go out with him. Understand?"

Dahlia just pursed her lips and shrugged, saying nothing. Seeing that her firm words had made as little impression on her godmother as a pebble thrown into the sea, Rorie was about to launch into another verbal declaration of her unshakable determination never to go on a date with Phillip Fairchild, when the doorbell rang.

"Well, we know who that is," Dahlia said with a beaming smile. "He's the only one who knows the way."

"He's not that smart. Dragon shows him the way," Rorie called after her as Dahlia hurried away.

"Dragon's in the backyard, dear, getting thoroughly brushed by Daisy and Daffy," Dahlia called back.

"Humph!" Rorie said to herself. "So he's a quick study? In other ways, he's far from perfect."

But whether or not he was perfect, Rorie's heart had begun to race at the thought of seeing Phillip again. She tried to concentrate on matching yarn, but the colors just blurred in front of her eyes.

Giving up, she moved to the full-length mirror attached to the closet door and observed her appearance. She had given in to the urge to wear her hair down, but she had dressed simply in a powder-blue sleeveless blouse tucked into a pair of stonewashed jeans. Pale pink lipstick and a touch of mascara were the extent of the makeup she wore. As she'd gotten ready that morning, she'd told herself she had no intention of dressing up for Phillip.

I don't care whether he thinks I'm pretty or not, she assured herself as she patted a wayward curl into place and rolled her lips together to evenly distribute her lipstick.

"Aurora?" It was Dahlia, calling her from the bottom of the stairs.

"Yes, Dahlia, I'm coming," she called back, steeling herself for the challenge of appearing distant and indifferent toward Phillip. She'd slipped a little yesterday, but another restless night of going over in her mind Kim's tearful revelations had made Rorie determined to be very cautious with Phillip. He might have saved her life, but that didn't mean he wouldn't break her heart.

Nevertheless, by the time she'd reached the bottom of the steps, her heart was hammering against her ribs harder and faster than ever. And when she walked into the parlor and saw Phillip standing by the window, casually dressed in a pair of tan chinos and a cream-colored banded-collar shirt, she felt goose bumps erupt all over her body. He smiled…and Rorie was helplessly dazzled.

"I'll leave you two alone," Dahlia said, quickly exiting.

Terrified, Rorie seemed about to detain Dahlia, but then turned back, realizing that she must face this moment sooner or later. And she owed it to Phillip to at least listen to whatever he had to say in defense of himself.

"You probably want to be alone with me about as much as you'd like to tumble down Niagara Falls in a barrel," he suggested drily.

Dangerous, but oh so thrilling… Rorie couldn't help comparing the two with disastrous results.

"I owe you the courtesy of listening, Phillip," Rorie said primly, moving to the sofa and sitting down with her back straight as a board and her hands clasped on her knees.

"But you don't expect to be swayed by my explanation about Kim, do you? You're very sure I'm the villain, aren't you?"

"I find it hard to believe that Kim would lie to me."

Phillip sat down in the chair by the sofa, propped his elbows on his knees and leaned forward. He was close enough that she could smell his cologne and see the silver flecks in his gray eyes. Too close for comfort...

"You hadn't seen her in years—until six months ago," he said.

"But she wouldn't lie to me," Rorie insisted.

"You're right. She wouldn't. And she wasn't lying to you when she told you those terrible stories about me."

Rorie blinked. "You mean you admit you treated Kim badly? That you used her and then abandoned her?"

"No, I did nothing of the sort. All I'm saying is that everything Kim said to you she *believed* to be absolutely true."

Rorie frowned. "I don't understand."

"Kim is delusional."

Rorie was disbelieving. "Delusional? You want me to believe she's *crazy?*" She stood up and began to pace the rug. "You're a piece of work, Fairchild! Kim and I were very close when we were kids. She was as sane as I am! What are you trying to pull?"

"I'm not trying to pull anything, Rorie," Phillip said seriously, watching her pace up and down. "I'm telling the truth. Kim and I did date. And we did get fairly close, for a time. But I never told her I loved her. She seemed like a really sweet girl at first, but then she got really possessive...*frighteningly* possessive. She was jealous of the most innocent conversations I'd have with other women."

"Your reputation with women might have made her feel a little insecure, Fairchild," Rorie suggested sarcastically, standing with her hands on her hips.

"That's understandable," he admitted. "But Kim's insecurities sort of took over her whole personality. She

spent every moment she could with me. She showed
up at work several times a day. I'd come home from
the office and find her in my condo.''

''You gave her a key?''

''No, I've never given any woman a key to my
condo. That's a serious step that implies love and commitment. Kim conned my secretary into giving her the
spare key he kept for me in his desk. Then she held on
to it. Short of changing the lock on my door, I didn't
know how to keep her out of my place. She'd have
dinner ready, then she'd stay the night...even when I
had to go out of town for meetings and wasn't even
there. She basically moved in with me without an invitation.''

Rorie changed position, folding her arms over her
chest and listening intently.

''Even though her jealous tantrums and possessive-
ness had killed whatever affection I'd felt for her, I
didn't want to hurt her. She seemed very...fragile.''
Phillip smiled sadly and shook his head. ''There I was,
the head of a huge company, managing hundreds of
people and issuing dozens of orders every day...but I
couldn't seem to stop a petite redhead from taking over
my life.''

Rorie sat down on the sofa again, folding one leg
under her. ''So what did you do?''

He looked grim. ''What I had to do. I'd told her
many times that there was no future for us, but I guess
I was too nice about it or too gentle. So I sat her down
one day and told her firmly and unequivocally that we
were through. My words left room for no misunderstanding about how I felt. She cried, but she seemed
resigned. She gathered her stuff and left, and I thought
it was over. I didn't ask for the key back, but I guess

I should have. Though I never caught her there, evidence began surfacing that she was still using the key to get into my condo. Small things, personal things started disappearing. Then, when I was out…whether I was out with a woman or having a business meeting…I'd see her."

"She was stalking you?" Rorie was horrified.

"Yes. That really unnerved me, so I had the lock changed on my door and hoped that that would finally put an end to things."

"Did it?"

"Unfortunately, no. She stormed into my office one day during a meeting with some of my European affiliates and screamed at me for changing the lock. It was horribly embarrassing for her when she finally calmed down and realized what she'd done."

"Poor Kim."

"Yes. I felt bad for her, but I was starting to feel pretty desperate about the whole situation for my sake, too. I considered getting a restraining order against her, but I didn't want to resort to that."

"What did you do?"

"I called her mother and talked to her about Kim's behavior. She was very understanding. In fact, she said she wasn't that surprised."

"Why?"

"Apparently Kim has done this sort of thing before."

"I had no idea!"

"How could you? Kim is perfectly normal…except that she becomes obsessive about men. She really believes everything she tells her sympathetic listeners. But, according to her mom the last time I talked to her, she's gotten professional help and is doing much better.

In fact, she says Kim might be getting engaged soon. I haven't seen her in months. That's why I was surprised when you brought her up.''

"Well, it was months ago that I talked to her about you," Rorie agreed, then she fell silent as she thought over everything Phillip had told her. She had to admit he was convincing.

"Now that I've explained myself, do you believe a single word I've said?''

"You'd have to be a dirty dog to make up such a story," she acknowledged grimly.

"I won't tell Dragon you said that," Phillip teased her, then grew immediately serious again. "I wouldn't have told you, I wouldn't have revealed any part of what I consider private and painful information about Kim and myself, if I didn't feel it was important to make you think a little better of me.''

She looked down, frowning at her clasped hands. "Because you want me to go out with you so you can pass the third test with flying colors, I suppose?''

He tilted her chin with his finger and compelled her to look at him. 'No, just so I can go out with you. Rorie, I like you. I've liked you from the day we met.''

"That was only three days ago," she said shyly. "And I was rude to you. I've been rude to you in just about every conversation we've ever had.''

He smiled. "But your softer qualities shine through. Your tender side is evident in the protective and respectful way you interact with your godmothers. And you couldn't have been more gentle when you tended my sore bum.''

Rorie was mortified to feel herself blushing. He was getting to her, and she hated that. "I was tricked into playing nurse by my matchmaking godmothers.''

He laughed softly, his breath fanning warmly over her face. "God bless 'em," he said affectionately. Then his smile disappeared and his gaze dropped to her mouth. "Briar Rose," he whispered. "I love that name. It fits you perfectly."

Rorie sat stiffly as she watched, half horrified, half crazed with excitement, as Phillip leaned closer and closer. His eyes drifted shut, the long lashes looking starkly black against his tanned cheek. With her eyes still determinedly open, she felt his lips touch hers. She tried not to respond, but her attraction to Phillip was too strong. Her eyes drifted shut, too.

Her response was tentative at first. She'd been kissed so few times in her life, and she'd never felt the urge to deepen the kiss beyond a little friendly lip pressing. But this time was different. She didn't want to like what was happening between her and Phillip, but the kiss seemed to take on a life of its own. Instead of drawing back after a few experimental seconds, she felt herself being drawn in deeper and deeper. She didn't want the kiss to end.

It didn't. Phillip parted his lips and slipped his tongue inside her mouth. The shock of such an intimate connection was electrifying...and so very *nice*. His large hands cupped her shoulders and Rorie's hands seemed to reach up of their own accord to wrap around his strong neck, pulling him closer.

He came closer. In fact, without even interrupting their kiss, he moved to sit on the sofa beside her and drew her into his arms. Rorie kissed him back as fervently, as intimately as he was kissing her. He gave a little moan and pulled her so close her breasts grew warm and achy against his hard chest.

Then, suddenly, she seemed to collect her scattered

senses and pulled away. Phillip looked surprised, dazed and disappointed.

"Why'd you stop?" He smiled crookedly. "I thought we were having a pretty good time just now."

"Well, I'm sure you *think* you know how to show a girl a good time," she murmured irritably, unwilling to concede his point. "Cocky, aren't you?"

"I wish you'd at least give me a chance to try to show you a good time, Rorie," he challenged. "Go out with me."

Rorie remained stubbornly silent. Phillip might have saved her life, and he might not have been the total bad guy in the Kim scenario, but he was still a reputed womanizer. She remembered too vividly all those beautiful faces and figures standing next to him in various newspaper photos. She was sure he'd kissed every one of them. He knew how to make women swoon, and he had a hell of a motive in this case to turn on the charm.

"I don't want to go out with you, Phillip."

"Why?"

"Because then you'll pass my godmothers' test." Of course, that was only partly true. She was afraid to go out with him. She was afraid he'd break her heart.

"Aren't you forgetting something, Rorie?"

"What?" she inquired suspiciously. She suddenly realized he was holding her hands and she slipped them free and scooted a few inches away.

He acknowledged her withdrawal with a rueful smile and an arch of his brow, but continued, apparently undaunted. "There's two parts to the last test. You have to agree to go out with me, but I also have to make sure you have a good time and come back happy. Remember?"

"That's true, but——"

"But what? You're afraid you'll enjoy our date, aren't you? In fact, you're so sure you'll have a good time that you don't *dare* take the chance."

"Don't be ridiculous, Fairchild," Rorie snapped. "You're not every girl's knight in shining armor. I can resist you and any charming little plan you might come up with for a night on the town."

"Prove it," he challenged. "Go out with me and prove I'm *not* your knight in shining armor."

"You're just trying to manipulate me," Rorie argued. "I won't be tricked into going out with you."

"This is not a trick," he countered. "It's a challenge. I challenge you to go out with me and have a *bad* time. You won't be able to do it, you know." He smiled with beaming self-assurance.

Suddenly Rorie didn't care whether she was being manipulated or not. At that moment, all she wanted to do was prove Phillip Fairchild wrong and wipe that smug smile off his face. If she was determined to have a bad time on a date, she was sure she'd manage it...even if she had to force herself by exercising all her willpower. And, just as Phillip had lots of motivation to make her happy on their date, she had lots of motivation to be miserable. She was determined to make him fail the last test and to lose some of that cockiness at the same time.

"Fine. I'll go out with you," she said, briskly businesslike. "But don't expect me to have stars in my eyes by the end of the evening. I'm not an easy sale, Phillip Fairchild."

"I know you're not, Rorie," Phillip assured her. "But that's part of your charm."

DRIVING BACK to his condo, Phillip felt like he was floating on air. Usually, when a woman played hard to get, as soon as he'd talked her into going out with him, the attraction waned. But with Rorie it was different. First of all, she hadn't been *playing* hard to get. She'd genuinely not wanted to have anything to do with him. And, secondly, he was more attracted to her than ever. Those kisses… Wow.

He'd had to come across like a conceited jackass to goad her into going out with him, but it was worth laying it on a little thick to get the opportunity of a lifetime, namely a date with Rorie McBride…and perhaps a priceless fertilizer formula in the bargain.

Grinning like a lottery winner, Phillip picked up his car phone and dialed Zach. "Zach, I have some arrangements I need you to make for a very special evening I have planned tonight. Everything has to be absolutely perfect. Do you have a pen and paper ready to take notes?"

"Ready, boss," Zach answered.

Several minutes later, his business concluded, Phillip was about to hang up when he remembered something else. "What about that information on Delphinia Devine?"

"Got it."

"Good! Bring it up to my condo. I should be home in fifteen minutes."

Replacing the telephone receiver, Phillip had to force himself not to drive over the speed limit. He was anxious to read over the information about Delphinia, but most of all he couldn't wait for the afternoon to go by so he could hurry back to the Farley house…and Briar Rose.

"NOT THAT PUMICE stone, you imbecile," Delphinia growled. "It's too rough on my delicate skin. Use the one with the pink handle."

On his knees at the end of the claw-footed tub, in white shirtsleeves rolled up to his elbows, his chauffeur's hat carefully laid on the closed toilet-seat lid, Simon obediently put down the pumice stone he had been using on his employer's foot and picked up the pink one.

With her dyed black hair pinned in a Medusa-like knot of slick tendrils atop her head, and a black mask over her eyes, Delphinia soaked in the tub, up to her sharp chin in purple-tinted bubbles. She drew long puffs on her cigarette and flicked the ashes haphazardly into the water, on the purple-carpeted floor, and on Simon. The only parts of her anatomy that showed above the bubbles were her head, her skinny neck, her shoulders and arms at the top of the tub, and her skinny ankles and feet at the bottom of it.

"Ouch!" complained Delphinia, drawing back her foot and splashing water and bubbles in Simon's face. "That hurt!"

Emboldened by the fact that she couldn't see him, Simon wiped the suds off his chin and scowled at his employer. "Madam, I am not schooled in the art of pedicure. I was hired to drive your car."

"I hired you to do whatever I need you to do, Simon," she drawled. "And you'll do it, or lose your job. After stealing jewels from your last employer, you're lucky to have any job at all."

"I explained about that," Simon said, affronted. "I was framed."

"Yes, yes. I know. Something about the cook being jealous of you. But then, no one is ever actually guilty of a crime these days, are they? If they don't blame it on a dysfunctional upbringing by their cruel parents, they can always say they've been framed, eh, Simon? Conspiracy! Conspiracy!"

Mortified, Simon said nothing.

"Besides, at the moment, I can't afford to hire someone to do my pedicures," Delphinia went on. "I need more money, Simon. *Lots* more money. That's why I must get my hands on the fertilizer formula—and soon. Very soon. Listening to the tapes last night was quite helpful. We have something on Fairchild now, but so far no opportunity to use it against him. Has the machine recorded any more conversations worth listening to, Simon?"

Simon rose, grimacing and pressing his hand to the small of his back. "I haven't had a chance to listen to them yet, madam, but I could bring the recorder in here and play them for you."

"I refuse to listen to my sisters nattering on about flower seeds and horned worms!"

"We can fast-forward through those parts," he assured her. "Shall I fetch the recorder, madam?"

"Yes. But hurry, Simon, I'm beginning to turn into a prune!"

Simon gave her a sneering look that seemed to suggest that he thought she already looked like one, and left to do her bidding.

Minutes later, he returned, plugged in the recorder and began playing the tapes. After fast-forwarding through most of the morning's conversations, he stopped at a part where Mr. Fairchild was talking privately with Aurora. The conversation was illuminating.

"He just told us all we need to know about his little fling with Kim Norville," Delphinia gloated, her head back, her scrawny arms resting on the lip of the tub. "Now, if only we knew where he plans to take Aurora on their date. If we can't reliably find out the time and place, we might have to follow them again."

"No more disguises, I hope," Simon grumbled under his breath. "I will not be Boris to her Natasha!"

"Quit talking to yourself, Simon," Delphinia advised him in a bored voice. "It's very unattractive and makes people wonder about your sanity. Now, fetch the tape from the bug we planted in his car, Simon," she ordered. "Perhaps he made arrangements for the date using his car phone."

Simon fetched the tape and played it, and Delphinia preened over the fact that she'd been right about him making date arrangements over the car phone.

"Now we have all the facts we need to cook Fairchild's goose," she gloated. "And I know the perfect person to wear the chef's hat! Call that actress woman who used to date Fairchild. The one who will do anything for a buck. As you may recall, Simon, she was very effective in tricking my last husband. What was the name…?"

"The name of your last husband, madam?" Simon inquired.

"No, simpleton! The name of the actress!"

"It's on the Rolodex, madam." *I'll look under "tart"*, he thought, snickering to himself.

"Tell her we've got another job for her. She'll probably jump at the chance to stick it to Fairchild. She has a vindictive nature, like me. Offer her the going price, but not a penny more."

"Very well, madam."

"But first hold up my towel while I get out," she said, pulling off her eye mask and rising from the foam.

"But don't look, Simon. I only allow lovers to see me naked."

Simon came forward with the towel held high, his eyes squeezed tightly shut. "I wouldn't dream of looking, madam," he said with heartfelt sincerity.

"HERE'S THE INFO about the Delphinia Devine person."

Phillip took the folder and laid it on the table, flipping through the papers with one hand and shaving with an electric razor with the other. "There's a lot here," he murmured, frowning. "It'll take me all night to read through it. Good work, Zach."

"No problem," Zach replied, flipping back his Hugh Grant hair and smiling. "She's quite the character, that one. It'll be entertaining reading."

Phillip looked up. "I'm sure it will. But I'm picking up my date in an hour. I suppose you didn't have any trouble making all the arrangements I asked for?" He peered at Zach, not the least bit worried about his secretary's answer. The kid was amazing. He was twenty-three, married with a small child, and was a full-time law student, but he still had the energy and organizational skills to make a great secretary.

Zach pulled a key out of his back pocket and handed it to Phillip. "Does that answer your question, boss— I mean, *sir?*"

"'Boss' is fine, Zach," Phillip told him with a smile. "Remind me to give you a raise."

"Must be a special lady," Zach offered, grinning. "Good luck, boss."

"I'll need it," Phillip said wryly. "Good night, Zach."

"Good night," Zach answered, then let himself out the door.

Phillip looked down at the small, ornate key resting in the palm of his hand. *My key to happiness,* he thought, his mind taking an unexpectedly poetic turn.

"You're right, Zach," he murmured. "She's a very special lady."

Phillip hurriedly finished dressing, checking his tie as he left the bedroom. He'd told Rorie to dress for dinner and dancing, and he couldn't wait to see her. She had a natural knack for style, and with a degree in fashion design and such a dynamite figure, she'd be a real knockout in an out-on-the-town kind of outfit.

Not that she didn't look scrumptious in jeans and a T-shirt. She'd probably look good in a gunnysack. Or in nothing at all...

The picture he'd just conjured up of Rorie naked made him slightly dizzy. To ground himself a bit before leaving to pick up his date, he flipped through the papers on Delphinia Devine, reading snatches here and there.

"Well, what do you know," he murmured as he read. "The old hag bugged her third husband's house so she'd get the goods on him before filing for divorce. Smart. Very smart. And very unscrupulous."

He read a bit more, then closed the folder. He called the valet and had his car brought around to the front of the building, then rode the elevator to the lobby.

THIRTY MINUTES LATER, standing at Aurora's front door, he congratulated himself on finding his way through the foliage even in the dark. Dragon had greeted him a few feet from the gate and now seemed ready to cover him with dog kisses.

"Sorry, old boy," Phillip said, pushing away the dog's face, then petting him apologetically on the head. "I'm saving myself for someone with breath a lot better than yours."

He rang the doorbell and was immediately admitted into the house by all three Farley sisters, their rosy faces wreathed in smiles.

"My, Phillip, how handsome you look!" Daffy enthused, waving a wooden spoon.

"Wait till you see Aurora!" exclaimed Daisy, clapping her hands like a child.

"Here she comes now," Dahlia observed, looking up the stairs with a proud smile.

Phillip looked up the stairs, too, and his heart skipped a beat. Aurora was a vision. She held on to the rail with one hand and had just extended her foot to take the first step down the stairs. But when Phillip's gaze met hers and he smiled, she froze in that position and smiled back.

Sleeveless and short with a gauzy, circular skirt, her dress was the pale peach of daybreak. The color made her skin look blushed and creamy, and her lipstick matched her dress perfectly. Her hair was loose and flowing down her back and as golden as sunshine. Her eyes were as blue as the sky.

Her long, shapely legs were sheathed in the sheerest hose, and she wore delicately strapped sandals with small heels. As she moved down the stairs, he noticed that her toenails and fingernails were painted pale peach, to match her dress. Dangling from each ear were tiny crystal globes on the most delicate gold chain imaginable.

Phillip gulped down a nervous swallow. He had a feeling he was in way over his head.

"Hi, Fairchild," Rorie quipped, a sparkle in her eyes to match those extraordinary earrings she was wearing.

"Aren't we on a first-name basis yet, Rorie?" he asked her. "How about just for tonight?"

"We'll see," she said coyly.

He took her elbow and was about to guide her out the door, when a whiff of her perfume made him stop in his tracks and stare at her incredulously. "You're wearing the perfume I gave you."

She shrugged and smiled. "Seemed a waste to let it just sit around."

He smiled back, too wise to question her further. He was satisfied just to know she'd accepted his gift, even though she acted so nonchalant about it.

"Remember, Phillip," Dahlia reminded him as they stepped off the porch, "in order to pass the test you must bring her back happy."

"I remember, Dahlia," he answered. "Never fear."

Rorie looked up at him and raised a beautifully arched brow. "Never say never, Phillip. That's what I said, and look where I am now."

Just where you belong, he thought. Albeit she was going out with him determined to be very hard to please, but at least he had a shot at putting stars in her eyes. Up to the challenge, he tucked her arm under his, and led her along the moonlight-dappled walkway.

The crickets were singing and Phillip's head was filled with the sweet scent of flowers and the even sweeter scent of Tears of Joy.

He'd bring her back happy, all right, he vowed. On a night like this, what could possibly go wrong?

Chapter Ten

They were headed south on Interstate 85 and had long ago passed any of the downtown Atlanta exits. Rorie was beginning to wonder exactly what Phillip had in mind.

"Um...where are we going?"

Phillip took his eyes off the road for a minute to turn and give Rorie a smile that could only be described as devilish. For about the hundredth time since she'd agreed to go out with him, she wondered what the heck she'd gotten herself into.

"We're going to the airport."

Rorie raised her brows. "Why? Is there a restaurant tucked between the United and Delta terminals that you really like?"

He chuckled. "Hardly. We're not eating at the airport. This may sound like a novel idea, but we're taking a flight out of the airport."

"A flight to *where*, Fairchild?"

"When are you going to start calling me by my first name?"

"The night is young."

"But I'm not. How long will I have to wait to hear you call me Phillip?"

"How can you possible say you're not young?" she chided him. "How old are you?"

"Thirty-three. Probably about five years older than you. Am I right?"

"A girl never tells. Let's just say there's not quite half a decade of difference in our ages."

Phillip cringed. "Ouch. When you call it half a decade, it sounds like a lot."

"You've managed to divert me from my original question, but I would still like to know where we're going."

"Savannah."

"Savannah! Why?"

"Savannah has beautiful beaches."

Rorie couldn't believe it. Ever since Phillip had come into their lives, she'd been thinking and dreaming of the beach. Frequently in her dreams she romped in the shallow surf or walked on the beach with Phillip...or found shells and made sand castles with a tall boy with dark, unruly hair. Each dream brought that boy more sharply into focus.

And now Phillip was actually taking her to the beach. It was almost too coincidental. In fact, it gave her goose bumps.

"Are you cold? I can turn the air conditioner off."

She turned and found him looking at her solicitously. And apparently he'd been looking at her closely enough to see the goose bumps rise on her arms.

"No, I'm not cold." In fact, she was feeling rather warm, and she had a feeling that by evening's end she'd be feverish. Whether it was washing the dog or being whisked away to Savannah for a romantic evening, spending time with Phillip always revved up her internal temperature.

"Don't you like the beach?" he asked her.

Rorie considered telling him no, she didn't like the beach. But while she was determined not to have a good time on their date, she decided she could at least be civil.

"I love the beach," she answered truthfully. "Before my parents died, we used to go there a lot. In fact we used to rent a little beach house in Savannah for a couple of weeks every summer and spend day after day picnicking, swimming, sleeping, playing. It was wonderful."

"It sounds wonderful."

A thought occurred to Rorie. An incredible, probably ridiculous thought. But she had to ask.

"Did you go to the beach a lot when you were a kid?"

"A *lot* would not be the correct term," he said, still looking straight ahead but smiling ruefully. "In fact, I only remember going to the beach once when I was a child. It was the summer I turned ten. Of course, as a teenager, I went with my friends all the time."

That shoots that theory, thought Rorie. She had been thinking that maybe her beach dreams were partly made up of memories, and that maybe, just maybe, Phillip had been that boy she'd played with so many years ago. But if he'd only been to the beach once during his childhood, the odds of him being her dream playmate were next to nil.

"Why didn't your parents take you to the beach more often?" she asked him.

"My father was a workaholic and he couldn't relax. A day at the beach, much less a week or two, would drive him crazy. But, don't get me wrong—" he slid her a quick glance "—I wasn't neglected or ignored as a child. My parents gave me everything I wanted or needed, and Dad was happy to spend time with me as long as the time spent was 'productive,' as he would say. You know the sort of stuff…helping me with my homework, watching the news together, taking tours of the corporate offices.''

Rorie winced in sympathy. "Sounds productive all right, but not much fun.''

Phillip chuckled. "He meant well. He just didn't know how to play. Mom was a little looser than Dad, but not much. After having a heart attack five years ago though, Dad has learned to relax and enjoy life somewhat. I just wish he'd wised up a few years earlier.''

Rorie thought she detected a note of wistfulness in Phillip's voice. "You were a lonely child, weren't you?''

He smiled grimly. "Hell, I'm still lonely, Rorie. But now I have only myself to blame.''

"Why?''

"I'd rather be alone than in a rocky relationship like so many of my friends. Sounds like an outdated concept, I know—it even sounds corny—but I guess I just don't want to get too involved until I'm sure I've met the right person.''

"How will you know the right person when she comes along?''

"I'll know.''

Rorie wished she had his confidence. She'd been waiting a long time for her prince to show up, but so far no one had even come close to filling the bill. Maybe he'd come and gone and she hadn't even noticed!

The sun was low in the sky by the time they arrived

at Hartsfield Airport. In a matter of minutes, they were boarding a small, sleek jet. The inside was luxurious and tastefully decorated, with large, plush, leather seats. They were greeted by the pilot and a small cabin crew, who were polite and pampering. Minutes later they took off, heading south, then the plane veered slowly to the east.

Craning her neck to catch the last golds and fiery reds of a stunning sunset, Rorie had to admit that, despite her determination to the contrary, she was having a good time...and not just because of her rich surroundings. Phillip was a charming and attentive companion. However, there was no way she was going to admit these revelations out loud. Besides, her opinion might change as the night wore on.

As they reached their cruising altitude, they unbuckled their seat belts and Phillip took her on a tour of the jet. "Why did I think we'd be going commercial?" she said wryly. "After all, you own a huge company. Obviously you'd have your own jet."

"I fly a lot to Europe to oversee our offices there. It just seemed to make sense to get a company jet. Saves a lot of time and hassle. It's a business expense that's worth every penny."

A business expense. Yes, the jet was used for business, thought Rorie. And that's exactly what Phillip was conducting at the moment...business. It was wise to remind herself of that fact. He was taking her out on a date to fulfill the last test to determine if he was worthy to buy the fertilizer formula. Sure, he'd said that he liked her and wanted to go out with her regardless, but would the idea have even occurred to him if not for the test?

"You're quiet, Rorie," Phillip commented, handing

her a glass of white wine the steward had brought from the bar.

Rorie took the wine and sipped it before answering with a sly smile, "I'm just savoring the moment. It's not often I get whisked away to Savannah on a private jet. Is this how you impress all your first dates?"

"Only my very special first dates," he replied suavely.

She arched a brow. "I'll bet there have been lots of those."

"Only one," was his prompt reply.

Rorie's betraying heart performed a cartwheel, but she taunted him, saying, "You expect me to believe that, Fairchild?"

"It's the truth," he said solemnly, holding up his glass in a toast.

No witty response came to mind, so Rorie touched her glass to his and took a hasty gulp of wine. Could he really be telling the truth?

They spent the last few minutes of the trip talking about general topics, while Rorie tortured herself by looking lingeringly at Phillip when he wasn't aware of her scrutiny. He'd worn a charcoal gray, silk-blend sport jacket she'd recognized immediately as an Armani, gray slacks and a jazzy burgundy-and-black geometric-patterned tie. The colors complemented his dark hair and cool, gray eyes. He looked and smelled like a million bucks. Which, of course, was no coincidence.

When they landed in Savannah, another white Mercedes just like the one Phillip drove in Atlanta was waiting for them. Within minutes they were speeding along a coastal highway to their next destination, which Phillip had mysteriously referred to only as a "seaside paradise."

As they drove up to the busy parking lot of a large, trendy-looking beachside restaurant, Rorie was a little disappointed. She had hoped that Phillip would realize that she would appreciate a more intimate atmosphere, where they could eat in peace. In such a hot spot, she was sure Phillip would be recognized and photographed, and maybe she'd end up in the paper, just another one of the Perfume Prince's dates, hanging on his arm like a glittery ornament. But at least this was something she could be unhappy about, which was exactly what she wanted…wasn't it?

However, after a short conversation with the valet, Phillip took Rorie's arm and…led her away from the restaurant!

"Where are we going?"

"I already told you. To a seaside paradise," he answered enigmatically.

"But—"

"Shh. Wait and see. Meanwhile, just enjoy the surroundings."

Rorie had to admit there was a lot to enjoy. They walked down a narrow, grassy path through colorful flowering shrubs toward the ocean. The sound of the surf got louder as they strolled along, their way illuminated by outdoor lights that resembled old-fashioned street lamps.

Rorie breathed in the salty tang of the ocean and the sweet scent of flowers that wafted in the warm breeze. She peered up at an ebony sky, a three-quarter moon, and stars so bright and big they looked close enough to reach out and touch.

Suddenly they came upon a wrought-iron gate decorated with fancy grillwork. Beyond the gate, Rorie could see a stretch of beach, a swell of deep purple ocean, and a Victorian-style cottage where the windows beamed with soft light.

"Is that where we're going to eat dinner?" she asked nervously. The way things were stacking up, she was going to have a very hard time trying to appear unimpressed and unhappy.

"If I can find the key," he said, groping in his inside jacket pocket.

She felt a moment's desperate hope. "Do you suppose you've lost it?"

"Not a chance," he said, producing the key with a flourish and inserting it into the lock. "I was only joking. There's no way I'd have misplaced this key. I wanted our first date to be special."

When he'd produced the key, Rorie found it interesting that she was both disappointed and elated. And what did he mean when he said "our first date," as if there would be others? Who was he kidding?

Phillip held her hand and they followed a cobbled walk over a small lawn to the cottage. Standing on the porch, Rorie looked up at the front facade of the quaint structure, admiring the gingerbread fretwork and the sand-dollar shingles. The tiny house was slate blue with white trim and shutters and a small tower similar to her own office turret. A grapevine wreath covered with dried larkspur and ivy hung on the door. Everything about the cottage was charming and welcoming.

"This place looks like it's straight out of Hansel and Gretel. It's enchanting," she said grudgingly.

"And only a stone's throw from the ocean," Phillip pointed out, turning her with a hand lightly placed at her waist. About fifteen feet from the door, the lawn ended and the sandy beach began. A little further down was the ocean, its foamy surf gleaming in the moon-light.

"Maybe after dinner we can take a walk on the beach," Phillip suggested.

Rorie nodded, feeling a little dazed. At this point she had an almost uncontrollable urge to bolt. Events were conspiring against her to make it impossible not to enjoy herself! And to top it all, considering the beach-setting and who she was with, it was as if the dreams she'd been having lately had suddenly come true.

"Let's go inside," Phillip invited, opening the door and cupping her elbow to guide her. "Dinner's probably waiting."

He was right. Dinner was waiting, and so was a tall, dignified-looking waiter—presumably from the restaurant—in a white jacket and black pants. Smiling respectfully, he stood by a small lace-and-linen-draped table in the middle of the room, which served as both the living room and dining area. Rorie assumed that the kitchen was down a small hallway she noticed, and that the narrow, curving stairway led to a bedroom. It was a perfect setup for honeymooners.

Honeymooners. The idea made Rorie feel warm all over. That's exactly what the cottage was primarily used for, she supposed. It was a private getaway for honeymooners or lovers. Maybe even old married folks came there to reignite the fire in their relationship. But how did she and Phillip fit into any of those categories?

Seeming to have read her mind, as Phillip pulled out her chair he whispered in her ear, "Don't worry. I only rented it for the evening and dinner, not the whole night. When the clock strikes midnight, we're out of here."

His warm breath against her neck sent a chill down

her back. She turned and looked into his eyes. In their depths she saw a lethal mix of humor and sensuality that took her breath away. For a moment, she wasn't sure whether or not she was glad they had the cottage only for the evening. She wanted to forget all about her godmothers' test, the dumb fertilizer formula and even Phillip's womanizer reputation, and give in to her desires.

Shaking herself out of the weak-willed stupor she'd fallen into, she quipped, "Thanks for the reassurance, Fairchild, but I'd have been very surprised if you'd been stupid enough to rent it for the whole night."

"Thank you…I think," he said, chuckling. "At least you don't think I'm stupid."

He sat down opposite her, and as the waiter poured their wine and explained the menu, Rorie's gaze wandered around the small room. It had been decorated in a country Victorian style. There was a lot of lace and antiques, but without the overall effect being too fussy or feminine. Fresh flowers abounded on the glossy surfaces of the cherrywood tables scattered here and there, and lovely art graced the walls. Again, the only word Rorie could come up with to describe the room was "enchanting."

In between courses of a fabulous dinner that Rorie only managed to eat a small portion of, the waiter retired to the kitchen. But after he served dessert, he wished them a good evening and left the cottage.

Rorie chewed nervously on her lip. They were alone.

"I guess we're on our own from now on," Phillip observed unnecessarily. "But, don't worry, we don't have dish duty."

Dish duty was the last thing Rorie was worried about. She'd take dishpan hands over a broken heart any day, and that's exactly where she was headed if she allowed herself to fall for the Perfume Prince. But every moment she spent with him made it harder and harder to control her feelings. She was madly attracted to him, and, worse still, now that she knew he wasn't the creep Kim had made him out to be, she *liked* him. Phillip could easily take those two facts and run with them.

"Don't you like mousse?" Phillip inquired, raising his brows and nodding toward the fluted glass full of dark, creamy chocolate.

"No," Rorie lied, thinking this an appropriate moment to start finding fault with something...*anything!*

He looked skeptical, but only said, "Would you like me to order you something else for dessert?"

"No. I'm too full." At least she was voicing a complaint...sort of.

He scooted out his chair, dropped his napkin on the table and stood up. As he towered over her, Rorie's gaze slowly climbed his tall, lean physique. By the time her eyes met his, she was breathless.

"I have a remedy for being too full," he announced, taking her hand and gently pulling her to her feet, then firmly into his arms. "Exercise."

"Wh—what kind of exercise?" she stammered. With her chest pressed against his, she was afraid he must be able to feel her wildly beating heart.

"Dancing. Remember? I promised to take you dancing."

"But there's no music." She looked around them, frantic for an escape from such a pleasurable embrace. "I positively hate dancing without music. And there's no room to maneuver in here. It's no fun dancing in cramped quarters."

As if he'd anticipated her objections and planned for them, he shrugged and smiled. "Then we'll go outside and dance under the stars. It's a private beach. No one will mind."

He took her hand and pulled her toward the door. "But that doesn't take care of the music end of it, Fairchild," she said. "We can't dance without music."

He said nothing as he led her outside onto the grass, then left her standing there for a moment to return to the porch.

"Kick off your shoes, Rorie, while I confer with the band," he called, bending down toward a wicker chair to turn on a boom box that was resting on the padded seat. Soft rock music, suitable for slow dancing, drifted into the night air.

"You think of everything, don't you?" she grumbled, automatically kicking off her sandals as he strode toward her with a sort of boyish cockiness that Rorie found irresistible.

"I try," he murmured modestly, pulling her into his arms.

Rorie's eyes couldn't help but close as she melted into Phillip's embrace. It seemed so natural, yet so thrilling, to be in his arms. *Too* thrilling. When she'd agreed to go out with Phillip, she'd been convinced that she could steel herself against his charm. Now she wasn't so sure.

He smelled so good. He felt so substantial, so *male,* so strong as he expertly danced her about the grass. Then, suddenly, he leaned forward and swooped her into a dip, holding her in a tilted position till she was light-headed and giddy.

"Are you having fun yet, Rorie?" he asked her with

a playful glint in his eyes that made her knees go weak. She tried not to smile, but ended up laughing instead, nervous excitement welling up in her like champagne bubbles. He laughed, too.

"I'm going to faint!" she warned him, so he pulled her up again and held her against him. Still breathless from laughing, they stared at each other till their smiles slipped away. His gaze drifted to Rorie's mouth and she knew that a kiss was imminent.

"Let's take that walk now," she abruptly suggested, pulling away and tugging him toward the sandy beach. The last thing she needed was smooching under the stars with Phillip Fairchild! There would be no way she could hide her enjoyment of *that*.

Although he looked a little disgruntled at first, he came willingly enough, then stopped at the edge of the lawn to say, "Let me take off my shoes and socks."

Rorie watched as Phillip took off his shoes and socks and set them on the porch. But he didn't stop there. He also took off his jacket and tie, rolled up his trouser legs, unbuttoned a couple of buttons on his shirt from the collar down, and turned up his cuffs. Mesmerized, she almost expected him to take off all his clothes. She knew exactly how he'd look naked, too…that is, minus the beesting swelling. He'd look fantastic.

"Ready?"

Rorie almost said, "For what?" but caught herself just in time. "I guess. Although, isn't it getting kind of late?" she answered instead, then cringed as she realized that she sounded scared.

Phillip said nothing. He simply draped his arm around her shoulders and moved with her toward the beach. They strolled silently along the shore for a few minutes—Rorie fighting her feelings the whole time—

then, of one accord, they turned and stared out over the vast ocean.

Standing at the edge of the water with the sea breeze in her hair, feeling the wet sand pull and shift under her feet and squish between her toes, Rorie was nearly knocked over by a sense of déjà vu. But why? It wasn't possible that she and Phillip had looked at the ocean together before…was it?

But the feeling persisted and got stronger. Not only did it seem as though they'd been there, done that before, but it felt as though they'd been destined to meet again.

Was all this meant to be? And did that mean she should give in to her feelings?

Meant to be. The words teased Rorie, making her very uneasy but no less drawn to the man standing next to her. She felt like she *belonged* with him. But how could that be? She hardly knew him! And she didn't even want to *like* him, much less fall in love with him.

"Rorie?"

Disturbed by feelings she didn't understand, Rorie looked up reluctantly. Moonlight illuminated Phillip's face enough for her to see the troubled look in his eyes and the slight frown of confusion that creased his brow. He was experiencing the same strange feelings she was.

"Lately, have you been dreaming about beaches?" she asked impulsively.

"Yes," he admitted. "You, too?"

"Yes. Was there ever a little girl in your dreams?"

"Sometimes."

She swallowed. "Do you…do you have a feeling of déjà vu right now?"

"Yes. And I've had similar feelings recently. Ever since you and I…" He paused, his frown deepening.

"Met...*again?*" she suggested in a whisper.

"Is it possible that on that one trip to the beach I took as a child I could have met you, Rorie?"

"It sounds impossible, but I suppose it *could* be true." She frowned, filled with uncertainly. "And if it's true, we must have made quite an impression on each other the first time we met."

He lifted his hands and dropped them lightly on her shoulders, looking earnestly into her eyes. "You made quite an impression on me the *second* time we met."

She shook her head, panicked. "No. I was rude and cold."

"But you thought I was a—"

"Scumbag."

He raised a brow. "I was going to say 'creep,' but 'scumbag' sounds even worse."

"I had good reasons to dislike and distrust you."

"I hope my explanation about Kim improved your opinion of me."

"I wouldn't be here with you now if it didn't, but—" She broke off and turned away.

His hands gripped her shoulders. "But what?"

"I wouldn't admit it, but I was already starting to like you...against my will...even before your explanation. My godmothers are generally very good judges of character. So's Dragon. But I just figured you could turn your charm off and on like a faucet and that you were scamming everyone."

"Everyone but you?"

She released a heavy sigh. "No...even me. You don't know how many times I've wanted you to...to..."

He turned her gently around and cupped her face with his hands. "To kiss you?"

Rorie felt all her willpower dissolve like sand in the sea. Her nod was barely perceptible.

"Probably not as many times as I've wanted to kiss you," he assured her in a husky voice, lowering his head to cover her mouth with his.

Phillip was stunned. He'd kissed Rorie once before, but this kiss was brimming with emotion and even more earthshaking than the first one. It was as if they'd crossed a threshold in their relationship, gone from strangers to lovers at warp speed.

He couldn't hold her close enough. She trembled, but still responded, slipping her arms around his neck and hanging on. Her lips were soft and inviting, her kisses as eager and hungry as his own. Her lips parted on a gasp, and he probed the sleek inner texture of her mouth with his tongue. Desire thrummed through his veins; he wanted her, needed her.

The feel of her against him was dizzying. He knew it was too soon, too fast, but he couldn't resist lifting his hand to cup the soft fullness of her breast. He felt her stiffen and he immediately removed his hand. But, as another heated moment of kissing passed, she caught his wrist and moved his hand back to her breast. Excited by her eagerness, Phillip brushed the pad of his thumb over her nipple. She moaned and every nerve in his body caught fire.

"This is crazy." He groaned against her neck. "I never meant for this to happen. Rorie, I—"

"Believe me...neither did I, Phillip," she said breathlessly, surprising and pleasing him with the use of his first name...and at such a moment. "But I want this as much as you do."

Reason vanished. Phillip couldn't deny his strong desire for her any longer...especially since she'd admitted to having the same feelings for him. It was too sweet, too satisfying to kiss her and caress her. He'd think later. Much later.

He lifted her in his arms and she clung to him, hiding her face against his shoulder as if she were shy or embarrassed. He kissed her forehead and compelled her to look at him, saying, "Are you really sure about this, Rorie? We can stop now. We can stop anytime you want." It would be damned difficult, but he'd find the strength somehow!

She looked up at him and her eyes glowed with warmth and desire. "I don't want to stop. I *can't* stop. I want you, Phillip. I really do."

And she meant it. Rorie had never been with a man, at least not completely. She'd been kissed and held and caressed, but she'd never wanted to go further. With Phillip it seemed natural…and inevitable. She'd fought the hard fight, but there was no denying fate.

Maybe the prince she'd been waiting for her entire life was only supposed to stay for a few glorious hours, she speculated hazily, then ride off into the sunset—with a fertilizer formula in his pocket—never to be seen again? It was a stretch for a fairy tale, but Rorie was in so deep now, she'd take whatever happy scenario she could get…no matter how short-lived.

He carried her to the cottage, stopping every few steps to kiss her. He maneuvered the door with his foot, then set her down just inside the room and took her into his arms again. They kissed passionately.

She couldn't get close enough. His tautly muscled body beneath her exploring hands was so pleasurable and thrilling. And his arousal as she pressed against him made her body respond with equal intensity.

He wanted her and she wanted him. She told herself

that that was all that mattered. Phillip may not have totally earned his playboy reputation but certainly he'd dated—and then forgotten—a lot of women over the years. Rorie couldn't fool herself into thinking that she was any more special than all of them.

Sure, while they'd stood on the beach together Phillip had indicated that he'd felt something special, some sort of déjà vu they both shared. But what, if anything, did that mean? And what would it mean to Phillip tomorrow when the enchantment of this evening was over?

Rorie didn't care. Tonight was not a night for reason or self-control. Tonight was the fulfillment of a dream, a fairy tale. Tonight she was a princess in the arms of her prince!

"Let's go upstairs, Rorie," Phillip whispered against her lips.

"Can we?" She looked at him uncertainly.

"Midnight is hours away," he told her, his eyes full of sensual promises.

"Hours away," she repeated with a trembling smile. It might seem like a long time to him, but to Rorie, anything less than a lifetime was too short to live a dream come true. But she would take what she could get. She took his hand and led him up the narrow stairs.

The bedroom was small but the four-poster bed, which was tucked into the tower portion of the room, was large. Moonlight streamed in through windows that were covered by sheer lace curtains. Like the rest of the cottage, the bedroom was full of antique furniture, fresh-cut flowers and beautiful art. But Rorie barely noticed her surroundings. To her the only thing in the room that really interested her was Phillip.

Without another word spoken between them, he took

her into his arms. Passion immediately flared between them again. His hands roamed her back and tangled in her hair.

"You have the most glorious hair," he whispered, threading his fingers through it and holding it up to the moonlight.

"Everything about you is glorious," she replied, smiling coyly as she caressed his broad shoulders. "And Nurse Ratched ought to know. I've seen just about everything."

He smiled back, a mischievous gleam in his eyes. "You don't seem like the kind of woman who would settle for 'just about' everything. Do you want to see...*everything?*"

She was grateful for the semidarkness of the room. Perhaps it hid her blush as she answered shamelessly, "What do you think?"

He chuckled. "I think we'd better get out of these clothes, Briar Rose."

She playfully slapped his arm. "How dare you use my godmothers' nickname for me at such a time?"

"I couldn't resist. It rhymed. Besides, it fits you perfectly. A soft, beautiful flower with thorns."

She was about to reply with something sassy, but he silenced her with another kiss, holding nothing back. By the time he released her lips, she was utterly breathless.

"Let's start with you, my rose," he teased, adeptly unzipping her dress in the back without turning her around. Instead he looked directly into her eyes, watching her response to everything he did.

A delicious shiver ran down Rorie's spine as the teeth of the zipper separated, exposing her skin to the cool air. She stood perfectly still as Phillip then nudged the dress off her shoulders. With a delicate swish, the pale peach dress fell into a pool of shimmering fabric at her feet.

Standing in her bra, panties, garter belt, and a tiny circle of a half-slip, Rorie thought she probably ought to be feeling a bit shy. She'd never been so provocatively attired in front of a man in her entire life. But she didn't feel shy. Not with Phillip. Despite her valiant efforts to avoid something like this happening between them, the whole situation, the whole night suddenly felt so right.

He stared at her, his eyes full of wonder and adoration. "You're so beautiful, Rorie."

"So are you," she answered, beginning to unbutton his shirt. "I remember."

Taking her time, Rorie helped Phillip out of his clothes till he was wearing nothing but boxers. He was gorgeous, all sinewy muscle and smooth, tanned skin. She quivered with desire.

"My turn now," he said in a husky voice, leading her to the bed and gently pushing her down to sit on the edge of it. "First your hose."

He got down on one knee and lifted her leg at the ankle. "By the way, I'm glad you didn't wear panty hose. I find garter belts incredibly sexy."

"I'm glad," she said in a small voice, her body tense with yearning.

"And your legs are so long and curvy." He circled her ankle with his fingers, then ran his hand up her leg and under her slip. He unsnapped the garter in front and in back, then rolled the hose down her leg with agonizing slowness, kissing the exposed flesh as he went along. He repeated the same wonderful torture on her other leg, tossed the hose on the floor, then pulled her to her feet.

Rorie was in a state of sensual bliss. Phillip made her feel so beautiful, so desirable.

And midnight was hours away.

Chapter Eleven

Phillip had divested Rorie of her hose in an erotic and leisurely fashion, but he made quick work of getting rid of her slip, bra and panties. And by the way she just as eagerly stripped him of his boxers, he could tell she was as impatient as he was to go on to the next phase of their lovemaking.

They tossed back the bedspread and blankets and tumbled onto the cool sheets to explore the wonders of each other's bodies. Delicious moments passed of caressing, stroking, kissing, tasting, murmuring. He was bowled over by her beauty and even more so by her enthusiasm. He wanted her more than he'd ever wanted a woman before.

"Phillip," she said faintly, urgently. "Make love to me."

Beyond the driving need to possess Rorie physically, Phillip felt a surge of emotions for her. Tenderness, protectiveness, *affection*... Could he be falling in love for the first time in his life?

But there was no time for analyzing feelings. She reached for him, wrapped her legs around his hips and clasped her arms around his shoulders, pulling him down and into her. He followed her lead, oh so willingly!

She gazed up at him as she rose to meet each thrust of his hips, and in her eyes he thought he saw the reflection of his own powerful emotions.

Her mouth opened on a gasp, her eyes drifted shut and her body stiffened and strained against him. He moved faster, responding to the signs that she was close to a climax. He was glad because he'd been struggling to hold back his own release for some time. She made him crazy. She made him ache and throb and want her like no other woman.

When her climax came, he came, too, his body convulsed with hot waves of pleasure that left him weak. He held her against him and they rode the tide of euphoria together, then, contented and thoroughly spent, they clung to each other and quickly drifted off to sleep.

WHEN RORIE WOKE UP next to Phillip, with the sound of the ocean in the background, she was sure she was dreaming. She turned her head on the pillow and feasted her eyes on the sight of her sleeping lover, his dark hair tousled from the combined onslaught of the sea breeze, sleep, and her eager fingers as they'd made love.

As they'd made love... Yes, she must be dreaming. She'd never let a guy get to first base before, much less hit a home run! But right in front of her eyes was the oh-so-solid and substantial proof that she hadn't been dreaming. And, of all men, he was the one she had sworn never to date, much less make love with! What had happened to her resolve tonight?

Unable to resist, Rorie lifted her hand and traced

with her fingertips the muscled line of his bare shoulder, the curve of his jaw, and the chiseled contours of his beautiful mouth, remembering their lovemaking and wishing there was time for more. Where was her resolve now? she asked herself ruefully.

She remembered, too, how effortlessly she'd lost her virginity last night, without the pain she'd heard about all her life. In fact, emotions and passions were running so high, Rorie didn't think Phillip even realized that he was her first lover. But she couldn't have asked for a better one. He had been tender at the right time and passionate at the right time.

She bent and kissed him gently on the lips.

Phillip's lashes fluttered and those gorgeous gray eyes of his—eyes that could be cool one minute and smoldering the next—opened and focused on her. His smile was sleepy and sexy as he reached for her and pulled her fast against him. They kissed deeply, and she realized quickly that he was as ready as she was for more lovemaking.

"We can't, Phillip," she murmured, pressing the palms of her hands against his hard, bare chest. Through the pads of her fingers she could feel the fast beating of his heart.

"Then you shouldn't have kissed me," he teased her.

"I was waking you up," she retorted. "Can you think of a better way to wake up? It's certainly *my* favorite."

"And I can't think of a better way to spend the next hour, either."

"Phillip, we can't!"

"Why can't we?" he challenged, trailing kisses down her neck and shoulder.

"Because it's nearly midnight and you need to drive me...I mean *fly* me home. Remember, you didn't rent the cottage for the night, only for the evening."

He propped his head on his fist and smiled down at her. "Actually, I did rent it for the night. The cottage is owned by the restaurant and they only rent it for full nights. Of course we don't have to *stay* the whole night."

She frowned. "But you said—"

"I know. I said I'd rented it only for the evening because I didn't want to make you nervous. I didn't want you to think I'd planned a full-scale seduction."

She stiffened. "Did you?"

He dropped a kiss on her nose, but quickly turned serious. "No, I didn't *plan* a seduction, but I'm certainly thrilled we ended up this way. Never in my fondest dreams did I think this would happen. I admit I lied, but I've come clean. Do you forgive me?"

She was staring at the lace edge of the sheet, so he reached down and tilted her chin with his forefinger so she'd look at him. Even though the lie was a small one, she wasn't sure whether or not she wanted to forgive him. He had told the lie to make her more relaxed...which was all part of his plan to win her over for the evening. She believed him when he said he hadn't planned a full-fledged seduction, but there was no denying he'd worked his wiles on her tonight and had told a fib to smooth things along.

However, since he really did seem contrite, and since it was hard to look into those melting gray eyes and think straight or stay angry, she gave a grudging smile and said, "All right, I forgive you. But you'd better not have told me any other little white lies."

"I haven't. Not a single one," he assured her.

"Good. I'm glad."

He grinned and his eyes gleamed with mischief. "Is glad the same thing as happy?"

She peered at him suspiciously. "I guess so. Why?"

"Your godmothers said I had to bring you back from our date happy in order to prove myself worthy to buy the fertilizer formula. Remember?"

"You're shameless!" she accused him, giving his shoulder a little shove. She knew he must be teasing, but for some reason his words sent a cold chill down her spine. Maybe the whole night *had* been nothing more than a business coup for him. For her it had been a beautiful dream. And now, like a splash of icy water, reality came crashing down around her. Wistfully, she decided to give in to the fairy tale a little bit longer. She'd deal with reality tomorrow.

He caught her wrist and pulled her into his arms. "Do *you* think I proved myself worthy, Rorie?"

"I haven't decided yet," she said, her heart thumping against her ribs and her nerves singing.

"Then maybe we should delay our trip home another hour or two and I'll help you make up your mind. What do you think?

"I think you talk too much, Fairchild."

He agreed, and for the next two hours they kept conversation to a bare minimum.

THEY ARRIVED at Hartsfield Airport at 3:00 a.m. and walked arm in arm, in a haze of happiness, through the main lobby toward the doors leading to the parking lot where Phillip had left his car. Even at such an early hour, the airport was still packed with droves of people. But Rorie was really surprised when one of those people stopped them by grabbing hold of Phillip's arm.

"Phillip!"

Phillip looked blankly at the beautiful woman, dressed in an elegant tailored pantsuit and carrying a suitcase. After a few beats, he said, "Brooke?"

"How ironic meeting *you* here," she drawled sarcastically, tossing back a mane of chestnut hair. "Glad to see you remember me, Phillip, but since it's only been a few days since I moved out, you sure as hell ought to remember me."

Rorie's heart seemed to stop beating. Her hands and feet and lips went ice-cold. Since she *moved out?*

Phillip darted a troubled glance toward Rorie, then turned back to the woman. "What are you talking about? I haven't seen you since—"

"Since you dumped me. Yeah, I know. I should have known I'd be like all the rest. But stupid me, when you gave me the key to your condo I figured—"

"He gave you the key to his condo?" Rorie repeated hoarsely. But Phillip had told her he'd *never* given his key to a woman! she thought desperately. Kim had pilfered hers from Phillip's secretary...or at least that's the way Phillip said it happened.

Phillip turned to her, angry and obviously very frustrated. "Rorie, I never gave this woman a key to my condo. I only dated her once or twice or— *Hell,* I don't remember! But I certainly never—"

"I'm glad I ran into you on my way out of town," the woman interrupted, rummaging in her purse, pulling out a key and dangling it in front of Phillip's nose. It swung back and forth like a hypnotist's pendulum, but Rorie could clearly see the Fair Lady Perfume logo on the key chain. "I was going to mail this to you, but giving it to you in person is much better. I've been wanting a long time to tell you what an S.O.B. you are.''

"Brooke, I don't know who put you up to this, but—"

"Is this the woman you told me about?" She gestured derisively toward Rorie. "The one that lives with three crazy old bats? Did your plan work?" She flitted a knowing eye over Rorie, making her blush. "Ah, but I can see that it did. She has that glow about her." She addressed Rorie. "How does it feel being romanced for a fertilizer formula?"

By now Phillip was so furious he was white around the mouth. "That's enough, Brooke." Ignoring the key, he turned to Rorie. "I haven't talked to this woman for months, Rorie. I don't know how she even knows about the fertilizer formula...unless Delphinia told her."

"But why is she here *now*, Phillip?" Rorie asked him, confused and hurting. "Delphinia didn't know your plans to take me to Savannah, did she? She would have had to know about your plans in order to set this up."

"I don't know how she found out, Rorie, but that's the only explanation for what's happening."

"Right," Brooke sneered. "I don't know who this Delphinia person is, all I know is that I don't want this key anymore." She held it between her thumb and forefinger as if it was covered with slime and offered it to Rorie. "Why don't you take it, honey? It will save Phillip the trouble of making another one for you."

Rorie was horrified. She didn't know what to think, how to react. The whole dreadful scene seemed like something out of a Woody Allen flick; a threesome having a painful confrontation in public. Only, in this case, there was nothing funny about it.

"I can't wait all day. I have a plane to catch," Brooke said in a tone of resigned contempt, dropping the key at Rorie's feet. "Good luck, honey. You'll need it."

The woman picked up her suitcase, and without a single glance back at them, walked away toward the escalator leading to a main terminal. Rorie watched her as she stepped onto the escalator and took something out of her purse that looked very much like a plane ticket. She seemed to scan it as if she were checking the departure gate and seat assignment. Rorie could not detect anything about her actions that seemed phoney or contrived. Either she was a good actor, or Phillip had been lying to her.

Phillip grabbed her arms and turned her to face him. His face was etched with concern, his eyes dark with anger and frustration. "Rorie, this is a setup. I swear it is!"

Rorie couldn't help it; she remembered the little white lie he'd told about only renting the cottage for the evening. And she tried to imagine how Delphinia could have arranged for one of Phillip's old girlfriends to run into them accidentally in the airport at three o'clock in the morning. It seemed so implausible.

And Brooke knew so much.... Surely not even Delphinia was so devious and desperate that she'd go to such lengths to discredit Phillip in her eyes. It seemed much more logical to believe that Brooke was telling the truth.

And if Brooke was telling the truth, that also led to speculation about Kim. Maybe she'd been telling the truth, too.

"Rorie?"

Rorie looked up into Phillip's anguished expression. She realized then that she was in love with him. Whether he was a liar and a user, or whether he was a victim of some outrageous plot, the bottom line was that she'd fallen in love with the man. He was the prince she'd been waiting for, only maybe he wasn't exactly the prince he ought to have been.

"You do believe me, don't you, Rorie?" Phillip demanded to know.

Rorie felt numb. "I don't know what I believe, Phillip," she answered truthfully.

PHILLIP WAS GLAD the Farley sisters weren't there to greet them when he walked Rorie to the door, then followed her inside. He had been half-afraid they'd wait up for their goddaughter and start worrying as the hours ticked by. But thank goodness they'd trusted him enough to go to bed. It was bad enough that Dragon was there, looking at him with big, adoring eyes.

He had another reason to be thankful the Farley sisters weren't around to witness the aftermath of his date with Rorie. She was obviously miserable. It showed in the way she walked, the way she held her head, the pained look in her eyes. She was hurt and confused, and he couldn't blame her. Brooke had played her part to the hilt, and very convincingly. Delphinia must have paid her well to put on such a show. And he must somehow have ticked Brooke off when they broke up, enough to make her eager to screw up his life for a bit of cold cash.

He was going to have to find a good woman and settle down, he reflected. Dating was proving to be too stressful! And maybe he'd found that good woman, but

now her former bad opinion of him had just received
enough fresh blood to nourish it back to full vigor.

"To say 'Thank you for the lovely evening' doesn't
seem quite right," Rorie said, looking at him with serious, disillusioned eyes, her arms crossed over her
chest in a protective, hands-off position.

"Rorie, I'm going to prove that Delphinia's behind
this mess."

She nodded, her expression listless and sober. "Yes,
I imagine you're pretty worried about failing the last
test."

"To hell with the test," Phillip growled. "I don't
care about the damn test. I care about you, Rorie, and
I care what you think of me!"

He reached for her, but she stepped back, hunching
her shoulders. He sighed. "Please don't write me off
yet. Give me a chance to prove I'm telling the truth."

"I want to believe you, Phillip, but I don't want to
get hurt."

"I swear I'll never hurt you intentionally, Rorie. And
I'll never lie to you."

She observed him sadly for a moment, tears welling
in her eyes. But she only said, "Good night, Phillip,"
and turned to walk up the stairs.

He watched her, fighting an urge to run after her and
lock her in a room with him till she believed he was
telling the truth. But all the evidence played against
him. For years he'd had a bad-boy reputation that the
media loved to embellish…a reputation that Kim had
reinforced with her obsessive pursuit of him and her
delusional thinking. And now another woman he'd
dated was claiming foul play.

Rorie hadn't known him long enough to trust him,
to have faith in him. He'd have to prove Delphinia was

behind it all, and he was determined to come up with the proof he needed as soon as possible, come hell or high water. He gave Dragon a distracted pat on the head, then turned and strode out of the house, finding his way easily through the thick foliage to the gate.

Phillip drove automatically to his condo, his mind sifting through everything that had happened over the past few days. He wished he'd completely read the file Zach had put together on Delphinia before leaving on his date with Rorie, but he'd do that as soon as he got home.

Phillip concentrated. He'd read snatches of the compiled information and it seemed like there was something in the back of his mind that kept nagging at him. Something about Delphinia that—

The proverbial lightbulb flashed on, flooding Phillip's mind first with suspicion, then with enlightenment. Of course! That was it! He couldn't wait to get home to test his theory.

Cordially waving aside the valet that was always on duty at the Grand, Phillip parked his car himself in the underground parking lot. It was well lit, and as soon as he turned off the engine, he started his search. Finding nothing under the dashboard, he opened the door and got out, then bent over the driver's seat and ran his hand underneath it, where the springs and other metal supports were located. *Bingo!*

Phillip picked off the small, round object and lifted it up to the inside car light to inspect it. He'd never used one before, but Phillip knew a bugging device when he saw one. Small and black with tiny holes in the front and a magnetic strip in the back, it was obviously a receiver. Delphinia, that old witch, had been bugging him! She'd eavesdropped on his entire conversation with Zach on the cell phone yesterday and heard all his plans for his date with Rorie!

The Farley house was undoubtedly bugged, too. That would explain why Simon had been on his hands and knees in the parlor the other day. Phillip would bet his life that Simon had been placing another receiver, just like the one he held in his hand, under the end table.

Phillip put the receiver back where he found it. He didn't want to tip Delphinia off too soon. In a few hours, after Rorie had a chance to sleep a bit, he'd return to the Farley house and search for other bugs. Then he'd have the goods to implicate Delphinia and prove his innocence to Rorie. He couldn't wait!

But Phillip sobered as he thought about how desperate Delphinia must be to resort to such devious methods to get the fertilizer formula. Apparently she needed the money badly.

She was desperate…and that made her dangerous.

Phillip clenched his jaw with determination. He would make sure Delphinia was stopped from ever bothering, harassing or hurting Rorie and her godmothers ever again.

Come hell or high water.

RORIE ENTERED the kitchen at the early hour of six, where her aunts gathered in their robes to drink coffee, read the paper, and discuss their gardening plans for the day before preparing breakfast at seven.

"Good morning," she called, forcing a cheerful note into her voice. Her godmothers looked up expectantly from their various occupations, bright smiles on their faces. But as soon as they saw Rorie's face, the smiles slipped away.

"Oh, my dear, what happened last night?" Dahlia immediately inquired.

"I was hoping I could at least look indifferent," she said ruefully. "But, as always, you guys can see right through me."

Rorie poured herself a cup of coffee and sat down at her usual place at the table. She'd pulled her hair back in a ponytail and was wearing the baby-doll pajamas she'd put on after Phillip brought her home that morning. She'd been hoping to get some sleep, but it had been a vain effort. Her godmothers stared at her, their expressions sad and concerned.

"I'm so disappointed!" Daisy said.

"I'm so *surprised!*" Daffy countered. "You looked so radiant last night when Phillip picked you up for your date. We felt sure you'd changed your bad opinion of him."

"I had...to a point," Rorie acknowledged. "But something happened...."

"Aurora, are you saying your opinion has changed again?" Dahlia asked her.

"I don't know, Dahlia," Rorie admitted, taking a sip of coffee. And again after a thoughtful pause, "I just don't know."

Apparently encouraged by her goddaughter's indecision, Dahlia reached over and patted Rorie's arm. "I don't know what Phillip has done to make you doubt him, my dear. And you don't have to tell us, either, if you don't want to. But I would advise you to give him the full benefit of the doubt. I don't know why, but I truly believe Phillip is a very worthy young man. And you must remember, appearances can be deceiving. Sometimes, if you truly...*care* about a person, you simply have to have faith in them."

"Listen to your heart, Briar Rose," Daisy advised her.

"Yes, listen to your heart, Briar Rose," Daffy echoed, smiling tenderly.

Rorie nodded and smiled wanly, but privately thought her godmothers' advice was simplistic and naive. She was the levelheaded one of the bunch, wisely acting on logic instead of emotion. How could she have faith in Phillip when the evidence implicated him so completely?

But if he's such a villain, why are you in love with him, Rorie? an inner voice chided her. For a levelheaded female, she'd definitely picked the wrong guy to fall for.

"I have to do some thinking, godmothers," she announced, rising from the table. "Unless you need the minivan for something, I'm going to drive to Grant Park. I'll probably just sit on a bench the whole time, but I'm taking my in-line skates in case I decide I need to move around. I probably won't be home till dinner."

"You're going alone?" Daisy asked worriedly.

"I'll be just fine," Rorie assured them.

"We'll fix you a lunch, my dear," Daisy offered, bustling to her feet.

"I'm not hungry—" Rorie began.

Dahlia cut her off, saying, "Nonsense. You can't skate or even think properly on an empty stomach. Run along and shower." She waved Rorie away. "We'll have a nice sack lunch prepared for you when you come downstairs again."

Rorie turned to go, then turned back. She impulsively gave Dahlia a long hug, saying, "Thank you for understanding." She hugged Daisy and Daffy, too, then hurried away, afraid she'd start blubbering like a baby. Her emotions were definitely on the surface these days! But after some quiet time for reflection, she might get her head on straight again.

"SHE'LL BE GONE all day," Delphinia said with satisfaction. "It's the perfect time to move in for the kill."

Simon eyed his employer with misgiving. He wouldn't have been surprised to see her rubbing her hands together like a villain in a silent movie. "Madam, you seem to take pleasure in this most unpleasant business," he suggested, bravely injecting his tone with a hint of disapproval.

"Why shouldn't I gloat a little, Simon?" Delphinia snapped, rising from the red chaise longue and walking to the window to move aside the heavy velvet drapes. She winced into the morning sunlight. "Don't I deserve to enjoy my victory? My plan worked! Briar Rose was completely taken in by Brooke's lies. Because of my brilliant plotting, Phillip Fairchild failed to pass my sisters' ridiculous tests!"

Simon turned down the volume dial on the surveillance equipment, which had been set up in the corner of Delphinia's bedroom. "But in the process, madam," he continued with a brooding frown, "you inflicted a lot of pain and suffering and nearly got Miss McBride run over by a car. And now her heart is broken."

"Details, Simon! Details!" Delphinia exclaimed. "What's important is that now that Fairchild's out of the picture, my sisters will feel obliged to sell the fertilizer formula to *me*."

"I don't know about that, madam," Simon demurred. "Why would they sell it to you now, when they wouldn't sell it to you before?"

Delphinia rounded on him, her face contorted with

rage. "Shut up, Simon!" she screamed. "If you can't be positive, just keep your stupid opinions to yourself!"

Simon trembled. "Yes, madam."

Delphinia calmed. "It's for your good as well as mine," she reminded him. "If I don't have any money, you don't get paid."

Simon sighed. "Yes, madam."

"Now go and fix me a protein drink for breakfast." He turned to go.

"And this time, Simon, don't forget to put my antioxidant tablets on the tray. How do you expect me to stay youthful if you don't take proper care of me?"

Simon stared at her for a long moment, a million scathing comebacks forming in his brain. But, in the end, he simply muttered, "Yes, madam," and hurried to the kitchen.

TWO HOURS LATER, Delphinia was seated on one of the sofas in her sisters' parlor, scattering ashes, as usual, and peering at them through narrowed, speculative eyes. Simon, as usual, stood at attention against the wall, nervously observing his employer as she prepared to launch her attack. It was like watching a lean and hungry cat in a pen with three plump pigeons.

"So, how are the tests going with Phillip Fairchild?" Delphinia boldly inquired, wasting no time with trifling chitchat.

The Farley females exchanged uneasy glances. Someone else in their position might have prevaricated or hemmed and hawed, but Delphinia's sisters answered with straightforward honesty.

"They're not going well at all," Dahlia admitted. "There have been a couple of mishaps associated with the tests. First, as you know, Phillip was stung by a bee. Then, when he and Aurora took Dragon to the groomers—'' She interrupted herself, eyeing Delphinia keenly. "But perhaps you heard about that incident?"

For the first time, Simon realized that Dahlia suspected her baby sister of having something to do with the various "mishaps" of the last week. He gulped noisily.

Delphinia screwed her face into an expression of false sympathy. "Yes, I *did* hear about it on the radio, and then later that night on the eleven-o'clock news. Dreadful! How could anyone *do* such a thing?"

"No one with a heart could do such a thing, that's for sure," Daisy observed.

Daffy emphatically nodded her agreement, but Dahlia just watched Delphinia with a thoughtful expression in her eyes.

"But I'm sure you didn't consider the beesting and the incident at the groomers to be entirely Phillip's fault," Delphinia smoothly put forth.

"No, of course not," Dahlia agreed. "That's why we passed him on those tests."

"I was sure you would," Delphinia purred. "But how did he fare with our lovely Briar Rose? Did she go out with him?" Delphinia sucked on her cigarette and flicked her ashes with a fair show of nonchalance as she awaited Dahlia's answer.

"She went out with him last night," Dahlia said.

"And? Did he bring her back happy?" Delphinia batted her fake lashes, assuming an expression of wide-eyed inquiry.

Dahlia seemed reluctant to answer, but Daffy, who was less astute than her older sister, blurted, "It went dreadfully! We don't know the details, but—"

"Rorie looked very unhappy this morning," Daisy continued in a rush of words. "We didn't see her when he first brought her home, of course, but we can only assume that she looked even more unhappy than she did this morning!"

"The *beast!* What did he do?" Delphinia inquired indignantly. "I was a little nervous about our sweet Aurora going out with a man of Phillip's reputation. And I must admit I was *very* surprised that you three encouraged him by giving him the run of the house!"

"As I said," Dahlia said stiffly, "we don't know all the details and can't judge *who's* to blame at present." Simon's blood ran cold as he noticed Dahlia's accusatory gaze boring into Delphinia, but his employer seemed oblivious to everything but her own agenda.

"Ah, well. Take it from me, sisters, men, as a rule, can't be trusted. *I* should know. And Phillip's obviously proved *he's* untrustworthy. He ought not to be allowed near your goddaughter again, *or* your fertilizer formula. Have you informed him that he did not pass your rigorous test?"

"We haven't seen Phillip since yesterday," Dahlia revealed.

Delphinia leaned forward. "But you *will* tell him he failed the test?"

Dahlia sighed. "Yes, I suppose we must. Although that's not the main thing we're concerned—"

Delphinia abruptly stood up and began her trademark pacing and posing. Her eyes glittered like a cat's might just before it sank its teeth into a pigeon's neck. "So, since Phillip won't be purchasing the fertilizer formula, surely you'll reconsider *me* as a buyer." She stopped in front of Dahlia and stared down at her with a bright, false smile and a menacing challenge in her eyes. "Won't you, sister dear?"

Simon held his breath.

Chapter Twelve

Dahlia squared her chin and glared back at Delphinia, a scrappy sort of foolhardy courage shining in her eyes. Simon wished he had half her gumption.

"Delphinia, the answer is no," she said firmly. "The answer will always be no. I'll never sell you the fertilizer formula, and no amount of underhanded shenanigans will make me change my mind."

Daisy and Daffy looked at Dahlia, obviously surprised by her reference to "underhanded shenanigans." Delphinia was surprised, too. But her surprise quickly changed to anger. Simon could see it building in her like a volcano priming for a blast of red-hot lava. He wanted to sink into the floor and disappear. Delphinia's outbursts of rage were extremely unpleasant. He squinted his eyes shut and waited...but nothing happened.

Braving a peek, he was amazed to see that Delphinia had somehow managed to bottle her anger. She'd removed herself to a far window and was puffing furiously on her cigarette. But Simon knew Delphinia well enough to realize that her unusual show of restraint hid a deeper, more devious motive.

Perhaps as suspicious as he was, Dahlia watched

Delphinia closely. Daffy and Daisy fretted silently, picking at their aprons with nervous fingers.

Presently Delphinia turned, a frighteningly calm expression plastered on her face. "Very well," she said in an emotionless voice. "Though I admit I resent it, I will respect your decision."

"That's very mature of you, Delphinia," Daisy observed with obvious relief.

"Yes, thank you for not pitching a fit!" Daffy added.

Delphinia scowled and Daffy scooted backwards into the sofa cushions.

"You'll be going now, I suppose?" Dahlia said with grave dignity, standing up to show her own eagerness for the end of such a painful interview.

"Yes, I'll be going," Delphinia answered coolly.

"I'll lead you through the yard," Daisy volunteered, anxious to rid the house of the black cloud Delphinia always brought with her.

No other words were exchanged between Delphinia and her sisters, and soon Simon was opening the door of the Rolls-Royce for her, then taking his place behind the wheel. He sat there, stiffly looking forward through the windshield, waiting for his employer to speak...or scream. She did neither and, for some time, sat so deathly still, Simon was growing quite alarmed. What was she hatching in that nefarious brain of hers?

"I have a plan, Simon."

Simon nearly jumped at the sound of her voice. It was low and controlled, but oh, so cunning. He looked at the rearview mirror into Delphinia's wicked black eyes, which were narrowed to slits, and at an evil grin.

"You...you do, madam?"

"Of course I do. You didn't think I'd let those loony

sisters of mine keep me from my ultimate goal, did you?''

"I must admit, madam, I was surprised at your, er, restraint when they refused to sell you the formula." Which was just as I predicted they'd do, he added to himself.

"Ranting and raving would be nonproductive at this point, Simon."

"I see," he said, dreading the point at which she decided that ranting and raving *were* productive.

"Drive to that deli on Clairmont. I want you to buy a two-pound hickory-smoked sausage."

It seemed she meant to put her plan, whatever it was, into immediate action. Simon did as he was told, tense with wondering what she might be up to. When he returned to the car with the sausage, he inquired, "What now, madam?"

"Drive back to my sisters' neighborhood, but park in our usual surveillance spot at the end of the street, under the trees," she ordered.

Again Simon did as he was told.

"Simon, have you ever heard me do my sweet-southern-miss impression?"

"Er...no, madam." He gave her a puzzled look in the rearview mirror. What other impression did she do? A Marilyn Monroe or a John Wayne? Now did not seem the appropriate time to do a comedy-club routine!

"Why don't ya know, I'm awfully *go-o-od* at it," she said, pitching her voice much higher than her usual husky tones, and drawing out her words till they were as sweet and loose as pulled taffy. Simon wanted to point out that most southerners didn't sound anything like the exaggerated drawl she was affecting, but he didn't dare. And since she was probably just trying to disguise her own voice, she was accomplishing that quite successfully.

"I think I'll just make a little ol' phone call to my sisters," she went on, seeming to take great delight in her phony accent. She picked up her cell phone and punched in the numbers, all the while smiling gleefully. But as the call went through and the phone began to ring at the Farley house, her smile disappeared and an expression of intense concentration came over her man-made features.

"Is this the Farley residence?"

Simon listened carefully.

"And is this Miss Dahlia Farley? Good, you're exactly the person I need to speak to. I'm calling from the Emergency Room at Piedmont Hospital."

Simon turned and stared at Delphinia, aghast. He had an inkling of what she was up to, and it was downright cruel!

"I have a young woman named Aurora McBride in the hospital with a serious injury. Looking through her wallet, we found a card that lists you as the next of kin—"

Delphinia paused as Dahlia obviously interrupted her with frightened exclamations and questions. Delphinia covered her mouth and giggled, throwing Simon an amused glance. Simon frowned.

"Please calm down, Miss Farley. She's not *dead!* Miss McBride merely fell down and broke her leg while in-line skating at Grant Park. Oh, and she also suffered a concussion and is still semiconscious. We think it would be best if you came down here. She's been murmuring your name and two others, as well. Is there a Daisy or a Daffy living there with you?"

Delphinia nodded into the phone, a satisfied smirk

on her face. "I think that's an excellent idea, Miss Farley. I'm sure that she'd love to see all three of you standing by her bed when she recovers consciousness. Goodbye now. See you soon."

Delphinia hit the "end" button on her phone and sighed happily. "Mission accomplished," she said in her normal voice. "Soon the three of them will be tearing out of the house and piling into a taxi headed for Piedmont Hospital to check on their sweet Briar Rose. And while they're gone…"

She rummaged in her purse and took out a large bottle of pills.

"Which are those, madam?" Simon couldn't help but inquire. She had so many medications and vitamins, he couldn't possibly guess which one she was holding at the moment. "I'll be no party to poisoning," he bravely informed her, amazed that he was actually standing up to her.

"I'm not going to poison anyone," Delphinia sniffed. "These pills are merely tranquilizers. I'm only going to put that beast of a dog to sleep for a couple of hours. Hand me the sausage, Simon. This was another useful thing we learned from bugging the house…Dragon's weakness for hickory-smoked sausage. No wonder those bland, puny wieners we used before failed to entice him!"

Simon handed her the paper bag with the sausage in it. Using her long, sharp nails, she began to imbed the pills in the sausage.

"Don't use too many, madam," Simon cautioned nervously. "You might put him to sleep permanently."

"The beast weighs three hundred pounds, Simon. It would take an entire bottle of these pills and a sledgehammer to put him to sleep permanently!"

Simon was silenced. She was probably right. "So, once he's asleep, I suppose we're going to steal the formula," he said gloomily.

"Absolutely. My patience has worn thin trying to reason with my sisters. And if I wait too long, Fairchild will wheedle his way into their goodwill again and nab the formula for himself and his stupid perfume company. You're quite sure you've got the route memorized, Simon?"

"Yes, madam. Just as you ordered me to do some months ago."

But then a frightening thought hit Simon, a thought he was surprised had not occurred to him before. "What will *you* do with the fertilizer formula, madam?"

"Sell it! What else?"

"But to whom, madam?"

"The highest bidder."

"What if he's a drug lord or a—"

"I can't police the world, Simon. It takes far too much time and effort just taking care of myself. There! That should be enough pills to do the trick. Has the taxi come yet?"

"No. Yes," he amended. "It's coming down the street now."

Just as Delphinia predicted, as soon as the taxi stopped at the curb, all three Farley sisters got in. Even from a distance, by the way they fidgeted and flurried about, Simon could tell they were upset.

As soon as the taxi turned and drove in the opposite direction toward the hospital, Delphinia exclaimed, "Now drive back to the house. Hurry!"

Filled with foreboding, but unsure of what else to do

besides obey his employer's orders, Simon drove back to the Farley house.

Once there, they got out of the Rolls and walked to the gate. Dragon rarely came to the gate, but simply waited for trespassers to come to him. But Delphinia wisely had no intention of finding herself on the same side of the fence with a three-hundred-pound dog that hated her guts. She eyed Simon speculatively, but he shook his head at her silent inquiry, drawing the line at the risk of being eaten alive for the sake of keeping his job.

"Call him, madam. Your distinctive voice will have him racing to the gate in seconds."

"No doubt intent on tearing my throat out," Delphinia muttered. Nevertheless, she leaned over the tall gate and called, "Dragon! Oh, Dragon! Come here, you loathsome beast!"

Dragon appeared instantly. He charged the fence, teeth bared, foaming drool dripping. As he snarled and barked furiously at them over the top of the gate, Delphinia and Simon backed away to a safe distance.

"Here, Simon, give him the sausage," Delphinia ordered, flinching at the sound of giant teeth snapping in the air.

Simon vehemently shook his head. "He'll take off my arm! Just chuck it over the fence, madam. I'm sure he'll go after it."

Delphinia was in too big a hurry to argue or bully or threaten, so she held the sausage high above her head and then flung it toward the fence. Her aim was a little off and she ended up hitting Dragon right between the eyes!

Such a blow to the head would have leveled most animals and people, but not Dragon. He did seem dazed for a moment, and he stopped barking. But he recovered quickly and seemed ready to resume his verbal abuse of the hated trespassers, when suddenly his head cocked to the side and he began to sniff the air vigorously.

"He's caught a whiff of it," Simon observed.

"It's so odorous, half the neighborhood has probably caught a whiff of it," Delphinia said dryly.

Dragon was torn between duty and gluttony, but the temptation was too great. He chose gluttony. After directing one last warning snarl at Simon and Delphinia, he got down on all fours and ripped into the sausage.

Fifteen minutes later, tiptoeing past Dragon's slumbering hulk of a body, Simon and Delphinia headed for the house. After two or three false turns, with Delphinia viciously scolding a nervous Simon at each mistake, they finally reached the porch.

As they expected, the front door was unlocked. After all, why lock the door when you have a watchdog like Dragon? Once inside, Simon looked around helplessly.

"What now, madam? Do you think they wrote the formula down somewhere? Or do they have it memorized?"

"I don't know. Let's make a quick search of the house first, looking in the obvious places paperwork might be stashed. But if we find nothing in ten minutes, we had better go straight to the greenhouse and scoop up a bagful of fertilizer. We can have it analyzed, then duplicated."

"I thought the fertilizer was combustible if not properly handled," Simon said anxiously.

"Surely we can properly handle the fertilizer, Simon. It's not as if we're going to bounce it around like a basketball!"

"You mean *I* can properly handle it," Simon murmured under his breath.

"Start looking, Simon. There, check that desk first. We don't have much time!"

RORIE PULLED UP to the curb right behind the Rolls-Royce. "What's *she* doing here?" she grumbled to herself. But she figured Delphinia had come to check on whether or not Phillip had passed the tests. Or perhaps she already knew Phillip hadn't passed.

Rorie had spent the last three hours at Grant Park, sitting on a bench and thinking. Just getting away from the constant sexual and emotional tension she'd felt while in Phillip's company enabled her to think more clearly. Adding to that the solitude and fresh air of the park, she'd managed to come to some conclusions.

Her first conclusion was that Phillip was probably right, and Delphinia was behind all the crazy things that had happened over the past few days. Rorie hadn't wanted to believe that Delphinia could harm her own sisters, but the greedy old witch apparently wanted the fertilizer formula badly enough to take that risk. It was less surprising that Delphinia would take the risk of harming *her,* because she knew Delphinia had never liked her.

The occurrence that was most difficult to accept as one of Delphinia's tricks was the scene with the woman at the airport. Rorie couldn't understand how Delphinia could have set up that encounter without being privy to their private conversations. And considering Phillip's reputation, any sane woman would have doubts...wouldn't she?

So maybe I'm insane, Rorie thought to herself. But she knew she wasn't insane; she was just in love. And while the facts were definitely pointing toward Phillip's guilt, her heart was telling her something else. It was telling her that Phillip was a good man and that he wasn't lying to her. And since her godmothers had advised her to listen to her heart, that's exactly what she was going to do. The wise Farley females had seldom led her astray before.

Rorie's last and most important conclusion of the morning was that she not only loved Phillip, but she believed in him and would trust him no matter how illogical such blind faith seemed at the moment. She knew that eventually his innocence would be proved. She just hoped he'd not completely given up on her. Maybe if he dropped by one more time to see her godmothers, they could talk and...

Rorie's own private genie must have been listening, eager to grant her her dearest wish. Just as she opened the car door and was about to step out, she saw in the rearview mirror Phillip's Mercedes pulling up behind the minivan. With her heart beating an excited rhythm, now she used the mirror to check her appearance. She'd left the house that morning with her hair in a ponytail and wearing absolutely no makeup. Little tendrils of hair had been pulled loose by the wind and her nose and cheeks were slightly sunburned from sitting on that bench for so long. And her clothes couldn't have been less glamorous; she was wearing a pair of cutoff jeans and an oversized white T-shirt.

She sighed, reconciled to the fact that she was going to have to greet Phillip not looking her best. But that didn't dull her own joy in seeing him, in knowing that he hadn't completely given up on her!

Phillip got out of the car and walked toward the open door of the minivan. It was Rorie; he could tell by the long, tan leg poised to step down from the driver's seat. His heart started beating with excitement. She probably still thought he was a scumbag, but now he had the proof to change her mind and expected to find more proof inside the house under the end table in the parlor.

She got out and turned to face him. She looked adorable. That demure ponytail she sometimes wore looked messy and windblown, framing her face with wisps and curls of golden hair. He stopped an arm's length away, admiring the fresh look of her with no makeup on, but with eyes like shining jewels and a blush of sun on the bridge of her nose and cheeks. But the most amazing, the most beguiling thing about her...was her smile.

"Rorie...?" He couldn't find the words. He asked the question with his eyes. She answered him by throwing herself into his arms.

Their kiss was long and passionate, an unspoken reconciliation and a new beginning decided on in the passing of seconds. But oh, what sweet seconds of bliss they were! Her warm, curvy body pressed against his, and her hands caressing him soothed away the worries of the past hours when he'd tried vainly to sleep. Now that Rorie was in his arms, all was right with the world.

When they finally pulled away for air, smiling like a couple of idiots at each other, he managed to say, "What's happened? Last night you—"

"I decided to trust you," she told him. "Let's get to the bottom of all this craziness together."

His heart swelled with happiness at her faith in him. "It won't take long, Rorie," he assured her. He glanced toward the Rolls. "I see Delphinia's here. I've got proof that she's the one we have to blame for what's happened over the past few days. I say we go inside right now and confront her."

"Lead the way," she said, and they headed for the gate arm in arm.

"It's odd that Dragon's not here to greet me," Phillip commented, lifting the latch on the gate and pushing in. "After that first day, he's always been waiting at the gate."

"Maybe he's inside the house," Rorie said, then frowned as she preceded Phillip through the gate. "No, not with Delphinia here."

"He must be in the dungeon," Phillip concluded, closing the gate behind them. "But not for long. We'll be getting rid of Delphinia in no time at—"

Phillip turned from relatching the gate and nearly ran into Rorie, who was standing stock-still in the middle of the walkway with her hand over her mouth. Following her horrified gaze, Phillip looked down at the ground and saw Dragon stretched out on the grass, looking dead as a doornail!

Phillip immediately stooped and checked Dragon's pulse at his neck. It was there, slow but strong. He held his ear near Dragon's mouth and felt and heard shallow breathing. He also smelled something. Garlic and...hickory?

"He's not dead," Phillip assured Rorie, glancing around the area. "I think he's been drugged."

"But will he be all right?" Rorie asked in a small voice.

"He's healthy and strong. He's in the shade. He'll sleep it off." Phillip saw a small chunk of something red under the edge of a bush and picked it up. It was a piece of sausage!

Phillip stood up quickly and grabbed Rorie's elbow. "We'd better get inside right away. Delphinia's up to something."

Phillip led the way unerringly through the maze of foliage to the front door. As soon as they were inside, Rorie called to her godmothers, but no one answered. They quickly separated, Phillip looking upstairs and Rorie looking down. But after checking all the upstairs rooms and finding them empty, Phillip came downstairs to find Rorie gone, too.

"What the hell is going on?" Phillip hissed under his breath. He saw the back door open and headed for it. Standing on the rear porch, he debated what to do. He was much less familiar with the backyard than the front. Which way did Rorie go? Could he find her before she found Delphinia? Would the Farley sisters be with their lethal little sister, or would Rorie be facing the wicked witch all by herself? Exactly how dangerous *was* Delphinia?

Phillip took the first path he could find in the forestlike yard. Since it had been cultivated for a garden, there was some sense to the arrangement and at least he wouldn't backtrack. "Where are you, Rorie?" he murmured, suddenly realizing just how important a woman nicknamed Briar Rose had become to his happiness.

RORIE WAS HEADED for the greenhouse. She figured Delphinia was after the fertilizer formula by hook or by crook, had her godmothers tied up by the potted petunias and was helping herself to the real stuff! She didn't wait for Phillip. She couldn't. She was too worried about her godmothers.

The greenhouse was in the farthest, most overgrown corner of the yard, where her aunts also kept a compost heap. She jogged all the way there, arriving out of breath and scared as hell, just in time to see Delphinia coming out of the greenhouse, rubbing her hands together and looking smug...till she noticed Rorie coming at her like a banshee.

"Where are they?" Rorie demanded, grabbing Delphinia's arms and giving her a shake. "Where are my godmothers?"

"Let go of me," Delphinia snapped. "You're hysterical!"

Rorie released her. "Just tell me where my godmothers are, Delphinia," she said through gritted teeth.

"How would I know where they are? When we got here, they were gone."

"You haven't done anything to them, have you?" she persisted, glancing suspiciously past Delphinia's shoulder toward the greenhouse door.

"Don't be ridiculous, Aurora," Delphinia drawled, rolling her eyes and ever so subtly shifting her stance so she remained squarely between Rorie and the greenhouse. "After all, they're my sisters."

Rorie narrowed her eyes. "What are you up to, Delphinia? Phillip and I saw what you did to Dragon."

Delphinia stiffened. "Fairchild's with you?"

Suddenly, Simon poked his head out of the greenhouse door. "If Mr. Fairchild's on the premises, maybe we'd better go, madam," he said nervously.

"Fine!" Delphinia spat, her innocent act abruptly abandoned. "But hold on to the fertilizer, Simon. We're not leaving without it!"

By now Simon was standing just outside the greenhouse door, clutching a plastic bag full of a dark, peat-like mixture that Rorie could only assume was her godmothers' famous fertilizer. He looked terrified.

Rorie stepped forward, holding out her hand. "I can't let you take that, Simon. In the wrong hands, the

fertilizer could be used illegally. And, as you know,
Delphinia won't care who she sells it to. Do you want
to be responsible for megasize drug crops?"

Simon bit his lip, his gaze darting back and forth
between Delphinia and Rorie.

"Don't listen to her, you idiot," Delphinia snarled.
"Take the fertilizer to the car *immediately!*"

Simon flinched and backed away a couple of steps,
clutching the bag tighter than ever.

"It's no surprise Delphinia has *you* 'holding the
bag,' instead of *her,* is it, Simon?" Rorie continued.
"I suppose you know it's very combustible." She was
trying to frighten him into giving the fertilizer to her.
She knew that her godmothers didn't add the secret
ingredient till just before putting it into the soil around
the plants, so this bag shouldn't be any more combustible than any other ordinary bag of fertilizer. But
Simon didn't know that.

He was hesitating. In another moment, Rorie was
sure, he would have handed over the bag, but suddenly
his eyes widened and he backed away several more
steps. Rorie looked over her shoulder and, sure enough,
there was Phillip, looking ready to bash heads.

"Drop the bag, you little weasel," Phillip ordered,
stepping forward menacingly.

"No! Give it to *me!*" Delphinia shrieked, making a
desperate lunge.

With two angry people headed in his direction, both
of them intent on wrestling out of his hands what he
thought was a bag of combustible fertilizer, Simon panicked. Tossing the bag over his head, he darted forward, pushing Delphinia out of his way and into the
compost heap, and skirting around Phillip.

Simon was about to zip past Rorie when she heard

a loud bang and a bright flash of light. Startled, she stumbled backward and fell. First there were stars, then an inky darkness descended over her like a great, black wave.

Linda Barlow

6 Lord bent him a noble man to have. Showing the speaker's unwanted and put. But there were they, the speedy dog legs deviate of the walkly ban't kidney warm.

Chapter Thirteen

Phillip watched helplessly as Rorie stumbled backward, tripped over a clay pot and knocked her head against the rim of a wheelbarrow. By the time he got to her, she was lying on the ground, unconscious.

Philip kneeled beside her, checked her pulse and breathing, then tried to revive her by talking to her.

"Rorie! Rorie, honey, speak to me."

She didn't respond. She had a lump on the back of her head, but there was only a little superficial bleeding. What worried Phillip the most was whether or not there was internal bleeding.

"Call 911, Simon!" he ordered as he cradled Rorie's head in his lap.

Simon stared horrified at Rorie's inert body, seemingly unable to move.

"Do it *now*, Simon!" Phillip snapped, sick with fear. "And wait out front so you can show them the way."

Jerked out of his trance, Simon had turned to go when Delphinia screamed from the compost heap, "First help me out of this, you imbecile!"

Phillip watched, frustrated, as Simon stopped in his tracks. If Simon didn't call 911, he'd have to leave Rorie and do it himself. But Delphinia's chauffeur and lackey only turned around long enough to throw his compost-covered employer a contemptuous glance and to say, "I quit, madam!" Then he hurried away toward the house.

"You can't quit! I won't allow it!" Delphinia screeched after him, looking ludicrous in a black designer sheath as she sat on her rear in the decaying garbage, a slimy, black banana peel on her shoulder instead of a diamond brooch. "Come back here, Simon!" she bellowed, pounding her fists into the compost.

"Shut up, Delphinia, or I'll have you arrested for trespassing…among other crimes you've perpetrated against this family," Phillip warned her. "And if there's anything seriously wrong with Rorie, I'll hold you personally responsible." He glared at her. "And, believe me, lady, if that happens, you're going to wish you'd never been born."

Phillip figured the loathing he felt for her and the urge he was barely controlling to wring her neck was evident in his eyes, because Delphinia did shut up. Turning his attention back to Rorie, he barely noticed as Delphinia Farley Cadbury Bolregard Devine struggled to her feet, scraped off what she could of the clinging, stinking garbage, and skulked out of the backyard.

In another minute, he heard sirens approaching. Minutes later Simon came running with the paramedics close behind. Philip stepped back as they put Rorie on a stretcher, his throat dry and his heart hammering with fear.

She has to be all right, he thought desperately. *I love her.*

PHILLIP RODE in the ambulance with Rorie, and they arrived at the Piedmont Hospital moments later. As the paramedics rolled Rorie inside on a gurney, he wondered how he was going to contact the Farley sisters when he didn't even know where they were. He had a feeling Delphinia had probably sent them on some wild-goose chase to empty the house, but he hadn't thought earlier about choking the information out of her. Too bad. He would relish getting his hands around her neck for any reason.

Rorie still hadn't regained consciousness, and Phillip knew that that was not a good sign. But he was fiercely keeping a rein on his fears and thinking positively. Rorie was a fighter. She wouldn't let a little bump on the head keep her down, he reasoned.

He started to follow the gurney down the hall, when a nurse touched his arm. "You'll have to stay in the waiting room, sir,' she told him, her expression sympathetic but firm. "We'll let you know what's going on. Are you related to the patient?"

"Yes. No." Frustrated, he ran a hand through his hair. "I'm...a friend."

"Do you know how to get in touch with her family?" she asked.

"I'm not sure where they are right now, but I'll try to find out," he said. "Is there a phone around here?"

"There's a phone in the waiting room you can use, and a pay phone right down the hall. After your make your calls, please give our admitting clerk all the information you can."

Phillip nodded and headed for the waiting room. When he opened the door, he saw three old ladies huddled around the phone.

"Dahlia! Daisy! Daffy!" he exclaimed.

They turned and stared at him. "What are you doing here?" Dahlia asked him.

"I was about to ask you the same thing. How did you find out Rorie was injured?"

"Well, we don't know if she's injured or not," Dahlia revealed, hurrying over with a concerned look on her face. "A young lady supposedly called us from this emergency room about a half hour ago and said that Rorie fell down while she was in-line skating, hit her head and broke her leg. But when we came in, they said no one bearing Rorie's description had been admitted all day! And that no one from the hospital had called us! So we've been calling other hospitals to see if she's been admitted there, but so far none of them—"

"Delphinia," Phillip murmured.

"What?" Dahlia said.

"Delphinia arranged for the phone call to get you out of the house. Rorie didn't break her leg and injure her head in-line skating at Grant Park."

"Well, that's a relief," Daffy said, patting her chest.

"There's more to the story, ladies," Phillip warned. "Maybe you'd better sit down."

ALTHOUGH THE FARLEY sisters were alarmed about Rorie's head injury, they were hopeful about the outcome. Like Phillip, they refused to entertain extravagant fears and had firm faith in Rorie's ability to recover. As for Delphinia's part in the incident, they received the news with soberness and sadness.

"I never wanted to believe she was a bad person," Daffy lamented.

"She's our sister," Daisy added miserably.

"But we can't let her be part of our lives anymore,"

Dahlia said firmly. "In exchange for our keeping quiet about her killer bees in brown-paper packaging and the cat escapade, not to mention trying to steal our fertilizer formula, she's not to come to the house or contact us in any way again. We'll pay her her share of the house Papa left to the four of us, then all ties will be broken. Do you agree, Phillip?"

"I think it's the right thing to do. She may not have purposely injured anyone, but her methods for getting what she wants are potentially dangerous—as we know—and bound to get more dangerous the more desperate she gets. I still intend to have words with the lady. I have proof of her guilt...to a point. I just wish I had more definitive proof, so I could be sure of scaring her away for good."

"I'll give you all the proof you need," came a voice from behind Phillip. He turned and saw Simon.

"You?" Phillip said incredulously. "You've been an accomplice!"

"Not willingly," Simon said meekly. "I needed the job, and I wasn't sure I could get another if I quit. I let her bully me. She scares the wits out of me, you know."

"She scares a lot of people," Dahlia said sympathetically.

"But it was still very wrong to help her plot against you," Simon continued. "I'm willing to tell the police everything, even if it implicates me. She has to be stopped."

"With you as a possible witness against her in court, I think the threat of exposure will be real enough to scare her into good behavior," Phillip said with grim satisfaction. "I'm sure her sisters would only send her to jail as a last resort."

"Well, let me know if I can do anything to help," Simon finished. "I'll be staying at the Clairmont Hotel till I find another position." He started to go, then turned back.

"I'd really like to know how Miss McBride gets along. Will you call me when there's a change in her condition?" he asked.

"I'd be happy to, Simon," Phillip assured him.

BUT, THREE HOURS LATER, there was still no change in Rorie's condition. An MRI had revealed some swelling of the brain at the site of the injury, but there was no subcranial bleeding or any other life-threatening or permanent damage.

"So, why doesn't she wake up, Doctor Williams?" Phillip asked the E.R. physician.

"I don't know," the doctor replied. "I'm going to admit her, and we'll keep a close eye on her till she regains consciousness. With these sorts of injuries, we just have to wait and see what happens."

"I'm sure she'll wake up very soon," Dahlia said, trying to hide her anxiety behind a brave smile.

"We can go up and see her as soon as she's settled into her room, can't we, Doctor?" Daisy inquired.

"I don't see why not," the doctor replied. "Now, which of you wants to sign the admission papers?"

The doctor directed Dahlia to the admissions office and Phillip sat down with Daisy and Daffy. He couldn't believe he was sitting in an emergency room, waiting for Rorie to be admitted to the hospital! He had every reason to expect her to recover from this accident, but his stomach churned and his legs felt like Silly Putty. The uncertainty of it all was nerve-shattering.

But everything else in Phillip's life had suddenly become crystal clear. After nearly losing her, he knew he never wanted to be separated from Rorie again. And as soon as she woke up, he was going to tell her that he loved her and wanted to marry her.

TROUBLE WAS, two days later, Rorie still hadn't woken up. The doctors were baffled. Her injuries just didn't seem to warrant such a long spell of unconsciousness. As far as they could tell, the brain swelling had gone down completely and nothing else seemed wrong. Her vital signs were excellent and she looked the picture of health. So why was she still sleeping?

"Phillip, why don't you go home and get some rest?" Dahlia suggested as she stood beside him at the foot of Rorie's hospital bed.

"I couldn't rest even if I did go home," Phillip said grimly. "I want to be here when she wakes up."

Dahlia nodded, as if she hadn't expected him to give any other answer. "Daisy and Daffy will be back soon with some lunch for you," she said. "I know the hospital food is dreadful and it may not tempt your appetite, but if you don't eat some of our fresh peach pie, Phillip, they'll have to start feeding you through an IV tube!"

Phillip turned and gave Dahlia a lopsided smile. "I won't waste away in just two days, Dahlia. Don't worry about me."

"But you're not getting any sleep, either."

"Sometimes I doze in the chair by her bed."

"When she wakes up, she won't even recognize you with those dark circles under your eyes. She, on the other hand, will be quite refreshed!"

"At least I've been showering and shaving," he defended himself. "These private rooms have all the amenities, and since Rorie can't take advantage of the shower, the nurses don't mind if I do.''

"No, you have the nurses wrapped around your little finger," Dahlia teased, but Phillip could only manage a weak smile in response. He fastened his eyes on Rorie again, willing her to wake up.

"She's so beautiful," Dahlia said with a sigh. "And she looks so peaceful and happy."

Phillip nodded. Dahlia was right. Rorie looked beautiful in her sleep. Daffy had braided her hair, and the long, golden plait fell over her shoulder and rested on her breast. Her skin glowed with dewy color and her lips seemed to curve ever so slightly up, as if she were enjoying a pleasant dream. Her godmothers had brought a nightgown from home that morning, the very same one she'd been wearing the night he'd followed her to the turret and found her spinning by candlelight.

"Yes, she's a real sleeping beauty," Dahlia said with another sigh. "Only I'd much rather she woke up so we could see those bright blue eyes of hers."

"Or hear her voice," Phillip added. "Even an insult from her would thrill me."

Dahlia patted him awkwardly on the shoulder. "Don't worry, Phillip. I'm sure Rorie will insult you many times before the two of you reach your golden wedding anniversary."

He turned to look at Dahlia, surprised. "So, you know how deeply I care about her?"

"I knew you two were meant to be together since the moment you showed up at our door," Dahlia said smugly.

"If you can see into the future like that, Dahlia, maybe you could set my mind at ease on one more point. When will Rorie wake up?"

Dahlia shook her head sadly. "That I don't know, Phillip."

LATER THAT EVENING, after the Farley sisters had gone home, Phillip sat in the chair by Rorie's bed in the semidarkness. He was nodding off when he heard a familiar voice call his name.

"Phillip?"

He startled and sprang to his feet, leaning over the bed to stare expectantly at Rorie. But she still appeared fast asleep.

"It was me, Phillip. *I* called your name."

Phillip turned toward the door and saw his mother standing there. In her pale blue suit and pearls, her perfectly arranged beauty-salon hair and small clutch purse, she looked like she'd come straight to the hospital from an afternoon tea and fashion show. But then his mother always looked that way. Meticulously groomed, proper and elegant. And reserved. Always reserved.

"I can see you're disappointed," she offered, stepping tentatively into the room. "You were hoping it was the young woman who was calling your name, weren't you?"

"No offense, Mom, but you're right," Phillip said, dragging his fingers through his hair. "I've been waiting for two days to hear her say my name."

She took another step into the room. "You must care about her very much."

"I do." He sank back wearily into the chair. "I just wish she'd wake up so I could tell her."

His mother raised a neatly arched brow. "She doesn't know?"

"I haven't had a chance to tell her. I didn't know

myself till *this* happened." He gestured helplessly toward the bed.

His mother nodded. "I see." She paused. "This must be very difficult for you. I wondered why you didn't call me or your father and let us know. We heard about it from Zach."

"I've been distracted—"

"We care about you, Phillip. If there's anything we can do..."

Phillip looked up at his mother. She might not be very demonstrative, but it was clear by the expression on her face that she was deeply sympathetic and concerned. He smiled. "Thanks, Mom, but there's nothing anyone can do. I'll be okay, and so will Rorie...sooner or later." Only he hoped it wasn't too much later.

His mother cocked her head to the side. "Her name is Rorie?"

"Yeah. Short for Aurora."

"Aurora," his mother repeated with a thoughtful expression. "I knew a little girl once name Aurora." Fixing her gaze on Rorie, she advanced into the room until she was standing at the foot of the hospital bed. As she stared at Rorie's face, her hand came slowly up to cover her mouth.

Phillip stood up. "What is it, Mom?"

"She looks just like her mother," she said in a trembling voice. *"Just like her."*

He walked to the bed. "You *knew* Rorie's mother?"

"Yes. Well, sort of. I met her during that one summer we vacationed at the beach in Savannah for a few days. On the last day, late in the afternoon, you and I were sitting on a blanket on the beach, dismally dreading the trip home. Your father, as usual, was making business calls. We were so sad to be going! But suddenly this lovely woman and her little girl spread out their blanket next to us. She immediately struck up a cheerful conversation with me and drew me out of my doldrums." His mother smiled wistfully. "As for you and the little girl…"

"What about me and the little girl?" Phillip asked eagerly. It seemed incredible, but he had a good idea where this story was going.

She turned to look at him fondly. "She was only about five, and you were nearly ten. You weren't interested in playing with a little girl her age, and you tried very hard to ignore her." She laughed, remembering. "But she was a determined little thing, and she chatted and cajoled till you agreed to walk with her on the beach. As she caught your big hand in her small one and dragged you reluctantly away, you threw me the most *miserable* look!"

"I think I can guess what happened," Phillip murmured sheepishly.

"Yes, the two of you had a wonderful afternoon together. You fed the seagulls, you helped her build sand castles, you waded in the surf. It was really amazing to watch how, over just a few hours, you became very protective of her. Her mother and I were convinced you and Aurora were destined to be married! We made plans to meet in Atlanta for lunch."

Phillip frowned as his mother's expression became suddenly sad. "You never saw Aurora's mother again, did you?"

"She was killed in a car accident shortly after we met. Aurora was sent off to be raised by a godmother—"

"*Three* godmothers," Phillip corrected.

"And I lost track of her." She reached out and

gently stroked Rorie's long braid. "Her mother was so beautiful, so vital and alive the last time I saw her." She turned to look at Phillip. "Don't you remember anything about that afternoon?"

"I didn't think so...till I met Rorie again. Then I started having feelings of déjà vu. And I'd have these dreams.... Rorie had been remembering, too. We'd just about decided that we must have met during that trip to the beach, but now you've confirmed it. It seemed too fantastic to believe. Who'd have ever thought we'd meet again?"

His mother placed her hand gently on his shoulder and smiled. "Maybe it was just meant to be."

MEANT TO BE, Phillip repeated to himself after his mother left. Well, if he and Rorie were meant to be, why was she still unconscious? He bent over the bed, his elbows propped on the mattress, holding Rorie's hand. He kneaded the slender fingers and turned her hand over to kiss the soft palm with an almost reverent intensity.

The doctors had encouraged him to talk to her, and he'd talked till he was blue in the face. Nothing seemed to stir her or pull her away from whatever pleasant dream she was enjoying.

"It's time to wake up, sleepyhead," he whispered, staring at her beautiful, peaceful face. "I've got things to tell you."

She slept on.

"My mother was here. She tells me we really did meet at the beach all those years ago. She recognized you because, apparently, you look just like your mother. And Aurora's not exactly a run-of-the-mill name, either."

Rorie gave a soft little sigh, barely breaking the even rhythm of her breathing.

"She says you and I are meant to be, Rorie, and I agree with her. What do you think, sweetheart?"

Rorie did not reply.

Shaking his head, Phillip felt as frustrated as he'd ever felt in the course of his—up till then—charmed life. He couldn't believe that he'd finally fallen in love, and the girl of his dreams was lying in an unexplainable coma. And he couldn't accept the fact that Rorie would never wake up, although that horrific thought *had* occurred to him. Many times. After all, there were unusual cases in every textbook.

Phillip hung his head, too tired to fend off the worries that he'd kept in cold storage for the past two days. What if she didn't wake up?

Phillip lifted his head and stared at Rorie. She was so beautiful....

His jaw hardened with determination.

"I'll never give up on you, Aurora," he vowed. "I just wish I knew what it would take to wake you up."

Then it came to him. As if she'd whispered it in his ear, Phillip recalled the words she'd said to him that night at their "seaside paradise," when she'd kissed him after their nap. *I was waking you up,* she'd said. *Can you think of a better way to wake up? It's certainly my favorite.*

It occurred to Phillip that while he'd kissed her hands, her cheek, and even the tip of her nose since the accident, he hadn't once kissed Rorie on the lips. Was it crazy to think he could get through to her by kissing her the way a lover kissed a lover? The way a man kissed a woman he was in love with?

Would the nurses think he was nuts or a sex-starved

lunatic if they caught him smooching with a woman in a coma?

He had to take that chance. Peering through the narrow window in the door, he checked to make sure no nurses were headed their way, then he hurried back to the bed and bent over Rorie.

"You said this was your favorite way to wake up, Briar Rose," he whispered. "So don't disappoint me."

He kissed her.

Phillip had been half-afraid Rorie's lips would be cold or stiff, but they weren't. They were as warm and soft as ever. He could almost imagine she was kissing him back, although he knew that was impossible. But it wasn't hard to imbue his one-sided kiss with all the love he felt for her, all the warmth and tenderness and commitment. If she was registering anything that was being said or done around her, she'd know with an absolute certainty that she was loved.

When he lifted his head, Phillip felt dazed. He could only imagine how much the kiss would have affected him had Rorie actually been awake and participating. If *that* didn't wake her up, nothing would.

"*Now,* Rorie. Now would be the time to wake up and say my name," he urged, fervently clasping her hands.

But her face remained quiet, her eyes closed. And instead of hearing Rorie's voice, he heard someone else's.

"Phillip Fairchild. I want to have a word with you."

The voice was all too familiar, and Phillip quickly turned. Sure enough, Delphinia stood just inside the door, all decked out in a black evening gown, long black gloves and a diamond choker. Or, considering her apparent financial woes, maybe the choker was cubic zirconium.

"How dare you come in here?" Phillip ground out in a low voice. "Get out!"

"Don't be nasty, Phillip," Delphinia advised as she slunk across the floor. "You're going to wish you'd been nicer to me when you hear what I have to say. Darling, I have a little proposition for you."

Chapter Fourteen

"I'm not interested in any proposition coming from you, Delphinia," Phillip informed her icily. "I can't believe you've got the gall to even show your face in this room."

Delphinia slid a glance toward the hospital bed. "Her accident was not my fault," she said disdainfully.

"Not directly, but you know you're as culpable as hell. Your efforts to sabotage my deal with your sisters put her in that bed as surely as if you'd hit her on the head yourself."

Delphinia sniffed. "Nonsense. What's wrong with a little healthy competition?

"As long as you play fair."

"I'm ambitious, just like you, Phillip. And that's why I'm here today. I want to strike a business deal with you."

Phillip was incredulous. "A business deal?"

She slunk a little closer and gave him what he supposed she intended as a provocative look. "I have a buyer for the fertilizer formula who will give you far more money than you could ever make by using it in your perfume business. Of course, we'd have to fly to South America to meet with him." She reached out and ran one of her bony fingers, tipped with a bloodred nail, down the front of his shirt, from collar to belt buckle. "I hear you have a private jet? Maybe we could...fly together?"

Fighting a wave of nausea, Phillip grabbed her wrist and squeezed hard. "You really are crazy, aren't you? I wouldn't go anywhere with you. And I wouldn't sell the formula to anyone that might use it illegally, no matter how much money they gave me. But you obviously have no scruples about that, or about anything else, do you, Delphinia?"

"You're hurting me," she informed him in a throaty voice.

When he realized she was enjoying the hard pressure on her wrist, he immediately let go and backed up a couple of steps till he was against the end of the hospital bed. "The only reason I haven't pressed charges against you is because of your relationship with Rorie's godmothers. But if she suffers any lasting effects from this accident, I'll make sure you become intimately acquainted with the inside of a jail cell."

"You have no proof."

"I found the bugging device in my car, and Dahlia found the ones you stashed in the house."

He thought he saw a flash of anxiety in her eyes. "You can't connect them with me."

"Yes I can. Simon has offered to supply me with all the proof I need to put you away, Delphinia."

Her eyes narrowed, the anxiety replaced by anger. "That little weasel. He hasn't the courage."

"You're mistaken, Delphinia. And to sweeten the deal for him, I'm going to find him a job with an *honest* employer...far away from you. I think the guy's got heart. He's called several times to check on Rorie. Simon's on my side now, but if you want to take the risk of being exposed as the witch you are, call my bluff and see what happens.''

They faced off. When it was obvious he wasn't going to budge, Delphinia, probably out of sheer desperation, tried one last time to seduce him. Advancing with a sultry roll to her hips, she grabbed his shirt front in both fists, then thrust her silicone breasts and her collagen-injected lips forward at the same time.

''Maybe I could make you change your mind, Phillip. Have you ever kissed a *mature* woman?''

Phillip was about to grab Delphinia and physically carry her out of the room and dump her in the hall, when a voice from behind him said, ''Get your hands off him or I'll throw this water pitcher!''

Phillip swung around and saw Rorie sitting up, holding the pink plastic water pitcher that had been resting on the tray beside her bed, and looking mad as hell.

''Rorie, you're awake!'' Phillip exclaimed.

''So the sleeping beauty has finally awakened,'' Delphinia drawled. ''A pity.''

''I can still throw this,'' Rorie warned. ''The plastic might not be heavy enough to do much harm, but don't witches melt when they get wet? I wouldn't take the chance if I were you, Delphinia.''

Delphinia sneered and slunk to the door. ''Your wit is as bland as your beauty, *Briar Rose*.'' She threw a scathing glance at Phillip. ''And your taste in women is deplorable. I do believe you deserve each other. Goodbye and good riddance!''

As the door swung closed behind her, Phillip muttered, ''One can only hope.'' Then he turned to Rorie. Her cheeks were pink and her eyes sparkled in the afterglow of her anger. She looked as fit as a fiddle, and, best of all, she was awake.

"You'd better set down that pitcher, Rorie, unless you want water spilled all over you when I hug you within an inch of your life."

Looking a little confused and dazed, Rorie nonetheless obediently set down the pitcher. Phillip wasted no time, but immediately sat down on the edge of the bed and drew her into his arms.

"Rorie. I can't believe it! Finally you're awake."

"How long have I been asleep?" she asked in a muffled voice against his shoulder. "And why am I in a hospital?"

He pulled away and smiled at her. "Do you remember falling down by the greenhouse?"

She knitted her brows. "Yes. Yes, I do. What happened?"

"You hit your head on a wheelbarrow and you've been unconscious for two days."

She blinked. "Two days? Good heavens, *why*?"

"That's what we all wanted to know."

"But, Delphinia…my godmothers…the fertilizer formula…"

"Your godmothers are safe, and so is the formula. Delphinia is out of our lives for good."

"I certainly hope we've seen the last of her," Rorie fervently agreed. "The old witch!" Suddenly her eyes widened and she got an abstracted look on her face.

"What is it, Rorie?" Phillip asked her.

"Calling Delphinia a witch made me remember a dream I was having. It was so strange, Phillip." She turned to him eagerly, her eyes aglow. "It was kind of like my own life, only exaggerated. You know, like a fairy tale."

He smiled, ready and willing to indulge her. "Tell me about it."

With a dreamy expression, she looked off into space. "I was a princess...and you were a prince. We were betrothed when we were children, but an evil witch cast a spell over me. She said that when I turned sixteen, I'd prick my finger on a spinning wheel and go to sleep for a hundred years. To protect me, my parents sent me away to live with my three fairy godmothers. But eventually I did find a spinning wheel and I did prick my finger and fall asleep. Against all kinds of odds, you rescued me and woke me with a kiss."

She turned back to Phillip. "When I woke up just now, I was dreaming that my prince—that you—were kissing me."

Feeling a tingling sensation all over, as if he'd just entered the twilight zone, Phillip inquired, "When exactly did you wake up, Rorie?"

"I think I was coming out of it when Delphinia showed up. I heard her say your name, then I pretty much heard everything else you two said to each other. But it was like I was struggling through a haze. When she started putting serious moves on you, though, that woke me up completely!"

Phillip did not doubt that it was his kiss that had awakened Rorie, but he wasn't sure she was ready to be blown away by such a revelation, or to hear how closely her fairy tale reflected real life. According to his mother's story, apparently they had been destined to be married since they were children, too, just like the prince and princess in her dream. Phillip had a proposal on the tip of his tongue, but for now, it was enough that Rorie was awake.

"When can I go home, Phillip?" she asked him, obviously full of restless energy.

"Don't get too excited, Rorie," Phillip cautioned her. "I'm sure you won't be able to go home till tomorrow. Now lie back and I'll call for the nurse and tell her you're awake, then I'll call your godmothers. If you settle down, maybe the doctors will let you have a little more company tonight."

Rorie eased back into the pillows with a big smile on her lips. "I'd like that."

A HALF HOUR later, Dahlia, Daisy and Daffy burst through the door, their rosy faces wreathed in smiles, and with baskets full of flowers and food hanging on their plump arms.

After being virtually smothered in hugs and kisses, Rorie asked the first question that came to mind. "How's Dragon?"

The godmothers were busily arranging flowers in vases and setting out peach pie and other luscious homemade tidbits on her bed tray. Soon the room would be transformed into a fragrant picnic area.

"He's just fine," Dahlia assured her, handing Phillip a thermos of coffee and a cup. "The tranquilizers Delphinia fed him wore off rather quickly, actually. He woke up much sooner than you did, lazybones!"

"That's good," Rorie said with a satisfied nod of her head. "I was worried about him."

"So were we," Daffy admitted. "Not only do we love the big old thing, but we need him to help make our fertilizer formula."

Phillip swallowed the coffee he'd been drinking and looked up, obviously puzzled. Rorie was mystified, too.

"In what way does Dragon help make your fertilizer formula?" Phillip inquired.

"He supplies the secret ingredient," Daisy answered, setting a small vase and a single, giant-size rose on Rorie's bedside table.

Rorie exchanged a bewildered glance with Phillip. "Dragon must have talents I'm not aware of, godmothers. Don't you need a thumb to hold a spoon and mix ingredients in a bowl?" she joked.

Dahlia pulled a chair up near the bed and sat down with a sigh. "I hadn't planned on talking about the fertilizer formula tonight, of all nights, but since my sisters brought it up..." She threw them a mildly admonishing glance. "You might as well know everything. As you already know, the fertilizer is just an above-average product without the secret ingredient."

"And we know firsthand that it's highly combustible," Phillip interjected. "But I thought you only added the secret ingredient at the last moment."

"We do."

"But then why did the bag Simon threw over his shoulder explode?"

"We had just mixed up a batch and added the secret ingredient when we were called to the hospital by Delphinia's imitation of an E.R. clerk. That's the batch Delphinia and Simon got into while we were gone."

"I see," Phillip said, nodding. He paused, then prompted them, saying, "So? Are you going to tell us what the secret ingredient is?"

"It's the compost," Dahlia said shortly.

"From the compost heap by the greenhouse?"

"The very same."

Phillip nodded again. "And the compost is special *because*..."

Daffy and Daisy giggled and Dahlia threw them another scolding glance. They muffled their giggles behind their hands while Dahlia puffed out her chest, lifted her chin, and said with great dignity, "The compost heap is special because that is where Dragon takes his, er, daily constitutional."

Rorie held back her own giggles as she watched Phillip's brows draw together in confusion. "His constitutional? You mean his walk? I don't get it, Dahlia."

"I think Dahlia means Dragon walks out to the compost heap every day—or perhaps more often—for a specific *purpose,* Phillip," Rorie said, trying to enlighten him without resorting to indelicate terms.

Phillip continued to frown, obviously straining his brain to decode all the double-talk. When it finally hit him, it was positively comical watching his jaw drop and his eyes widen with amazement. "You mean, Dragon goes to the compost heap to—"

"Yes," Dahlia confirmed with a vigorous nod of her head, seeming eager to avoid saying what Dragon actually did at the compost heap.

"And the secret ingredient in your fertilizer is—"

"Yes, yes," Dahlia agreed with more vigorous nodding. "Dragon's additions to the mix have been invaluable. Without his, er, contribution, the fertilizer formula wouldn't be half as effective."

Rorie could see that Phillip was stunned. She was surprised, too, but a part of her found the whole thing hilarious. She wanted to laugh, but she was afraid Phillip wouldn't think it was as funny as she did.

Obviously, the fertilizer formula was worthless without the secret ingredient, and the secret ingredient depended on a dog who would not live forever. Not to mention the problem one would have mass-marketing the stuff. Even if only a tiny amount of the secret ingredient was needed for each batch, a lone dog would have a pretty hard time supplying the world with his own brand of magic fertilizer!

Phillip looked at her, and he must have detected the merriment in her eyes she was trying so hard to squelch. She watched as the merriment rose in his eyes, too, and soon they were both laughing till their sides ached. The godmothers laughed, too, never able to resist a good joke...especially if they were the perpetrators.

When the laughter died down, Phillip wiped his eyes and confronted Dahlia. ''You were going to sell me the fertilizer even though you knew it would be worthless for the purposes I had in mind?'' he admonished her with a good-natured smile.

''We never intended to sell you the fertilizer formula,'' Dahlia revealed, completely unashamed. ''Did we, girls?''

Daisy and Daffy shook their heads.

Phillip half laughed, half choked. ''Then why, for crying out loud, were you testing me?''

''We were testing you to see if you were worthy of acquiring our most precious possession.''

''Yes, but wasn't that the fertilizer formula?''

Phillip seemed really stumped. So was Rorie.

''No.'' Dahlia smiled at Rorie. In fact, all three of her godmothers were smiling at her. ''Though it would be incorrect to actually call her our possession, Rorie is the most precious thing in our lives. It would also be incorrect to imply that you could actually acquire her—after all, it wouldn't be politically correct to say it in such terms, now would it? But we were testing you, Phillip, to see if you were worthy of being Rorie's *husband*.''

Rorie wished she could sink into the floor! Her godmothers were unabashed matchmakers, but actually assuming that Phillip would marry her simply because they'd decided he was worthy of such a prize was too embarrassing for words!

Oh, she *wished* it were possible! She wished it more than anything in the world. She loved Phillip and would like nothing better than to be loved by him in return and to become his wife, but they'd only known each other a few days. Unless the blessed union had been foreordained, it was crazy to think they could come to the point of matrimony so soon.

Feeling herself blushing, Rorie hung her head, unable to look at Phillip.

''Well?'' she heard him say.

''Well what?'' Dahlia responded.

''Did I pass?''

Rorie's head reared up. She stared at Phillip, but she could only study his profile. He was looking at Dahlia, waiting for her answer. It seemed incredible, but was it possible that he *wanted* to pass the tests?

''With flying colors,'' Dahlia assured him with a wink and a wide smile. ''Don't you agree, sisters?''

''Unquestionably,'' Daisy said.

''Indubitably,'' Daffy agreed.

''And with that endorsement, Phillip, I think we'll leave you and Aurora alone. We brought enough to supply all the patients on this floor with flowers. We'll be back later. You know what to do in our absence, I gather?'' Dahlia looked at Phillip over her glasses.

''Indubitably,'' Phillip replied with a grin.

In less than a minute, the godmothers had gathered

their baskets of flowers and scurried out of the room, leaving Rorie alone with Phillip. Hardly knowing what to expect, she met his gaze shyly.

He got up from his chair and came to sit on the bed beside her. While Rorie held her breath, he took her hands and lifted them to his mouth, grazing the knuckles softly with his lips, then kissing them. She watched adoringly, fascinated by the shadow of his lashes on his chiseled cheekbones and the silky curls of dark hair that fell over his forehead.

When he lifted his gaze and smiled at her, she thought her heart would melt. "A hospital room is hardly a fairy-tale setting for a proposal, is it?" he said softly.

Rorie had no idea what to reply. She wanted to tell him that any setting was magical when he was there. Instead, she merely gulped nervously and waited. Was it possible that, *finally*, her prince had come?

"By all indications, Rorie, you and I are meant to be together. In fact, my mother visited earlier...while you were sleeping...and confirmed what you and I had suspected all along. We *have* met before. We did spend a day at the beach together when we were children. Our mothers decided then and there that we ought to marry someday, and, if your mother had lived, I'm sure they would have contrived to get us together. But fate took care of that anyway, didn't it?"

"Oh, Phillip," Rorie murmured, her eyes welling with tears.

"You're everything I've ever wanted, Rorie. I love you and I want to marry you. Will you?"

Filled with happiness, Rorie couldn't help a teasing reply. "Are you sure you don't just want me for my godmothers' fertilizer formula, Fairchild?"

He chuckled and squeezed her hands. "I might want a little help from the fertilizer for one specific project I have in mind."

She raised a brow. "Oh?"

"Yes, I want to develop a fragrance called Briar Rose. Inspired, of course, by you, my darling. I'll need the biggest, most fragrant, most beautiful roses to distill, and then I'll add just a pinch of something sharp and potent to give it an edge. Do you approve?"

Rorie laughed. "Completely."

"Shall we seal the deal with a kiss?"

"Which deal, Fairchild? The marriage deal or the fertilizer deal?"

His eyes gleamed with a mixture of mischief and love. "Why, both of course."

She punched him in the arm. Then she kissed him.

And she just knew in her heart that they were destined to live happily ever after.

EVER HAD ONE OF THOSE DAYS?

TO DO:

☑ late for a super-important meeting, you discover the cat has eaten your panty hose

☑ while you work through lunch, the rest of the gang goes out and finds a one-hour, once-in-a-lifetime 90% off sale at the most exclusive store in town (Oh, and they also get to meet Brad Pitt who's filming a movie across the street.)

☑ you discover that your intimate phone call with your boyfriend was on company-wide intercom

☑ finally at the end of a long and exasperating day, you escape from it all with an entertaining, humorous and always romantic Love & Laughter book!

ENJOY
LOVE & LAUGHTER™
EVERY DAY!

For a preview, turn the page....

Here's a sneak peek at
Colleen Collins's RIGHT CHEST, WRONG NAME
Available August 1997...

"DARLING, YOU SOUND like a broken cappuccino machine," murmured Charlotte, her voice oozing disapproval.

Russell juggled the receiver while attempting to sit up in bed, but couldn't. If he *sounded* like a wreck over the phone, he could only imagine what he looked like.

"What mischief did you and your friends get into at your bachelor's party last night?" she continued.

She always had a way of saying "your friends" as though they were a pack of degenerate water buffalo. Professors deserved to be several notches higher up on the food chain, he thought. Which he would have said if his tongue wasn't swollen to twice its size.

"You didn't do anything...bad...did you, Russell?"

"Bad." His laugh came out like a bark.

"Bad as in *naughty*."

He heard her piqued tone but knew she'd never admit to such a base emotion as jealousy. Charlotte Maday, the woman he was to wed in a week, came from a family who bled blue. Exhibiting raw emotion was akin to burping in public.

After agreeing to be at her parents' pool party by

noon, he untangled himself from the bed sheets and stumbled to the bathroom.

"Pool party," he reminded himself. He'd put on his best front and accommodate Char's request. Make the family rounds, exchange a few pleasantries, play the role she liked best: the erudite, cultured English literature professor. After fulfilling his duties, he'd slink into some lawn chair, preferably one in the shade, and nurse his hangover.

He tossed back a few aspirin and splashed cold water on his face. Grappling for a towel, he squinted into the mirror.

Then he jerked upright and stared at his reflection, blinking back drops of water. "Good Lord. They stuck me in a wind tunnel."

His hair, usually neatly parted and combed, sprang from his head as though he'd been struck by lightning. "Can too many Wild Turkeys do that?" he asked himself as he stared with horror at his reflection.

Something caught his eye in the mirror. Russell's gaze dropped.

"What in the—"

Over his pectoral muscle was a small patch of white. A bandage. Gingerly, he pulled it off.

Underneath, on his skin, was not a wound but a small, neat drawing.

"A red heart?" His voice cracked on the word *heart*. Something—a word?—was scrawled across it.

"Good Lord," he croaked. "I got a tattoo. A heart tattoo with the name Liz on it."

Not Charlotte. Liz!

Let's Celebrate!

LOVE & LAUGHTER™

invites you to
the party of the season!

Grab your popcorn and be prepared to laugh as we celebrate with **LOVE & LAUGHTER**.

Harlequin's newest series is going Hollywood!

Let us make you laugh with three months of terrific books, authors and romance, plus a chance to win a FREE 15-copy video collection of the best romantic comedies ever made.

For more details look in the back pages of any Love & Laughter title, from July to September, at your favorite retail outlet.

Don't forget the popcorn!

Available wherever
Harlequin books are sold.

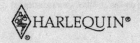

HARLEQUIN®

LLCELEB

And the Winner Is...
You!

...when you pick up these great titles
from our new promotion at your
favorite retail outlet this June!

Diana Palmer
The Case of the Mesmerizing Boss

Betty Neels
The Convenient Wife

Annette Broadrick
Irresistible

Emma Darcy
A Wedding to Remember

Rachel Lee
Lost Warriors

Marie Ferrarella
Father Goose

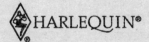 

HARLEQUIN WOMEN KNOW ROMANCE WHEN THEY SEE IT.

And they'll see it on **ROMANCE CLASSICS**, the new 24-hour TV channel devoted to romantic movies and original programs like the special **Harlequin** Showcase of **Authors & Stories**.

The **Harlequin** Showcase of **Authors & Stories** introduces you to many of your favorite romance authors in a program developed exclusively for Harlequin readers.

Watch for the **Harlequin** Showcase of **Authors & Stories** series beginning in the summer of 1997.

If you're not receiving *ROMANCE CLASSICS*, *call your local cable operator or satellite provider and ask for it today!*

Escape to the network of your dreams.

ROMANCE CLASSICS

Harlequin American Romance
cordially invites you to

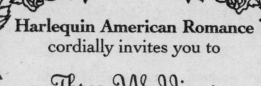

Three Weddings
& A HURRICANE

AT THE PARADISE HOTEL
MAUI, HAWAII
(Weather permitting)

with a special appearance by Hurricane Bonnie

Three couples + one hurricane =
lots of romance!

Don't miss this exciting new series blowing your
way from American Romance:

#691 MARRY ME, BABY
by Debbi Rawlins (August 1997)

#695 QUICK, FIND A RING!
by Jo Leigh (September 1997)

#698 PLEASE SAY "I DO"
by Karen Toller Whittenburg (October 1997)

Available wherever Harlequin books are sold.

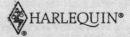

HE SAID

♥

SHE SAID

Explore the mystery of male/female communication in this extraordinary new book from two of your favorite Harlequin authors.

Jasmine Cresswell and Margaret St. George bring you the exciting story of two romantic adversaries—each from their own point of view!

DEV'S STORY. CATHY'S STORY.
As he sees it. As she sees it.
Both sides of the story!

The heat is definitely on, and these two can't stay out of the kitchen!

Don't miss **HE SAID, SHE SAID.**
Available in July wherever Harlequin books are sold.

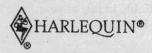

HARLEQUIN®